THE EYE IN THE MUSEUM

THE EYE IN THE MUSEUM

J. J. Connington

COACHWHIP PUBLICATIONS
Greenville, Ohio

The Eye in the Museum

First published 1929.
2016 Coachwhip edition

ISBN 1-61646-338-4
ISBN-13 978-1-61646-338-0

CoachwhipBooks.com

CONTENTS

Introduction, by Curtis Evans 7
1 · At the Struan Museum 23
2 · A Case of Heart-Failure 43
3 · The Verdict 54
4 · The Case Against Joyce 60
5 · Superintendent Ross 75
6 · Digitalis Purpurea 84
7 · The Man with the Aliases 100
8 · Nine to Eleven P.M. 123
9 · Mrs. Fenton's Husband 139
10 · I.O.U. 153
11 · The Financial Side of the Case 165
12 · The Light in the Museum 176
13 · "Kowtow! Kowtow to the Great Yen How!" 179
14 · The Eye in the Museum 187
15 · The Race to the Sea 200
16 · The Case for the Prosecution 211
17 · The Springs of Action 222

INTRODUCTION
CURTIS EVANS

Alfred Walter Stewart (1880-1947)
Alias J. J. Connington

During the Golden Age of the detective novel, in the 1920s and 1930s, "J. J. Connington" stood with fellow crime writers R. Austin Freeman, Cecil John Charles Street, and Freeman Wills Crofts as the foremost practitioner in British mystery fiction of the science of pure detection. I use the word "science" advisedly, for the man behind J. J. Connington, Alfred Walter Stewart, was an esteemed Scottish-born scientist who held the Chair of Chemistry at Queens University, Belfast for twenty-five years, from 1919 until his retirement in 1944. A "small, unassuming, moustached polymath," Stewart was "a strikingly effective lecturer with an excellent sense of humor, fertile imagination, and fantastically retentive memory," qualities that also served him well in his fiction. During roughly this period, the busy Professor Stewart found time to author a remarkable apocalyptic science fiction tale, *Nordenholt's Million* (1923), a mainstream novel, *Almighty Gold* (1924), a collection of essays, *Alias J. J. Connington* (1947), and, between 1926 and 1947, twenty-four mysteries (all but one true tales of detection), many of them sterling examples of the Golden Age puzzle-oriented detective novel at its considerable best. "For those who ask first of all in a detective story for exact and mathematical accuracy in the construction of the plot," avowed a contemporary

London Daily Mail reviewer, "there is no author to equal the distinguished scientist who writes under the name of J. J. Connington."[1]

Alfred Stewart's background as a man of science is reflected in his fiction, not only in the impressive puzzle plot mechanics he devised for his mysteries but in his choices of themes and depictions of characters. Along with Stanley Nordenholt of *Nordenholt's Million*, a novel about a plutocrat's pitiless efforts to preserve a ruthlessly remolded remnant of human life after a global environmental calamity, the most notable character that Stewart created is Chief Constable Sir Clinton Driffield, the detective in seventeen of the twenty-four Connington crime novels. Driffield is one of crime fiction's most highhanded investigators, occasionally taking into his hands the functions of judge and jury as well as chief of police. Absent from Stewart's fiction is the hail-fellow-well-met quality found in John Street's works or the religious ethos suffusing those of Freeman Wills Crofts, not to mention the effervescent novel of manners style of the British Golden Age Crime Queens Dorothy L. Sayers, Margery Allingham, and Ngaio Marsh. Instead we see an often disdainful cynicism about the human animal and a marked admiration for detached supermen with superior intellects. For this reason, reading a Connington novel can be a challenging experience for modern readers inculcated in gentler social beliefs. Yet Alfred Stewart produced a classic apocalyptic science fiction tale in *Nordenholt's Million* (justly dubbed "exciting and terrifying reading" by the *Spectator*), as well as superb detective novels boasting well-wrought puzzles, bracing characterization, and an occasional leavening of dry humor. Not long after Stewart's death in 1947, the Connington novels fell entirely out of print. The recent embrace of Stewart's fiction in recent publishing is a welcome

[1] For more on Street, Crofts and particularly Stewart, see Curtis Evans, *Masters of the "Humdrum" Mystery: Cecil John Charles Street, Freeman Wills Crofts, Alfred Walter Stewart and the British Detective Novel, 1920-1961* (Jefferson, NC: McFarland, 2012). On the academic career of Alfred Walter Stewart, see his entry in *Oxford Dictionary of National Biography* (London and New York: Oxford University Press, 2004), vol. 52, 627-628.

event indeed, correcting as it does over sixty years of underserved neglect of an accomplished genre writer.

Born in Glasgow on September 5, 1880, Alfred Stewart had significant exposure to religion in his earlier life. His father was William Stewart, longtime Professor of Divinity and Biblical Criticism at Glasgow University, and he married Lily Coats, a daughter of the Reverend Jervis Coats and member of one of Scotland's preeminent Baptist families. Religious sensibility is entirely absent from the Connington corpus, however. A confirmed secularist, Stewart once referred to one of his wife's brothers, the Reverend William Holms Coats (1881-1954), principal of the Scottish Baptist College, as his "mental and spiritual antithesis," bemusedly adding: "It's quite an education to see what one would look like if one were turned into one's mirror-image."

Stewart's J. J. Connington pseudonym was derived from a nineteenth-century Oxford Professor of Latin and translator of Horace, indicating that Stewart's literary interests lay not in pietistic writing but rather in the pre-Christian classics ("I prefer the *Odyssey* to *Paradise Lost*," the author once avowed). Possessing an inquisitive and expansive mind, Stewart was in fact an uncommonly well-read individual, freely ranging over a variety of literary genres. His deep immersion in French literature and supernatural horror fiction, for example, is documented in his lively correspondence with the noted horologist Rupert Thomas Gould.[2]

It thus is not surprising that in the 1920s the intellectually restless Stewart, having achieved a distinguished middle age as a highly regarded man of science, decided to apply his creative energy to a new endeavor, the writing of fiction. After several years he settled,

[2] The Gould-Stewart correspondence is discussed in considerable detail in *Masters of the "Humdrum" Mystery*. For more on the life of the fascinating Rupert Thomas Gould, see Jonathan Betts, *Time Restored: The Harrison Timekeepers and R. T. Gould, the Man Who Knew (Almost) Everything* (London and New York: Oxford University Press, 2006) and the British film *Longitude* (2000), which details Gould's restoration of the marine chronometers built by in the eighteenth-century by the clockmaker John Harrison.

like other gifted men and women of his generation, on the wildly popular mystery genre. Stewart was modest about his accomplishments in this particular field of light fiction, telling Rupert Gould later in life that "I write these things [what Stewart called tec yarns] because they amuse me in parts when I am putting them together and because they are the only writings of mine that the public will look at. Also, in a minor degree, because I like to think some people get pleasure out of them." No doubt Stewart's single most impressive literary accomplishment is *Nordenholt's Million*, yet in their time the two dozen J. J. Connington mysteries did indeed give readers in Great Britain, the United States, and other countries much diversionary reading pleasure. Today these works constitute an estimable addition to British crime fiction.

After his 'prentice pastiche mystery, *Death at Swaythling Court* (1926), a rural English country house tale set in the highly traditional village of Fernhurst Parva, Stewart published another, superior country house affair, *The Dangerfield Talisman* (1926), a novel about the baffling theft of a precious family heirloom, an ancient, jewel-encrusted armlet. This clever murderless tale, which likely is the one that the author told Rupert Gould he wrote in under six weeks, was praised in *The Bookman* as "continuously exciting and interesting" and in the *New York Times Book Review* as "ingeniously fitted together and, what is more, written with a deal of real literary charm." Despite its virtues, however, *The Dangerfield Talisman* is not fully characteristic of mature Connington detective fiction. The author needed a memorable series sleuth, more representative of his own forceful personality.

It was the next year, 1927, that saw "J. J. Connington" make his break to the front of the murdermongerer's pack with a third country house mystery, *Murder in the Maze*, wherein debuted as the author's great series detective the assertive and acerbic Sir Clinton Driffield, along with Sir Clinton's neighbor and "Watson," the more genial (if much less astute) Squire Wendover. In this much praised novel, Stewart's detective duo confronts some truly diabolical doings, including slayings by means of curare-tipped darts in the double-centered hedge maze at a country estate,

Whistlefield. No less a fan of the genre than T. S. Eliot praised *Murder in the Maze* for its construction ("we are provided early in the story with all the clues which guide the detective") and its liveliness ("The very idea of murder in a box hedge labyrinth does the author great credit, and he makes full use of its possibilities"). The delighted Eliot concluded that *Murder in the Maze* was "a really first-rate detective story." For his part, the critic H. C. Harwood declared in *The Outlook* that with the publication of *Murder in the Maze* Connington demanded and deserved "comparison with the masters." "Buy, borrow, or—anyhow get hold of it," he amusingly advised. Two decades later, in his 1946 critical essay "The Grandest Game in the World," the great locked room detective novelist John Dickson Carr echoed Eliot's assessment of the novel's virtuoso setting, writing: "These 1920s . . . thronged with sheer brains. What would be one of the best possible settings for violent death? J. J. Connington found the answer, with *Murder in the Maze.*" Certainly in retrospect *Murder in the Maze* stands as one of the finest English country house mysteries of the 1920s, cleverly yet fairly clued, imaginatively detailed and often grimly suspenseful. As the great American true crime writer Edmund Lester Pearson noted in his review of *Murder in the Maze* in *The Outlook*, this Connington novel had everything that one could desire in a detective story: "A shrubbery maze, a hot day, and somebody potting at you with an air gun loaded with darts covered with a deadly South-American arrow-poison—*there* is a situation to wheedle two dollars out of anybody's pocket."[3]

Staying with what had for him worked so well, Stewart the same year produced yet another country house mystery, *Tragedy at Ravensthorpe*, an ingenious tale of murders and thefts at the ancestral home of the Chacewaters, old family friends of Sir Clinton Driffield. There is much clever matter in *Ravensthorpe*. Especially fascinating is the authors inspired integration of faerie folklore into his plot. Stewart, who had a lifelong—though skeptical—interest

[3] Potential purchasers of *Murder in the Maze* should keep in mind that $2 in 1927 is worth over $26 today!

in paranormal phenomena, probably was inspired in this instance by the recent hubbub over the Cottingley Faeries photographs that in the early 1920s had famously duped, among other individuals, Arthur Conan Doyle.[4] As with *Murder in the Maze*, critics raved this new Connington mystery. In the *Spectator*, for example, a reviewer hailed *Tragedy at Ravensthorpe* in the strongest terms, declaring of the novel: "This is more than a good detective tale. Alike in plot, characterization, and literary style, it is a work of art."

In 1928 there appeared two additional Sir Clinton Driffield detective novels, *Mystery at Lynden Sands* and *The Case with Nine Solutions*. Once again there was great praise for the latest Conningtons. H. C. Harwood, a critic who, as we have seen, had so much admired *Murder in the Maze*, opined of *Mystery at Lynden Sands* that it "may just fail of being the detective story of the century," while in the United States author and book reviewer Frederic F. Van de Water expressed nearly as high an opinion of *The Case with Nine Solutions*. "This book is a thoroughbred of a distinguished lineage that runs back to 'The Gold Bug' of [Edgar Allan] Poe," he avowed. "It represents the highest type of detective fiction." In both of these Connington novels, Stewart moved away from his customary country house milieu, setting *Lynden Sands* at a fashionable beach resort and *Nine Solutions* at a scientific

[4] In a 1920 article in *The Strand Magazine* Arthur Conan Doyle endorsed as real prank photographs of purported fairies taken by two English girls in the garden of a house in the village of Cottingley. In the aftermath of the Great War Doyle had become a fervent believer in Spiritualism and other paranormal phenomena. Especially embarrassing to Doyle's admirers today, Doyle also published *The Coming of the Faeries* (1922), wherein he argued that these mystical creatures genuinely existed. "When the spirits came in, the common sense oozed out," Stewart once wrote bluntly to his friend Rupert Gould of the creator of Sherlock Holmes. Like Gould, however, Stewart had an intense interest in the subject of the Loch Ness Monster, believing that he, his wife and daughter had cited a large marine creature of some sort in Loch Ness in 1935. A year earlier Gould had authored *The Loch Ness Monster and Others*, and it was this book which led Stewart, after he made his "Nessie" sighting, to initiate correspondence with Gould.

research institute. *Nine Solutions* is of particular interest today, I think, for its relatively frank sexual subject matter and its modern urban setting among science professionals, which rather resembles the locales found in P. D. James' classic detective novels *A Mind to Murder* (1963) and *Shroud for a Nightingale* (1971).

By the end of the decade of the 1920s, the critical reputation of "J. J. Connington" had achieved enviable heights indeed. At this time Stewart became one of the charter members of the Detection Club, an assemblage of the finest writers of British detective fiction that included, among other distinguished individuals, Agatha Christie, Dorothy L. Sayers and G. K. Chesterton. Certainly Victor Gollancz, the British publisher of the J. J. Connington mysteries, did not stint praise for the author, informing readers that "J. J. Connington is now established as, in the opinion of many, the greatest living master of the story of pure detection. He is one of those who, discarding all the superfluities, has made of deductive fiction a genuine minor art, with its own laws and its own conventions."

Such warm praise for J. J. Connington makes it all the more surprising that at this juncture the esteemed author tinkered with his successful formula by dispensing with his original series detective. In the fifth Clinton Driffield detective novel, *Nemesis at Raynham Parva* (1929), Alfred Walter Stewart, rather like Arthur Conan Doyle before him, seemed with a dramatic dénouement to have devised his popular series detective's permanent exit from the fictional stage (read it and see for yourself). The next two Connington detective novels, *The Eye in the Museum* (1929) and *The Two Tickets Puzzle* (1930), have a different series detective, Superintendent Ross, a rather dull dog of a policeman. While both these mysteries are competently done—the railway material in *The Two Tickets Puzzle* is particularly effective and should have appeal today—the presence of Sir Clinton Driffield (no superfluity he!) is missed.

Probably Stewart detected that the public minded the absence of the brilliant and biting Sir Clinton, for the Chief Constable—accompanied, naturally, by his friend Squire Wendover—triumphantly returned in 1931 in *The Boathouse Riddle*, another well-constructed criminous country house affair. Later in the year came *The Sweepstake Murders*, which boasts the perennially popular tontine multiple murder plot, in this case a rapid succession of puzzling suspicious deaths afflicting the members of a sweepstake syndicate that has just won nearly 250,000 pounds.[5] Adding piquancy to this plot is the fact that Wendover is one of the imperiled syndicate members. Altogether the novel is, as the late Jacques Barzun and his colleague Wendell Hertig Taylor put it in *A Catalogue of Crime* (1971/1989), their magisterial survey of detective fiction, "one of Connington's best conceptions."

Stewart's productivity as a fiction writer slowed in the 1930s, so that, barring the year 1938, at most only one new Connington appeared annually (because of the onset of serious health maladies, Stewart was unable to publish any Connington novel in 1936). However, in 1932 Stewart produced one of the best Connington mysteries, *The Castleford Conundrum*. A classic country house detective novel, Castleford introduces to readers Stewart's most delightfully unpleasant set of greedy relations and one of his most deserving murderees, Winifred Castleford. Stewart also fashions a wonderfully rich puzzle plot, full of meaty material clues for the reader's delectation. *Castleford* presented critics with no conundrum over its quality. "In *The Castleford Conundrum* Mr. Connington goes to work like an accomplished chess-player. The moves in the games his detectives are called on to play are a delight to watch," raved the reviewer for the *Sunday Times*, adding that "the clues would have rejoiced Mr. Holmes' heart." For its part, the *Spectator* concurred in the *Sunday Times*' assessment of the novel's masterfully-constructed plot: "Few detective stories show such sound reasoning as that by which the Chief Constable brings the crime home to the culprit." Additionally, E. C. Bentley, much

[5] A tontine is a financial arrangement wherein shareowners in a common fund receive annuities that increase in value with the death of each participant, with the entire amount of the fund going to the last survivor. The impetus that the tontine provided to the deadly creative imaginations of Golden Age mystery writers should be sufficiently obvious.

admired himself as the author of the landmark detective novel *Trent's Last Case*, took time to praise Connington's purely literary virtues, noting: "Mr. Connington has never written better, or drawn characters more full of life."

With *Tom Tiddler's Island* in 1933 Stewart produced a different sort of Connington, a criminal gang mystery in the rather more breathless style of such hugely popular English thriller writers as Sapper, Sax Rohmer, John Buchan and Edgar Wallace (in violation of the strict detective fiction rules of Ronald Knox, there is even a secret passage in the novel). Detailing the startling discoveries made by a newlywed couple honeymooning on a remote Scottish island, *Tom Tiddler's Island* is an atmospheric and entertaining tale, though it is not as mentally stimulating for armchair sleuths as Stewart's true detective novels. The title, incidentally, refers to an ancient British children's game, "Tom Tiddler's Ground," in which one child tries to hold a height against other children.

After his fictional Scottish excursion into thrillerdom, Stewart returned the next year to his English country house roots with *The Ha-Ha Case* (1934), his last masterwork in this classic mystery setting. (For elucidation of non-British readers, a ha-ha is a sunken wall, placed so to delineate property boundaries while not obstructing views.) Although *The Ha-Ha Case* is not set in Scotland, Stewart drew inspiration for the novel from a notorious Scottish true crime, the 1893 Ardlamont murder case. From the facts of the Ardlamont affair Stewart drew several of the key characters in *The Ha-Ha Case*, as well as the circumstances of the novel's murder (a shooting "accident" while hunting), though he added complications that take the tale in a new direction.[6]

[6] At Ardlamont, a large country estate in Argyll, Cecil Hambrough died from a gunshot wound while hunting. Cecil's tutor, Alfred John Monson, and another man, both of whom were out hunting with Cecil, claimed that Cecil had accidentally shot himself; but Monson was arrested and tried for Cecil's murder. The verdict delivered was "not proven," but Monson was then—and is today—considered almost certainly to have been guilty of the murder. On the Ardlamont case, see William Roughead, *Classic Crimes* (1951; repr., New York: New York Review Books Classics, 2000), 378-464.

In newspaper reviews both Dorothy L. Sayers and "Francis Iles" (crime novelist Anthony Berkeley Cox) highly praised this latest mystery by "The Clever Mr. Connington," as he was now dubbed on book jackets by his new English publisher, Hodder and Stoughton. Sayers particularly noted the effective characterization in *The Ha-Ha Case*: "There is no need to say that Mr. Connington has given us a sound and interesting plot, very carefully and ingeniously worked out. In addition, there are the three portraits of the three brothers, cleverly and rather subtly characterised, of the [governess], and of Inspector Hinton, whose admirable qualities are counteracted by that besetting sin of the man who has made his own way: a jealousy of delegating responsibility." The reviewer for the *Times Literary Supplement* detected signs that the sardonic Sir Clinton Driffield had begun mellowing with age: "Those who have never really liked Sir Clinton's perhaps excessively soldierly manner will be surprised to find that he makes his discovery not only by the pure light of intelligence, but partly as a reward for amiability and tact, qualities in which the Inspector [Hinton] was strikingly deficient." This is true enough, although the classic Sir Clinton emerges a number of times in the novel, as in his subtly sarcastic recurrent backhanded praise of Inspector Hinton: "He writes a first class report."

Clinton Driffield returned the next year in the detective novel *In Whose Dim Shadow* (1935), a tale set in a recently erected English suburb, the denizens of which seem to have committed an impressive number of indiscretions, including sexual ones. The intriguing title of the British edition of the novel is drawn from a poem by the British historian Thomas Babington Macaulay: "Those trees in whose dim shadow/The ghastly priest doth reign/The priest who slew the slayer/And shall himself be slain." Stewart's puzzle plot in *In Whose Dim Shadow* is well-clued and compelling, the kicker of a closing paragraph is a classic of its kind and, additionally, the author paints some excellent character portraits. I fully concur in the *Sunday Times* assessment of the tale: "Quiet domestic murder, full of the neatest detective points. . . . These [characters] are not the detective's stock figures, but fully realised human beings."[7]

Uncharacteristically for Stewart, nearly twenty months elapsed between the publication of *In Whose Dim Shadow* and his next book, *A Minor Operation* (1937). The reason for the author's delay in production was the onset in 1935-36 of the afflictions of cataracts and heart disease (Stewart ultimately succumbed to heart disease in 1947). Despite the grave health complications that beset him at this time, Stewart in late 1936 was able to complete *A Minor Operation*, a first-rate Clinton Driffield story of murder and a most baffling disappearance. A *Times Literary Supplement* reviewer found that *A Minor Operation* treated the reader "to exactly the right mixture of mystification and clue" and that, in addition to its impressive construction, the novel boasted "character-drawing above the average" for a detective novel.

Alfred Stewart's final eight mysteries, which appeared between 1938 and 1947, the year of the author's death, are, on the whole, a somewhat weaker group of tales than the sixteen that appeared between 1926 and 1937, yet they are not without interest. In 1938 Stewart for the last time managed to publish two detective novels, *Truth Comes Limping* and *For Murder Will Speak*. The latter tale is much the superior of the two, having an interesting suburban setting and a bevy of female characters found to have motives when a contemptible philandering businessman meets with foul play. Sexual neurosis plays a major role in *For Murder Will Speak*, the

[7] For the genesis of the title, see Macaulay's "The Battle of the Lake Regillus," from his narrative poem collection *Lays of Ancient Rome*. In this poem Macaulay alludes to the ancient cult of Diana Nemorensis, which elevated its priests through trial by combat. Study of the practices of the Diana Nemorensis cult influenced Sir James George Frazer's cultural interpretation of religion in his most renowned work, *The Golden Bough: A Study in Magic and Religion*. As with *Tom Tiddler's Island* and *The Ha-Ha Case* the title *In Whose Dim Shadow* proved too esoteric for Connington's American publishers, Little, Brown and Co., who altered it to the more prosaic *The Tau Cross Mystery*.

ever-thorough Stewart obviously having made a study of the subject when writing the novel. The somewhat squeamish reviewer for *Scribner's Magazine* considered the subject matter of *For Murder Will Speak* "rather unsavory at times," yet this individual conceded that the novel nevertheless made "first-class reading for those who enjoy a good puzzle intricately worked out." "Judge Lynch" in the *Saturday Review* apparently had no such moral reservations about the latest Clinton Driffield murder case, avowing simply of the novel: "They don't come any better."

Over the next couple years Stewart again sent Sir Clinton Driffield temporarily packing, replacing him with a new series detective, a brash radio personality named Mark Brand, in *The Counsellor* (1939) and *The Four Defences* (1940). The better of these two novels is *The Four Defences*, which Stewart based on another notorious British true crime case, the Alfred Rouse blazing car murder. (Rouse is believed to have fabricated his death by murdering an unknown man, placing the dead man's body in his car and setting the car on fire, in the hope that the murdered man's body would be taken for his.) Though admittedly a thinly characterized academic exercise in ratiocination, Stewart's *Four Defences* surely is also one of the most complexly plotted Golden Age detective novels ever written and should delight devotees of classical detection. Taking the Rouse blazing car affair as his theme, Stewart composes from it a stunning set of diabolically ingenious criminal variations. "This is in the cold-blooded category which . . . excites a crossword puzzle kind of interest," the reviewer for the *Times Literary Supplement* acutely noted of the novel. "Nothing in the Rouse case would prepare you for these complications upon complications. . . . What they prove is that Mr. Connington has the power of penetrating into the puzzle-corner of the brain. He leaves it dazedly wondering whether in the records of actual crime there can be any dark deed to equal this in its planned convolutions."

Sir Clinton Driffield returned to action in the remaining four detective novels in the Connington oeuvre, *The Twenty-One Clues* (1941), *No Past Is Dead* (1942), *Jack-in-the-Box* (1944) and *Commonsense Is All You Need* (1947), all of which were written as

Stewart's heart disease steadily worsened and reflect to some extent his diminishing physical and mental energy. Although *The Twenty-One Clues* was inspired by the notorious Hall-Mills double murder case—probably the most publicized murder case in the United States in the 1920s—and the American critic Anthony Boucher commended *Jack-in-the-Box*, I believe the best of these later mysteries is *No Past Is Dead*, which Stewart partly based on a bizarre French true crime affair, the 1891 Achet-Lepine murder case.[8] Besides providing an interesting background for the tale, the ailing author managed some virtuoso plot twists, of the sort most associated today with that ingenious Golden Age Queen of Crime, Agatha Christie.

What Stewart with characteristic bluntness referred to as "my complete crack-up" forced his retirement from Queen's University in 1944. "I am afraid," Stewart wrote a friend, the chemist and forensic scientist F. Gerald Tryhorn, in August, 1946, eleven months before his death, "that I shall never be much use again. Very stupidly, I tried for a session to combine a full course of lecturing with angina pectoris; and ended up by establishing that the two are immiscible." He added that since retiring in 1944, he had been physically "limited to my house, since even a fifty-yard crawl brings on the usual cramps." Stewart completed his essay collection and a final novel before he died at his study desk in his Belfast home on July 1, 1947, at the age of sixty-six. When death came to the author he was busy at work, writing.

More than six decades after Alfred Walter Stewart's death, his "J. J. Connington" fiction again is available to a wider audience of classic mystery fans, rather than strictly limited to a select company of rare book collectors with deep pockets. This is fitting for an individual who was one of the finest writers of British genre fiction between the two world wars. "Heaven forfend that you should imagine I take myself for anything out of the common in

[8] Stewart analyzed the Achet-Lepine case in detail in "The Mystery of Chantelle," one of the best essays in his 1947 collection, *Alias J. J. Connington*.

the tec yarn stuff," Stewart once self-deprecatingly declared in a letter to Rupert Gould. Yet, as contemporary critics recognized, as a writer of detective and science fiction Stewart indeed was something out of the common. Now more modern readers can find this out for themselves. They have much good sleuthing in store.

THE EYE IN THE MUSEUM

CHAPTER I
AT THE STRUAN MUSEUM

"Not so very far to walk, was it?"

Leslie Seaforth swung open the big door in the wall and ushered his fiancée into the grounds of the Struan Museum. As the latch clicked behind them, the girl took a step or two up the path and looked about her in unconcealed surprise.

"What a lovely place, Leslie! I'd no notion we'd come to anything like this at the top of that miserable little back road. Just look at those flower-beds; the tints are simply gorgeous."

Seaforth, having fastened the door, came forward to the girl's side again. He was under thirty, six or seven years older than Joyce. Among his acquaintances he had the reputation of being a good friend or a bad enemy; and in his natural expression there was a trace of hardness which might easily deepen into ruthlessness. It vanished as he watched Joyce Hazlemere's delight in the scene before her.

"Funny you never thought of coming up here before," he pointed out. "Rather like the Londoners who never go near the Tower. Within ten minutes' walk of your house; and the very place for you when the home atmosphere grows a bit too sultry for your nerves."

At this last phrase, Joyce's brows contracted for an instant, but she recovered herself almost at once.

"I expect that dingy little lane put me off," she said, lightly. "And the notice-board at the end of it isn't enticing. 'The Struan Museum. Admission, *3d.* Season Tickets, *2s. 6d.*' Do any human beings ever buy season tickets for museums? Museums always sound so fusty, somehow, and full of all sorts of frightfully educational things that bore you stiff even to look at. I'm thankful I never went in very heartily for museums. Do you sell many season tickets, really?"

Seaforth disclaimed any definite knowledge of the matter.

"Old Jim Buckland, the Keeper, could tell you," he answered. "I'm only a sort of Secretary to the Struan Trust, you know. Touches his cap to me, Jim, of course; but he believes in his heart that the real Panjandrum is the cove who takes the threepences at the door. Come to think of it, I don't remember passing any rush-order for reprinting season tickets lately. Even the threepences are few and far between. One or two kids turn up now and again. Come here to gloat over some Chinese prints showing select tortures, and go away again sated with horrors. Expect they wake screaming in the night at the thought of those pictures."

"Don't be gruesome, Leslie. I think we'll give those pictures a miss. I don't want to wake screaming in the night."

She turned away to gaze across the gardens. Seaforth made no effort to distract her attention. He was quite content to wait beside this fair-haired girl, whose hazel eyes sent a thrill through him every time he met their glance. Though in the last two years his memory had stored up pictures of her in every attitude, he always seemed to find something fresh in her. Wonderful luck he'd had, he reflected for the thousandth time. Joyce had come back from the Continent to live with that aunt of hers; and six weeks after he'd seen her for the first time, they were engaged. As soon as he saw her, he'd known what he wanted; and he'd got his own way even quicker than he had hoped. These were the sort of recollections one could find some pleasure in. It was the later stages that didn't bear thinking about. To stand aside and see Joyce worried and badgered, and to be unable to lift a finger to help—that was a nasty experience. Curse this money question!

Joyce, looking around, saw his expression and guessed the cause.

"This looks just like the garden of an old private house," she commented, with the evident intention of rousing him from his thoughts.

"Why not? Old Struan lived here; the Museum's his house. Collecting was his hobby. He didn't know a good thing from a bad one, though; just gathered in everything that came along and labeled it. Sort of human raven or jackdaw, you'd think, to judge from the results."

Joyce looked up at the house among the trees.

"What's that funny tower sort of thing on the roof?" she demanded.

"Another of old Struan's curiosities. Let you see it when we go up, if you like. Next to the Chinese tortures, it's the kids' greatest joy. They love it."

Joyce turned her hazel eyes on him in mock perplexity.

"I suppose it's this legal training of yours, Leslie. You sometimes talk a lot without conveying much to a plain person like me. What *is* the thing?"

"A *camera obscura*, they call it."

"That helps a lot. Thanks ever so much."

"Easiest way's to show you the thing; saves explanations. What about moving along now? Sort of official visit, this, you know. Old Jim Buckland's been seedy lately, and the doctor told him to go away for a change. Jim hates it; but he hands over the Great Seal and the petty cash to-day, and I pass 'em on to Mrs. Jim. She's to take in the threepences while he's on leave."

Joyce gave a final glance over the gardens. Flowers meant more to her than museums.

"Well, suppose we go on?" she conceded.

They turned toward the house.

"By the way," Seaforth requested, "treat old Jim nicely, Joyce. He's a devil of an old fusser and all that. Wrapped up in the collection and thinks no end of it. One can hardly shake him off when he starts. But he's really a decent old bird and burns to show off all the rubbish in the place to visitors. So few people ever put their noses over the door that he fairly spreads himself if he gets a chance."

Joyce agreed with a nod, and they made their way up to the Museum. Seaforth rang the bell, and in a few moments the door was opened by a pleasant-faced white-whiskered man in an official braided jacket.

"This is Miss Hazlemere, Buckland," Seaforth explained. "No objection to her having the run of the gardens any time she wants to, I suppose?"

"Pleased to meet you, Miss." Buckland made a ceremonious gesture which was saved from any touch of the ludicrous by his naturally old-fashioned manner. "If you want to visit the gardens, just come in when it suits you. Nice view we get over the town on a sunny day, Miss, very pretty indeed. We've got garden seats here and there, if you want to sit down. Just come in when it suits you. You needn't see me unless you want to."

Seaforth fished a sixpenny-bit from his pocket and solemnly handed it over. The keeper received it with equal formality.

"Would you sign the Visitors' Book, Miss? Here's a new pen. We've got quite a lot of distinguished signatures—I can show you Lord Gleneagle's, if you like. Foreign gentlemen, too. We've had three or four of them. Americans mostly. Greatly interested, they were. The last one we had was a very nice gentleman. He sent me a postcard from America afterwards."

Joyce wrote her name in the book, and the old man blotted the ink with scrupulous care when she laid down her pen. Bearing Seaforth's injunctions in mind, she put a question:

"Did you ever pay a visit to the British Museum?"

Old Jim's pleasure at this opening was refreshing.

"The British Museum, Miss? Yes, I was there once. A very fine collection, I thought it, very good indeed. Not but what we've got some things here that they can't beat. Our five-legged stuffed calf, now: I saw nothing so strange as that in London. And Signor Antonio Manetti's pottery collection, too. Mr. Struan picked that up very cheap, a great bargain. Phoenician, some of it; Greek and Roman specimens, too; and there's a Cyprian vase that's reckoned to be over two thousand years old. I'll let you see it. You shouldn't miss it."

A fresh thought struck Joyce.

"I suppose all this talk about the Portland Vase must have interested you?"

"The Portland Vase, Miss?"

Evidently the name suggested nothing to old Jim.

"Yes. Don't you remember all the talk about it in the newspapers when the Duke of Portland took it away from the British Museum?"

Old Jim shook his head.

"No, Miss. You see, I never read the newspapers. I haven't opened one for years. No time for reading. The collection keeps me busy; what with dusting it, and writing fresh labels, and looking after it generally, it's as much as a man can do to keep pace with the work. And now, Miss, if you'll allow me, I'll just show you round, so that you won't be missing any of our best things."

"Not much time to spare, this visit," Seaforth interjected warningly as he glanced at his watch. "Just show Miss Hazlemere one or two of the most interesting things, Buckland. She'll come again and see more another time."

"Just as you say, sir," the keeper acquiesced in a slightly wounded tone. "I'll just show her Mr. Struan's Eye and one or two of the other gems of the collection. Then she can come later on and go over the rest at her leisure, if that suits her."

"Mr. Struan's Eye?" asked Joyce, with a slight shudder. "That sounds rather grisly. I'm not sure I'd like it."

Buckland's white-fringed face was creased by a reassuring smile.

"Oh, no, Miss, it's not what you think it is. Quite a work of art, you'll see. Now, if you'll be so good as to follow me, I'll take you to it first of all."

Joyce made a grimace at her fiancé behind the keeper's back; but she obediently followed the old man through what had been the hall of the mansion and into one of the rooms filled with glass cases.

"This is Mr. Struan's Eye," said old Buckland, halting before one of the cabinets and tapping the glass.

Joyce came up beside him and glanced at the object which he indicated.

"Why it's a glass eye!" she exclaimed.

"Yes, Miss. They haven't its match in the British Museum, I can assure you. I made special inquiry about that, when I was there. Very interested they were to hear about it, too."

His voice unconsciously took on the sing-song tone of the guide who has exhibited and described the same object times without number.

"Mr. Struan, Miss, had the great misfortune to lose the sight of his right eye when he was a boy. A playmate one day threw quicklime into his face and destroyed the eyeball. It had to be removed, Miss; a very serious and dangerous operation in those days when they had no anaesthetics. And Mr. Struan was very conscious of the disfigurement it left. He was a very fine gentleman, and he was very sensitive about the matter.

"Then, about the year eighteen hundred and fifty, a Frenchman of the name of Poissonceau invented the artificial eye made from glass; and a Mr. Müller of Lauscha—that's in Germany, Miss—began to make these new artificial eyes. Mr. Struan heard about this; so he traveled night and day until he got to Lauscha. He was so quick about it, that this Eye before you is the third one that Mr. Müller made—which means that it's a specimen of real historical interest and almost unique, as you can understand.

"Naturally, Mr. Struan's Eye caused great interest and excitement in this neighbourhood when he came back from Germany. People used to wait in the street for him to go by, so that they might have an opportunity of examining it."

He paused for a moment to allow his audience time to assimilate the information he had given them.

"This Eye, Miss," he went on, "has another claim to the attention. It was this very Eye that gave Mr. Struan the idea of founding his Museum. He'd got this great curiosity in his possession, and he soon set about finding other things to go with it. And then, when he died and there was no further need for his Eye, it was directed in his last testament that this valuable object should be placed in the collection: the foundation and the copestone in one, as might be said. Take a good look at it, Miss; it's well worth your attention."

Bored but still polite, Joyce pretended to make a close examination of the rather primitive sample of glass-work, until old Jim was satisfied that she had appreciated all its virtues.

"And now, Miss, I'd like to show you something else that you won't find in the British Museum. Mr. Struan was a great traveler in his day; and he collected specimens of the waters of all the great rivers: the Rhine, the Danube, the Volga, the Rhône, the Jordan, and some others. Here they are in these jars on this shelf. Very interesting and instructive."

He smiled with a child-like air of cunning.

"Now I'll tell you something I don't tell the public. The Volga water's not just all I'd like it to be. A little accident happened to the jar, once upon a time; and we had to fill it up to the level with some ordinary water. But, of course there's no real deception, Miss. There's water from the Volga in the jar, quite correct, just as it says on the label."

Attracted, despite her boredom, by the old man's simple pride in this collection of rubbish, Joyce allowed him to lead her from place to place and show her what he regarded as the star pieces of the Museum: the broken orrery with its tarnished brass planets, the dingy bird of Paradise, the flint arrowheads, the stuffed crocodile, and Signor Antonio Manetti's pottery. Only when old Jim attempted to display the Chinese prints did she object firmly.

Seaforth intervened when the old man seemed anxious to press the point.

"Don't think that's the sort of thing Miss Hazlemere would care to see, Buckland."

"You think not, sir? Not the one they call 'The Human Pig'? It's very curious and interesting; and not nearly so nasty as some of them."

"No, certainly not 'The Human Pig,'" Seaforth interrupted in a tone that put an end to argument. "What Miss Hazlemere wants to see is the *camera obscura*. I'll show it to her myself. Don't you bother to come up."

Old Jim's face fell. Evidently he felt sorely disappointed at being robbed of the chance of acting as showman.

"You're sure you can work it yourself, sir?"

Seaforth's curt nod convinced him that there was no appeal, so he gave in with a good grace.

"You'll find the *camera obscura* most interesting, Miss," he assured Joyce. "I often go up there and have a look round the town myself, when I can spare ten minutes or so. It keeps me in touch, more or less, now that I can't walk far and get about as I used to do. It's almost as good as being in the streets yourself and meeting all your friends. A wonderful invention, Miss, very curious. That's another thing they haven't got in the British Museum. When you come down again, Miss, you'll find me here. You must see the five-legged calf before you go; it wouldn't do to miss that."

He hovered uncertainly as though he were still in hopes that his services might be required; then, as Seaforth led the girl towards a spiral staircase, he turned away with the air of a dog dismissed and sent home in the middle of a walk.

At the head of the spiral, Seaforth opened a door and stood back to allow Joyce to go in before him. She found herself in almost complete obscurity. All she could distinguish was a white table-top, its mat surface shining faintly in a pale beam of light which fell vertically upon it from the top of the tower away above their heads. Then, as her eyes grew accustomed to the gloom, she perceived what she took to be some wheels and cables on the wall beside the table.

Seaforth's arm guided her toward the faint glow of the illuminated table-top; and when she reached it, her exploratory forefinger discovered that the four-foot disc was whitened with a coating of distemper. Seaforth, by her side, reached up to the controls; and she heard from the cupola of the tower above them a sound of some heavy body moving on rollers. Then, so unexpectedly as to take her aback, a brilliant picture flashed out upon the pallid surface under her eyes.

"Why, it's the main street!" she exclaimed. "I can see the people walking about there, as clearly as if I were just beside them. And what lovely colours! Why, the leaves on the trees seem greener than real leaves. I can see them fluttering."

For a moment or two she gazed at the picture without speaking, so interested was she in watching the objects moving in the field of vision.

"This beats the cinema hollow," she continued, when she had grown accustomed to the apparatus. "It's ever so much more vivid. I don't wonder that the old man likes to come up here, just to watch it. Oh! There's Dr. Platt in his car."

The image of a young man in a two-seater slid swiftly across the disc as she spoke, and vanished out of the picture. His appearance seemed to have started a train of thought in Seaforth's mind.

"What on earth persuades that aunt of yours to employ Platt as family doctor?" he asked in a tone which showed that he hardly expected an answer. "I've seldom struck a medical with a worse manner. Gives you the impression of an absolute rabbit, somehow. No confidence in himself."

Joyce was still intent on the ever-changing picture of the street.

"Oh, he lives just along the road," she suggested. "It's handy, if anything goes wrong, you know. Though of course Dr. Hyndford's house is right opposite, across the river; and we could get him to come over in his canoe just as easy as we can get Dr. Platt. I wonder why Aunt Evelyn doesn't think of that. She's friendly enough with Dr. Hyndford, and he's a better doctor, too."

"Curious," Seaforth replied, without encouraging her to pursue the subject further.

More than once, the idea had crossed his mind that perhaps the objection came from the doctor's side. The General Medical Council deals severely with physicians who are too intimate with their women patients; and from that point of view it was probably safer for Dr. Hyndford to have nothing to do with Mrs. Fenton professionally. He had little to gain by acting as her medical adviser; and there was no need for him to run the risk of being struck off the Register.

"Now we'll have a look at something else," Seaforth proposed, beginning to shift the controls.

As he moved them, the picture of the street seemed to flow sidelong from the table, vanishing with disconcerting smoothness into the air beyond, while on the opposite side of the disc fresh images sprang into life out of the void and slipped swiftly across the field of vision.

"A bit further round," Seaforth said, "and you'll see something you know well."

He turned the lenses in the cupola further, seeking for the object. He meant to show her an arbour in Mrs. Fenton's garden, the place where they had sat when he asked her to marry him.

"Go a bit slower, Leslie, please. The way that picture slides across the table's almost uncanny. It makes me a bit giddy to watch it. I suppose it's because one's so close to it that it seems far more vivid than the cinema."

"Just coming to it. . . . Wait. . . . There!"

But as he brought the lenses to rest, he saw that his little effect was ruined. The arbour was in the picture; but he had not foreseen that it might be occupied. In one of the chairs lolled a hard-faced woman of about forty: expensively dressed, carefully finished, but looking every day of her age despite all the effort she made to compete with the younger generation. A notebook and pencil lay to hand on the cane table beside her; and a pink newspaper spread disordered sheets on the floor where she had dropped it. With her hands indolently clasped behind her head, she leaned back in her chair and addressed the second occupant of the arbour; and the picture on the disc, large and clean-focused, was so clear that the two watchers in the tower could see the movement of her thin flexible lips as she spoke.

The second figure on the screen was a clean-shaven, heavy-featured man, some five or six years older than the woman. In his younger days he had been athletic; but as middle age drew on, muscle had been replaced by flesh; and now without being ungainly, he had lost all spring in his movements. As he lounged in his chair, listening to Mrs. Fenton, his grey flannels and well-worn Panama gave no clue to his profession. Joyce saw him shake his head decidedly, as though negativing some suggestion which her aunt had made.

At the side of the picture, a neat maid came through the open French window of the house and approached the arbour. Mrs. Fenton turned in her chair, took what appeared to be the brown envelope of a telegram, tore it open eagerly, and then, after a glance at the message, threw it angrily on the floor.

"Another of her bets gone wrong," Seaforth interpreted sardonically.

"Yes," Joyce confirmed ruefully. "And that means you'd better not come to dinner to-night. There's no use asking for trouble; and she'll be in one of her usual tempers, if I know the signs. You can take me on the river afterwards, though, if you like. Don't come up the backwater; it's not worth while. I'll be at the foot of the garden at nine o'clock and you can come alongside and pick me up."

"Dinner would be no great catch anyhow, I expect," Seaforth admitted, with an attempt to be philosophical. "I can't stand a woman who drinks nothing but stiff whiskey and soda with her food. Her being a relation of yours makes it worse instead of better."

He began to manoeuvre the controls.

"I've had about enough of that little idyll. Suppose we hunt for something else."

The image of the garden swept across the disc and as it vanished they saw for a moment a picture of Dr. Hyndford's canoe moored on the bank. Then, suddenly, the whole field was filled with a vision of smooth-flowing water, coursing swiftly across the disc.

"Why, it's just like standing on a bridge and watching the river flow under your eyes," Joyce exclaimed. "It looks so near that it seems funny it makes no noise when it ripples. . . . Oh, there's the Hyndfords' motor-boat, moored out in midstream. See the swirl of the water along the side; it's fascinating, somehow, to watch it."

Seaforth moved the controls at random and a fresh scene appeared on the screen.

"What's that?" Joyce asked, and then answered herself as she recognised it. "Oh, it's the garden of the Hyndfords' house, of course. I know it by that big bed of foxgloves. . . . And there's Mr.

Hyndford pottering about as usual. He's the decent one of the family, Leslie. I like him. Somehow he always gives me the impression that he's a bit nervous of that brother of his. You know those light-blue eyes the doctor's got—sort of eyes that seem to bore into you when they look at you. I've noticed sometimes that Mr. Hyndford hates to have them turned on him; and I don't wonder at it a bit. I don't like them myself."

Seaforth evidently felt that they had seen enough of the Hyndford family. With some touches on the controls, he brought the lenses to bear again upon the main street of the little town. For a few moments Joyce watched the picture without comment; then the sight of a familiar figure made her speak again.

"Look!"

Her extended finger threw its sharp shadow on the table as she pointed out a thin, slightly stooping figure which was walking with long strides along the pavement.

"There's Mr. Corwen, Leslie. Isn't it funny to see someone you know, walking along without the faintest notion that he's being overlooked? It makes me feel I'll never be able to move about in town after this without wondering whether someone up here isn't watching me.... He's going towards your office. Let's follow him up."

Seaforth obediently manoeuvred the controls so as to keep the lawyer in sight until he reached his destination and disappeared through a door which had a large brass plate beside it.

"It looked just as if he'd popped through the table," Joyce remarked, as the door closed behind the lawyer in the picture. "I suppose it's because this thing's so near, that one gets that queer feeling. After all, it's just a sort of cinema. Perhaps the bright colours make it look more like the real thing. I got quite a start when he vanished through that door."

After a momentary pause, she added:

"I do wish he'd hurry up and give you a partnership, Leslie."

This was evidently a sore point with both of them, as Seaforth's tone betrayed when he answered.

"James Corwen is a very nice man—but it hurts him damnably to part with a stiver. I'd chuck the whole business and go elsewhere to-morrow, if it weren't for the prospects. It'll be a thundering fine connection to drop into. And he's promised to take me in. He'll keep his word all right, some time, no fear on that score. But in the meanwhile—"

He broke off as though comment was needless.

"Seen enough, now?" he asked a moment later.

"I think so," Joyce decided. "I want to have a look at the gardens before we go. Why don't you get keen on flowers, Leslie? You don't seem to have the faintest interest in them; I can't think why. The only person I know who's really keen on gardening is Mr. Hyndford. He picked up a lot about it when he was out in the East; and he'll talk by the hour about plants if you get him on to the subject. Perhaps that's one reason I like him."

Seaforth showed no desire to pursue the subject. "Well, if you want to look round here, let's go down," he suggested, opening the door for the girl.

They descended the spiral stair; and as Joyce blinked in the bright afternoon light which flooded the Museum, she found old Jim beside her. He had come to the tower foot when he heard their steps.

"I heard you coming down, Miss, and I thought you'd like to see some of the other things, now, before you go. I'd like you to have a proper impression of the collection, Miss, seeing that it's your first visit to the Museum. Lots of interesting things still to see, if you'll let me take you round."

"Miss Hazlemere wants to look round the flowers in the garden, Buckland, before she goes. We haven't much time, so I'm afraid there's nothing further doing here to-day. She'll be up again, sometime."

Old Jim seemed to consider this poor consolation for a lost opportunity.

"You see, Miss, I'm going off first thing tomorrow; and I don't know when the doctor'll allow me to get back again. It would be a pity if you were to go round the place here without someone to explain all the valuable exhibits to you; you'd lose half the pleasure of it, Miss, that way."

Joyce exchanged a swift glance with her fiancé.

"Well, then, I tell you what I'll do," she promised. "I'll not put my foot over the door of the Museum till you come back again; then you can show me round properly. I'll keep to the gardens, if I come up at all."

"The very thing, Miss," old Jim agreed, somewhat comforted by this solution. "And did you like the *camera obscura*, Miss? Very interesting. Some evening you must come up and see the town by moonlight through it. That always makes a pretty picture."

"Very well, then. We'll wait till you come back again."

Old Jim conducted them ceremoniously to the door, but if he had hopes that Joyce would relent, he was disappointed. When they were out of earshot, she turned to Seaforth.

"Your friend's an old dear and all that, of course; but one could imagine that his cage ought to be labeled 'Bores (dangerous).' If it weren't that his pride in that awful collection's rather touching, I could have screamed and bitten him more than once. And now, let's have a look at the flowers."

For a time they wandered through the alleys of the old garden, Joyce engrossed in the contents of the flower-beds, whilst Seaforth concealed his complete lack of interest to the best of his power. At last, however, he succeeded in decoying her to a sheltered seat from which they could look over the sunny little town.

"You'd better keep something in reserve," he suggested. "You can come up here any time, now you know the way."

Joyce sighed faintly.

"It'll be some place where one can get away from things," she said, thoughtfully. "You know, Leslie, the longer it goes on, the worse it gets. You're a man, and you can't understand what it's like for me, living with Aunt Evelyn. If you were a girl, how would you like to be under the thumb of a woman of over forty who was jealous of your looks and hates you because she knows that at her age she can't compete with a girl amongst men? She can make you feel it in all sorts of ways."

"I suppose she can," Seaforth confirmed gloomily.

"And she's spiteful to the backbone, Leslie. Look at the way she's treating her husband. He wants a divorce, and I don't blame him a bit for that. At first I was rather against him. I didn't understand how the land lay, then; but now I do. He wants to shake off Aunt Evelyn and marry that girl, you know; and out of sheer spite, Aunt Evelyn won't divorce him. She's got enough evidence to do it if she wanted to; he'd be only too glad if she would. But just out of sheer malice she's letting things slide—just to keep him and the girl from putting things right."

"If I were in his shoes, I think I'd try to turn the tables on her. Surely it wouldn't be difficult as things are."

Joyce shook her head.

"Dr. Hyndford, you mean? Well, I'm as positive about that as I am about anything; but if you put me into the witness-box to-morrow, I couldn't give you a single bit of real evidence that would prove anything."

She paused for a moment as though thinking along a fresh line.

"All the same, I believe there may be something in it," she added. "Do you know, I saw Mr. Fenton in town yesterday. Of course he didn't come near us. It's just possible that he's come to look into things on the spot and see if he can pick anything up."

Then, again abruptly, she changed the subject. "Have you gone over those papers again, Leslie? Isn't there any way out?"

Seaforth made a gesture that suggested hopelessness.

"I got out the papers in the office yesterday and went over the whole thing afresh. No loophole anywhere. Your father's first will was all right, except that it didn't cover the very case that turned up."

"I never blamed Daddy," Joyce protested. "It was a dreadful affair."

Seaforth nodded sympathetically.

"Would probably have been all right, even then," he said, "if only Corwen had been here when the motor-smash happened. He's got his wits about him. But with Corwen off on a holiday, and old Millom in charge—"

"How I do hate that silly old man, even if he's been in his grave for years! I've his muddling to thank for all I've had to stand."

Joyce bit her lip to restrain herself. There was no need to speak of the matter; it was familiar to them both in its smallest detail. Joyce's father was ten years older than his wife; and his first will had been drawn up on the assumption that she would survive him. Then came the motor-accident; Mrs. Hazlemere was killed instantly, and her husband was hurt so badly that he could not live more than a day. Half mad with pain and incapable of thinking things out properly, he had just been able to realise one thing: that his current will made no provision for the upbringing of his little daughter, since in it her mother's survival had been taken for granted. Old Millom, the almost superannuated senior partner in the firm of Millom & Corwen, had lost his grip on business; and, instead of suggesting a codicil to the existing will, he had allowed the pain-racked dying man to dictate a completely fresh instrument.

Joyce's parents had meant to send her to school on the Continent—so down went some clauses providing for that. When she came back from school, where was she to go? Her aunt was the only relation she had; at that time Mrs. Fenton had not separated from her husband; she seemed the proper person to bring the girl up—so down went the provision that Joyce was to live in Mrs. Fenton's house until she was twenty-five.

A man suffering acute physical pain cannot think of every detail; and old Millom, almost senile, lacked the mental alertness which would have enabled him to foresee eventualities. Between them, they forgot the possibility that the girl might want to marry; and so, into the will went a clause providing that Mrs. Fenton was to draw the full thousand a year income from the estate until her niece was twenty-five, and that out of this she was to furnish Joyce with clothes and pocket-money.

Then the fatal blunder had been made. Old Millom, with an ill-placed revival of a lawyer's caution, realised that there should be some control over Joyce, something to ensure that she would conform to the terms of the will. And so he suggested the proviso that, if Joyce failed to abide by the conditions of the will, her money should revert to her aunt. Joyce's father, suffering agonies from his injuries, had trusted to Millom's experience; and thus, between the dying man and the legal pantaloon the fatal clause had been inserted without consideration.

"Old Millom's to blame, right enough," Seaforth agreed bitterly. "That clause bears the stamp of his mint. Your father couldn't be expected to see what it might lead to—has led to. Mere words to him, most likely, when old Millom proposed it. And *he*'d no right to suggest it—fancy a lawyer interfering in the making of a will and shoving things in that his client would never have passed, if he'd been able to consider them. That's how it stands, though, no matter how it was done. You're tied to your aunt till you're twenty-five, or else she gets every penny."

"We couldn't upset the will, could we?"

"Wills take a lot of upsetting. Besides, if we tried that, your aunt would fight to the last ditch—and all the costs would come out of the estate. If she really turned spiteful, the expenses might swallow up everything.

He broke off with a gesture of irritation.

"We can't marry on my screw. Old Corwen won't give me a partnership for years yet. Let's talk about something else, Joyce. That subject just makes us feel like a pair of rats in a trap."

His attempt to divert the girl's thoughts proved a complete failure. In Joyce's character there was a tough streak which helped her to hold her emotions in check for long periods; but when the explosion came at last it was all the greater for the previous constraint. She had endured as much as she could bear at the hands of her aunt and now her long-pent-up feelings demanded vocal expression.

"That just shows how little you understand what it's really like," she exclaimed bitterly. "It's easy enough for you to say: 'Let's change the subject.' It's only something one talks about, so far as you're concerned. *You* haven't to go back to that house and see the beastly business begin all over again: the jealousy, the pin-pricks, and all the rest of it. You haven't to watch her scattering *your* money in betting, while she makes a scene over every three guineas spent on a new hat. You haven't to stand that doctor hanging round the place with his air of being more at home there than you are yourself and discussing betting from morning to night—bets that are to come out of *your* money. It's easy enough for you!"

She broke off, as though to give him a chance of saying something; but Seaforth had seen a flame in the hazel eyes which he knew was a danger-signal, and he wisely kept silence. Joyce clenched her hands till the knuckles turned white.

"She's even taken to blaming me for these heart-attacks of hers. The worry I give her is what brings them on, she insists. You've no idea of what it's like, this continual nagging."

"I've a fair notion," said Seaforth in a grim tone.

"You haven't! You think you have, that's all. It's a very different thing when you've got to go through it, like me. I don't know when I hate her most: when she's her sneering natural self; or when she's had a glass or two and got to the stage when she's sort of hearty and overflowing with a loathsome geniality or joviality, or whatever you call it; or when she gets beyond that stage and grows angry and suspicious."

Suddenly she seemed to make up her mind to tell him something further.

"I hadn't meant to say anything about this to you, Leslie. It's the last straw. It'll give you some real notion of things. Last night, when I came in, there she was with a decanter and a syphon beside her. She was stupid with drink; I could see that at a glance and I tried to get away upstairs. You know the state I mean, when they repeat the same silly sentence over and over again and work themselves up into a passion because they think you're not paying attention. At last I went to the door. Then she lost her temper completely and broke out. I tried to calm her down. I expect the maids know all about it, but there's no use letting her scream bad language for everyone to hear. It was no good. She raged at me—a regular virago, Leslie, pouring out the worst abuse she could think of. I opened the door; and as I turned to go out of the room, she staggered out of her chair and struck me in the face. She struck me, Leslie! I can't go on. I can't stand it any longer. You'll have to think of something, Leslie. I'm at the end of my tether."

She dropped her head on Seaforth's shoulder and broke down completely. With his arm about her, he tried to soothe her; and at last she looked up again and felt for her handkerchief.

"There! I'm better now," she assured him. "Silly of me to go on like that. I'm all right again."

But the stormy light was still in her eyes, and next moment she exclaimed ragefully:

"I don't think much of the way things happen. Why should people like Mother and Daddy be cut off like that, when things like Aunt Evelyn seem to thrive on weak hearts? I can't see it."

Seaforth's anger had flared up at her story, but he kept himself in hand for fear of exciting Joyce still further at the moment.

"*That* would be a solution of the whole trouble," he said, slowly.

"What? What do you mean?"

"If she died in one of her heart-attacks," he explained deliberately. "Then, I expect, you'd come into your money straight away; and everything would be plain sailing."

"I wish she would," Joyce exclaimed vehemently. "If she were out of the way— Why, it would almost be worth it."

"A benefit to the world if someone poisoned her, you mean?" Seaforth completed her thought. "She'd be a perfect case for a pure-minded murderer. No loss to anyone. But that sort of thing's a bit risky, though. Perhaps she'll save trouble by going off in one of her heart-attacks."

Joyce's expression hardened at his words.

"If I have another scene like that one last night," she said sombrely, "I'll lose control of myself. I could have killed her then, when she struck me. Suppose I had struck back? With that heart of hers, anything might happen, you know. It would be a way out of this trap."

She pondered for a moment or two, as though turning the idea over in her mind.

"You're a lawyer, Leslie. What would happen suppose I lost my temper and struck back, and she . . . well, if her heart failed under the strain? They couldn't do anything to me, could they? It would be just an accident, wouldn't it?"

CHAPTER II
A CASE OF HEART-FAILURE

DR. PLATT, having finished a cigarette, dropped the remains on the ash-tray beside him and put his hand into his pocket in search of his case. Arresting the gesture half-way, he glanced at the thriller on his knee and noted that he had only another ten pages to read. Was it worth while starting a fresh smoke before going to bed? Undecided, he looked up at the clock and found that it was shortly after midnight. He drew out his case, extracted a cigarette; then, after a momentary pause, slipped it back into its place and returned the case to his pocket.

Dr. Platt's professional advancement had been hindered by two unfortunate personal characteristics: he had a weak chin and he could never make up his mind. To camouflage the former, he had early in life acquired the habit of pinching his lower lip between his right finger and thumb; and despite his later efforts to rid himself of this idiosyncrasy, his hand still had a tendency to creep up to his face in moments of doubt.

The mental characteristic had been touched off with brutal directness by Dr. Hyndford on one occasion. "Suppose I'm called in by a man with a sore throat. I look him over and I say: 'You've got a touch of tonsilitis, evidently. Nothing to worry about. Do so-and-so, and you'll be as right as rain in no time.' But if Platt were called in, he'd say: 'It seems to be a case of tonsilitis—but one can never be sure.' He'd fiddle with his chin, look a bit perplexed, and finally recommend gargling as if it were a major operation that he was afraid of. No good, that sort of thing, you know, not a damned bit of use. But here's a tip for you, if you've got to deal with Platt. While he's floundering around trying to make up that mind of his, suggest something. He's a weak man. Weak men of his type hate following advice. Want to show they've a mind of their own, I suppose. So he'll come down against your suggestion at once, and then he'll stick to that like grim death. There's your tip. It's what I always do myself."

Dr. Platt, cigaretteless, finished his thriller and rose to his feet with a stifled yawn. He put the book on a shelf and examined the window-catches, preparatory to going upstairs to bed. As he turned from the windows, his telephone bell rang, and crossing the room he picked up the receiver.

"Dr. Platt speaking," he announced, with some foreboding, for he hated to be called out at night.

"I'm Seaforth, speaking from Mrs. Fenton's house," the voice at his ear explained. "Come round at once. Something's happened."

And before Dr. Platt could collect himself sufficiently to make any inquiries, the wire went dead.

Dr. Platt loathed emergencies of any sort, because they demanded rapid decisions; and the breathless message over the 'phone annoyed him by its vagueness.

"Silly ass!" he grumbled, as he put down the receiver and went in search of his hat. "Something's happened! Why couldn't he tell me what it was, so that I'd be prepared?"

He hesitated for a moment whether to change into his shoes or not, then decided to go as he was. He picked up his bag from the hall-table, opened the front door, and went out into the warm night flooded by the full moon. It was only a five-minute walk to Mrs. Fenton's, so it was unnecessary for him to take out his car. He closed the door behind him and set off.

The road, stretching in gentle curves between the lines of trim villas, was almost as bright as in day-light. Wakened up by the fresh air and exercise, Dr. Platt stepped out briskly, while turning over in his mind the possibilities which might await him at The Cedars. A hundred yards from his own house, he came suddenly upon a pair of lovers clasped in the shade of an overhanging tree; but except for them, no one seemed to be abroad at that hour. Stanningmore folk went to bed early as a rule, and patrolling constables were few.

One other person was wide awake, however. Marton of Starfield Towers was an enthusiastic amateur astronomer; and on nights when the sky was clear, he was generally to be seen in the open air, peering through his four-inch telescope and making sketches of the planets by the aid of a dim and carefully shaded lantern. Tall trees in neighbouring gardens had made it impossible for him to set up a permanent observatory with a clear field of view; and he was forced to drag his telescope laboriously from place to place as the celestial objects changed their positions hour by hour through the night; but a minor drawback of this sort had no power to damp his enthusiasm.

As Dr. Platt reached the gate of The Cedars, his eye was caught by the glint of the moonlight on the long brass barrel of Marton's instrument, perched on its tripod stand in the middle of the lawn of Starfield Towers, which stood just across the road from Mrs. Fenton's house. The sound of the doctor's footsteps in the quiet night had evidently roused the attention of the astronomer, for he lifted his head from the eyepiece and stared inquisitively at the dark figure with the bag in its hand. Then, recognising an acquaintance, he straightened himself up.

"Is that you, Platt? You're out late, surely. Is anyone ill, over there?"

"No," Platt assured him sarcastically. "Only a burst pipe would bring me out at this hour. Don't you know I do a bit of plumbing in my spare time?"

Marton was neither abashed nor offended.

"Of course, of course," he conceded. "Silly question, that of mine. Pointless, in fact. But who's ill? It's nothing serious, I hope."

"I don't know," Dr. Platt retorted in a tone that had more than a touch of peevishness in it.

He put his hand on the latch of the gate and was just on the point of going in, when another of Marton's recognitions of the obvious reached him.

"Ah, I see. A sudden call, eh?"

The clang of the gate as it swung back, covered any remark that Dr. Platt may have chosen to utter. Just as he made his first steps up the path towards the front door of The Cedars, the amateur astronomer in Marton came uppermost.

"Drop across here when you come out again, and have a look at Jupiter," he called hospitably. "It's looking splendid to-night—very clear seeing. I haven't had as good a night for three weeks back. Jupiter's well worth seeing, well worth seeing. The belts are quite plain, marvellously clear."

Dr. Platt, more annoyed than ever at this last-moment interruption of his train of thought, made no reply beyond a vague gesture. The clang of the gate had evidently been heard in the house, for as he moved up the path, the front door opened and Seaforth's tall figure appeared in silhouette against the golden light of the hall.

"That you, Platt? Glad I got hold of you at once. Don't expect you can do anything to help, though."

Then, as the doctor entered, he added:

"Mrs. Fenton's dead."

Dr. Platt was obviously taken off his guard by the news. This was not one of the possibilities which he had been turning over in his mind as he came along.

"How do you know she's dead?" he demanded. "Her heart wasn't normal, of course; but . . . well, last time I examined her she seemed more or less all right. Most likely it's just a fainting fit. Get some brandy in case we need it. Where is she?"

Seaforth treated the request for brandy with unconcealed contempt and led the way towards the back of the house where Joyce Hazlemere, white and shaken, was standing waiting beside an open door.

"In there," Seaforth directed, curtly.

Entering the drawing-room, Dr. Platt saw Mrs. Fenton's figure stretched on a settee on the other side of the room. If ever a woman looked dead, it was the one before him. The body was perfectly composed, with no trace of any death-struggle. Death might have come to her in sleep, so far as the appearances went. At the first glance, Dr. Platt was inclined to agree with Seaforth. But he had been contradicted by a layman, and that rankled in his mind. He determined to go into the matter thoroughly.

Putting down his bag, he took the wrist of the body and endeavoured to detect the pulse; but after a short trial he gave up the attempt.

"Like a looking-glass to test the breathing?" Seaforth inquired, as though wishing to be helpful.

Dr. Platt shook his head. When he was there as an expert, he objected to ignorant laymen thrusting their advice upon him. Without answering, he opened his bag and took out his stethoscope. But the stethoscope failed to reveal any action of the heart. Dr. Platt considered for a moment, mechanically replacing his instrument in his bag.

"Have you a piece of thread or some thin twine?" he demanded impersonally at last.

"I'll get you some," Joyce volunteered. "How much do you need?"

"Six inches or so would be enough."

Joyce nodded and vanished through the door. He heard her racing upstairs.

Hitherto his attention had been concentrated on the body before him; but by her intervention, Joyce had brought herself into Dr. Platt's field of consciousness; and while he waited for the twine, his thoughts wandered to the girl. Somehow, he felt there was something rather abnormal about her. Without being able to define precisely the idea which had entered his head, he had a vague impression that she was not displaying exactly the kind of emotion which might have been expected in the circumstances. She was badly shaken, evidently; her face betrayed that plainly enough, apart altogether from secondary signs. But somehow, he got the impression that shock and grief were not intermingled in this case as in the usual sudden death. Shock had left its mark plainly enough; but Joyce Hazlemere had suffered it dry-eyed. In the face of death, one might have looked for some decent display of sorrow, even if it were made merely for the sake of appearances; but there had been no trace of anything of the sort. The girl seemed almost callous. As for Seaforth, he too seemed quite unmoved by regret—rather ruder than usual, if anything. Dr. Platt contented himself with docketing his observations in his memory as an example of the curious manner in which some people react under strain.

"Will this be enough?" Joyce asked, as she returned with a short piece of twine.

As Dr. Platt took it from her, Seaforth interjected a suggestion couched in a tone which made it almost equivalent to an order.

"You'd better get off to bed, Joyce. No point in hanging about here, is there? I'll look after things. Or, if you're going to sit up, you'd better wake one of the maids. Get some coffee, or something."

Dr. Platt surprised an exchange of glances between the two. Then Joyce seemed convinced, for she nodded in acquiescence and slipped out of the room.

"No need for her here," Seaforth pointed out. "Bit of a shock for her. Better out of it. Now what are you going to do, Platt?"

Without troubling to answer, Dr. Platt knelt down beside the settee, wound the piece of twine tightly round one of Mrs. Fenton's fingers and knotted it securely. Then, leaving it in position, he took the temperature of the body and made a careful general examination so far as that was possible. After a minute or two, he seemed to think that sufficient time had elapsed for his experiment to reach its end, and he stooped over the settee to examine the ligatured finger.

"That test gives a positive result," he admitted in a grudging tone, "but one never can tell. If the heart were still working, the finger ought to go red and then blue when it's tied up. I don't see any change."

Again he considered for a moment before speaking.

"One might try it," he said at last. "There's nothing like being sure of things. Is there any sealing-wax to be had? You know your way about the house."

"There used to be some in a drawer of that writing-desk," Seaforth answered, going over to a small escritoire which stood in one corner of the room.

He pulled out a drawer, hunted for a moment among the contents, and finally produced a stick of sealing-wax, which he handed to Dr. Platt with a certain air of perplexity. The doctor pulled out a box of vestas and went over to the settee. Seaforth, completely puzzled, moved across the room to his side.

"What's this game?" he inquired, as Dr. Platt began to slip aside the upper part of Mrs. Fenton's evening frock.

"I want to get at the skin of the chest," was the reply. "There! That'll do."

To Seaforth's increasing surprise, the doctor put a match to the sealing-wax, held it there until the wax burned with a good flame, and then deliberately allowed a drop to fall on the dead woman's skin, removing it almost as soon as it had landed. Then putting down the stick of sealing-wax, he examined the skin carefully.

"She's dead," he announced at length. "You probably didn't notice it; but a blister formed where the hot wax fell and it burst almost at once, leaving a colourless background. That's fairly conclusive."

He moved over to the fireplace and leaned against the mantelpiece.

"It's very curious," he commented, "Her heart was not all one would have liked, of course; but one would hardly have expected this, somehow. One never can be sure, naturally, especially in cases of this sort. . . . How did it happen?"

Seaforth shook his head.

"I don't know," he said, slowly. "She was all right at dinner-time, Miss Hazlemere says. I came round after dinner to take Miss Hazlemere on the river, but I didn't see Mrs. Fenton then. We stayed out on the river pretty late; and when we got here again, Miss Hazlemere said she was going straight to bed, so I didn't come up to the house. I just put her ashore at the foot of the garden."

He paused for a moment, as though picking his words with some care.

"Before I'd gone very far, I heard Miss Hazlemere calling me back; so I got ashore, of course, and met her on the bank. It seems she'd gone in by the front door and had looked into this room on her way upstairs to get a book. The lights were on, and there was Mrs. Fenton, just as you saw her yourself when you arrived. Bit of a shock, Miss Hazlemere got, naturally. So she ran down the garden, and called after me. She was upset, of course. I came up, had a look at the body, and rang you up at once. You know the rest."

Again Dr. Platt was half-conscious of something that jarred on him. The blunt matter-of-factness with which Seaforth told his story seemed a shade out of place in such surroundings. Dr. Platt did not sentimentalise over patients himself to any extent; but he expected better things from their relations.

"Syncope, I suppose?" Seaforth demanded, interrupting the doctor's chain of thought.

But Dr. Platt, passing from questions of psychology, had returned to the medical aspect of the case; and it was clear that he could not make up his mind what view to take.

"Syncope?" he asked, fretfully. "What do you mean by that? If you mean heart-stoppage, anyone can see her heart's stopped. What I'm not sure about is why it stopped."

He pondered for a moment or two, and then added:

"I examined her not so long ago. There was nothing organically wrong with her, so far as one could make out. Her heart was working perfectly; sometimes her pulse dropped, but the rhythm wasn't interrupted. She complained of indigestion occasionally, and that sometimes affects cardiac action. It's surprising to find a sudden collapse like this."

He relapsed into a brown study. Seaforth, repressing his impatience, waited for a further pronouncement.

"Of course, from the history of the case," Dr. Platt continued after a prolonged pause, "heart-block was always a possibility. It didn't occur to me as likely, though, from what I saw of her. Very difficult to tell what may happen in some cases."

Seaforth nodded indifferently.

"Well, I suppose that's all we can do at present," he suggested, with the idea of dislodging the doctor. "Lucky you've been attending her, Platt. There'll be no bother about a death certificate."

Dr. Platt's hand stole up towards his mouth, but he stopped the gesture midway.

"I'm not so sure about that," he said, undecidedly. "I wasn't here when she died, you know."

"But, Good Lord, man! you can sign a certificate even if you've never seen the body at all. Half the certificates in the world are signed that way. What's to hinder you doing it in this case? She was your patient."

There was more than a hint of dictation in Seaforth's tone, and Platt reacted in his usual manner.

"I don't think I can reasonably sign a certificate in this case, Seaforth. I really don't know the cause of death."

"You know her heart was weak. She's died suddenly. Surely it's plain enough. What's to prevent you signing?"

Dr. Platt's mouth made one or two movements reminiscent of a nibbling rabbit; but almost immediately he covered them by his lifted hand. This was an emergency which he had certainly not foreseen. However, he had taken his line now, and he proposed to show that this bullying lawyer couldn't browbeat him.

"There ought to be a P.M.," he declared, with a parade of resolution.

Seaforth was taken aback and showed it.

"A post-mortem?" he exclaimed. "What on earth do you want that for?"

"To find out the cause of death, of course," Dr. Platt explained, with the air of making things quite clear to an inferior intellect.

"But surely you're satisfied that she died of heart-failure? What more do you want?"

"I want to see the state of her heart."

Seaforth was obviously staggered by the finality in the doctor's tone. He had always had a certain contempt for Dr. Platt, regarding him as something of a shuffler; and this sudden stiffening was a phase which he had not met before in the course of their very slight acquaintanceship. His tone grew polite, and even solicitous, as he endeavoured to get a reversal of the doctor's decision.

"But, look here, Platt, just think what you're doing. You won't be able to keep a P.M. quiet. Someone will get to know about it and pass the word round. You know how people talk if they get a shadow of an excuse. Insist on a post-mortem, and you'll never persuade people it's a mere formality. Every gossip-engine in the place will start working at full steam. Suspicious death, and all that sort of stuff. What's the use of risking chatter of that sort? Think of Miss Hazlemere's feelings."

His appeal failed completely. By this time, Dr. Platt's weak character had landed him in a position from which he could not see his way to withdraw with any credit. In reply to Seaforth's arguments, he merely shook his head stubbornly.

"I didn't see her die."

A further thought seemed to occur to him.

"You know, Seaforth, I'm not satisfied with what I've seen tonight. The whole thing begins to look a bit fishy, if you ask me. None of my business, of course; but I must keep myself clear whatever happens. I shall have to report the death to the coroner."

Dr. Platt observed with increasing suspicion that this announcement seemed to cause Seaforth acute dismay.

"The coroner? What the devil's the coroner got to do with it?"

Dr. Platt threw a glance at the body on the settee as though to protest against the violence of Seaforth's language in the presence of the dead.

"I'm going to report it to the coroner," he repeated mulishly. "I've got my own position to safeguard, remember. Just the other day I read in the papers a case where a medical got rapped over the fingers for being too slack with death certification. It turned out to be a case of poisoning, eventually. I shouldn't care to be in that doctor's shoes: and I don't mean to be, either. You may take that as certain. What sort of figure would I cut, if I gave a certificate and it turned out that there had been any foul play?"

"Foul play?" Seaforth demanded with a white and angry face. "What do you mean by 'foul play'?"

Dr. Platt glanced at the formidable figure before him, and he seemed a shade less certain of himself as he replied:

"Nothing. Nothing of that sort. Just a mere hypothetical case, of course."

And with that he secured his bag and walked out of the room, leaving Seaforth only too conscious that he had handled the whole affair disastrously.

CHAPTER III
THE VERDICT

THE INTEREST AROUSED by the affair at The Cedars found its reflex in the *Stanningmore Gazette*, which published a fairly full report of the proceedings at the coroner's inquest.

THE CEDARS MYSTERY

The inquest was resumed at Stanningmore yesterday on Mrs. Evelyn Fenton, of The Cedars, Stanningmore, who was found dead in suspicious circumstances as already reported.

The first witness called was Miss Joyce Hazlemere. She stated that she was the niece of the deceased, with whom she had lived for about two years. At dinner-time on the evening of the tragedy, her aunt seemed quite normal. They had the same dishes at dinner. Mrs. Fenton, in addition, had a whiskey and soda. Witness had felt no ill-effects from the food. During the meal, there had been a slight altercation between her aunt and her on account of Miss Hazlemere's having arranged to go out on the river with Mr. Leslie Seaforth that evening. Such altercations were not uncommon. Witness explained that she and Mr. Seaforth were engaged. The altercation came to nothing.

Dr. L. Radstock (the coroner): When did you get engaged to Mr. Seaforth?—Eighteen months ago. There was no secret about the engagement.

The witness described how Mr. Seaforth had brought his canoe to the foot of the garden after dinner and they had gone off together in it. They came back shortly after midnight, and she came ashore, leaving Mr. Seaforth in the canoe. She went up to the house, found the French window of the drawing-room closed, and walked round to the front door. Thinking that a book she was reading might be in the drawing-room, the witness went in there in search of it and found her aunt dead. The body was lying on a settee. There was no sign of any struggle and the lights were on. She made sure that her aunt was really dead and then ran out to recall Mr. Seaforth. She estimated that between leaving Mr. Seaforth and seeing him again about five minutes elapsed.

Mr. Seaforth was called next. He corroborated the evidence of the previous witness, so far as the facts fell within his knowledge. When she recalled him, they went together up to the house. He inspected the body and at once rang up Dr. Platt.

Dr. Hubertus Platt was then called. He stated that he had been Mrs. Fenton's medical adviser for about five years. When he first knew her, she had been perfectly healthy except for minor ailments. In fact, two years ago she had effected a small insurance and had been passed without difficulty by the company's doctor. Some fifteen months ago, her heart started to give trouble; there were attacks from time to time, none very serious. There was nothing organically wrong with her heart, so far as he had discovered. She complained of indigestion at times; and indigestion sometimes caused cardiac irregularity. The witness described how he had been rung up by Mr. Seaforth. When he first saw the body, Mrs. Fenton might have been dead for ten minutes or for an hour—he could not say exactly. From what he knew of the history of the case, he saw no reason for this sudden collapse. It surprised him so much that he refused to give a certificate.

The coroner questioned Dr. Platt about the treatment he had been giving Mrs. Fenton, and Dr. Platt explained what drugs he had prescribed.

The coroner: Did Mrs. Fenton suffer much from coughs or colds?—She was rather subject to them.

The coroner: Did you ever hear of Paronax?—That is an American quack cough-and-cold cure. I never prescribed it to Mrs. Fenton. I am quite positive about that. It was advertised occasionally when it first came out; but I have seen no advertisement of it recently, not for a year at least.

The coroner: You were not aware that Mrs. Fenton was using it?—No, I knew nothing about it.

The next witness was Lucy Stifford, the house-parlourmaid at The Cedars. She stated that she had seen bottles labelled Paronax in Mrs. Fenton's bedroom. The medicine seemed to be used only at intervals, and fresh bottles appeared when the old ones were emptied. She identified one bottle as having been found in Mrs. Fenton's room after her death. Witness had put her initials on it when asked by the police to do so, to make sure there was no mistake.

She stated further, in answer to the coroner's questions, that Miss Hazlemere and her aunt were not on good terms, largely owing to Mrs. Fenton's fault. She mentioned that Mrs. Fenton was addicted to whiskey and that the habit had grown on her in the last two years. Mrs. Fenton was difficult to get on with.

Dr. Amyas Keymer, the well-known expert, was then called. He had carried out the post-mortem on Mrs. Fenton. His attention had been drawn to two rather faint marks, one on each side of the throat of the deceased, slightly in front of the ear and just below the jaw.

The coroner: These marks could not be due to an attempt to throttle the deceased?—No. Even a fair pressure at these points would fail to constrict the windpipe.

The coroner: Would there be an immediate mark on the skin in consequence of the pressure?—From an examination of the tissues. I infer that only light pressure was used. In this case, no immediate development of a mark was likely; but after death the mark would appear.

Pressure at these points, the witness continued, would affect the vagus nerves and the internal carotid arteries. The vagi control the action of the heart, and pressure on these nerves might stop the heart-beat. Pressure on the internal carotid artery might stop the flow of blood to the brain. He understood that in jiu-jitsu, advantage was taken of these facts to knock a man out, which showed how dangerous pressure on these regions might be.

The coroner: It would need special anatomical knowledge to put one's finger on the proper spot?—Undoubtedly. The ordinary man would not know either the danger or the exact spot to press. He would almost certainly resort to mere throttling.

The coroner: Would heavy pressure be required? Would it need a strong man to exert it?—Oh, no. In this case, no great pressure had been used. The faintness of the marks and the state of the compressed tissues showed that clearly.

Dr. Keymer then gave further results of his postmortem examination of the deceased. There was nothing abnormal in the stomach surface, no trace of any strong irritant poison. In the stomach contents he had found traces of veronal which he had identified microscopically and also by a chemical test. Veronal was used as a sleep-producing drug; and the normal dose was five to ten grains. The toxic dose might be as low as fifteen grains. In his opinion, there was not a toxic dose in the stomach. In one case, a person had taken 150 grains of veronal (about one-third of an ounce) and recovered after it. The toxic dose varied so much that it was difficult to assert anything; but in his view the veronal had nothing to do with Mrs. Fenton's death directly.

The foreman of the jury asked if veronal was a scheduled poison. Could it be bought by anyone without prescription?

Dr. Keymer said veronal had been transferred from Part II to Part I of the schedule of poisons under the Pharmacy Act in 1917. In reply to the foreman, he explained that the effect of this provision was that nobody could buy veronal unless he was known to the druggist supplying it or was introduced to the druggist by someone known to both buyer and seller. In either case, the buyer would have to give his name and address, state the purpose for which the veronal was to be used, and sign the Poison Book in which these entries were made.

Continuing his evidence, Dr. Keymer stated that in addition to veronal, the stomach contained something else. From the fact that the heart of the deceased seemed anatomically normal when he examined it and from the undoubted fact that the deceased suffered from a functional abnormality of the heart, he had been led to look for something in the stomach contents. He had not been able to isolate any of this second material in a pure form; but on injecting an extract of the stomach contents into various frogs, he had observed that the frogs' hearts were slowed down. The evidence pointed to digitalis. That was as far as he cared to go.

The foreman of the jury asked if Dr. Keymer thought there was a fatal dose of digitalis in the stomach.

Dr. Keymer: I cannot give a definite answer to that, for this reason. Digitalis is a cumulative poison. It is not destroyed or excreted rapidly by the body, so that a second dose coming soon after the first one might bring the total in the stomach above the fatal amount, although if taken independently the two doses would each be well below the toxic quantity.

The foreman: Is digitalis a scheduled poison?

Dr. Keymer: It is. It was added to the schedule in 1925.

The foreman: That is, previous to any incident which has been dealt with in the evidence?—Yes.

The coroner: Can you say anything definite as to the real cause of death?—The veronal had nothing to do with it. With digitalis, one can never be sure, owing to the cumulative action of the drug; but if death had been due to the digitalis, I should have expected some symptoms which were not observed, such as sickness, dilation of the eye-pupils, and some inflammation of the stomach coatings. Pressure on the vagi and the internal carotids would undoubtedly produce death.

Dr. Platt was then recalled. He stated that he had never prescribed digitalis in any form to Mrs. Fenton. Questioned by the coroner, he admitted that what he had taken for heart weakness might have been due to the administration of digitalis—the symptoms would correspond.

The coroner: When did these symptoms appear first?—About fifteen months ago.

The next witness was John Knowle, a pharmaceutical chemist. He stated that he was Mrs. Fenton's druggist. No one else in Stanningmore supplied medicine to The Cedars. He had never supplied any veronal. As to Paronax, he had never had an inquiry about it from anyone in the town. It was a purely American concern and had little sale in this country, so far as he knew. He was quite positive that he had never supplied either of the scheduled poisons to anyone at The Cedars; his books proved that.

Duncan Holland was then called. He described himself as an analytical chemist specialising in food and drugs. He had analysed the contents of two bottles. One was a bottle of Paronax with the seal intact, bought by himself in presence of a witness at a druggist's in London. It contained no digitalis. The other bottle had been supplied to him by the coroner. He identified the bottle (the same one as was referred to in the maid's evidence as having been found in Mrs. Fenton's bedroom). It contained digitalin, the active principle of digitalis tincture. In answer to the coroner, he stated that a tablespoonful of this Paronax—the dose recommended on the label—would not contain anything like a fatal dose of digitalis. When asked if several doses taken in succession would have a fatal effect owing to the cumulative nature of the poison, he declined to give an explicit answer to a hypothetical question.

The witness then described the results of analysing the whiskey from the decanter found on the drawing-room table beside Mrs. Fenton's body. It contained no veronal, nor was there any digitalin in it. It appeared to be plain whiskey.

Dr. Keymer (recalled) was questioned as to the possibility of a fatal dose having been taken in the cough mixture (Paronax). He refused to commit himself definitely on this point and repeated that the amount detected by him in the deceased's stomach was not on the scale of a fatal dose, so far as his experience went.

The coroner, in his summing up, cautioned the jury not to go beyond the evidence in forming their opinion. It was not necessary for them to name any specific person in their verdict. Their duty was to discover, if possible, the cause of death; and an open verdict would be sufficient.

The jury, after rather prolonged consideration, returned a verdict of wilful murder by some person or persons unknown.

CHAPTER IV
THE CASE AGAINST JOYCE

JAMES CORWEN was the leading solicitor of the district; and his physical appearance was almost as well known to the townsfolk of Stanningmore as the dial of the Town Clock itself. The rather massive features, the deep legal lines from nostrils to mouth, the determined lips, and the unemotional eyes, would have marked him out in a crowd. But if a stranger, struck by his face as he passed in the street, had asked a native what manner of man James Corwen was, he would have gleaned very little. "A sound lawyer . . . hard where money's concerned . . . rather a dry stick . . . keeps to himself."

The last phrase might have suggested a reason for the paucity of the remainder. The fact was that very few people could claim to know Mr. Corwen in his hours of leisure. Though he knew more about the private affairs of Stanningmore people than any other individual in the town, he had probably fewer social contacts than anyone else. A confirmed bachelor, he seemed to feel no need of society in the ordinary sense of the term. People had ceased to trouble him with invitations. His own entertaining was confined to three cronies who came to his big comfortable house on Tuesday and Friday evenings, when they played bridge for three hours with the accuracy and taciturnity of automata. How he spent the remaining five evenings of the week no one knew.

Into the sequel to the affair at The Cedars he had been drawn neither willingly nor reluctantly but in the purely professional capacity of Joyce Hazlemere's lawyer. Throughout the inquest he had listened to the various witnesses with a superficial indifference which concealed completely anything that passed through his mind. Occasionally he made a note of some point; but in general his attitude was that of a man invited to the first night of a boring play which he must sit through out of courtesy to his host.

The verdict—"Murder by some person or persons unknown"—had been almost a foregone conclusion on the evidence; and when the foreman had announced it, most people present would have been quite prepared to substitute the name of Joyce Hazlemere for the more general term used by the jury.

Returning to his office, James Corwen had put the matter completely out of his mind while he devoted himself to going through the business which had accumulated during the time he had spent at the inquest. When he had completed his task, he signed some documents and rang for his clerk.

Groombridge, who came at the summons, was a monk-like person who had been a clerk in the firm even before James Corwen's name was put on the plate outside the door. "A fossil from the Millomian strata," Corwen had once defined him, in a rare moment of expansion; and if there was any contempt in the phrase, it was directed at the original head of the firm and not at Groombridge. The solicitor was quite content with his subordinate. Groombridge was completely devoid of ambition, asked for no increases in salary, did his work with the accuracy of a machine, and had a thorough understanding of his employer's ways in business.

James Corwen looked up as Groombridge came into the room; but the routine of years made it unnecessary for him to say anything. A gesture of his hand indicated the signed documents on the table; and the clerk picked them up without a word concerning them. But at this point came one of the rare divergences from routine. Groombridge produced a paper which he had brought with him when he was summoned.

"Would there be any objection to my photographing that, sir?" he inquired, handing the document to his employer.

James Corwen's cold eyes showed a faint trace of amusement, but the emotion did not extend to the rest of his features.

"Is it another rare specimen for the graphology collection?" he inquired with more than a touch of tolerant contempt in his tone. "A curious fad, that of yours. Why not try stamp-collecting for a change? You might make some money out of stamps."

Groombridge's face suddenly lighted with a flash of real enthusiasm; the mere mention of the subject seemed to waken him from his customary circumspection. To him, graphology was more a passion than a hobby; and the correspondence of the solicitor's office furnished him with endless material for research, since few of the clients used typewriters. For a quarter of a century he had been amassing specimens of manuscript to illustrate some theories which he had formed; and his humble ambition, unmentioned to a human soul, was to write a book on the subject when he had gathered sufficient evidence in support of his views. *Some Minor Characteristics of Handwriting*, by Benjamin Groombridge, Notary-Public. He had fondled the idea so long in his mind that now he could almost see the first copy in his hand: a big solid volume bound in dark blue, with gold lettering on the back, and crammed with enthralling illustrations.

"I'm afraid postage-stamps don't attract me, sir," he said, in a tone which showed that he suspected Corwen was ironical. "They're not practical, like manuscript."

His employer's dry sense of humour was tickled by this suggestion.

"Practical?" he echoed. "Postage-stamps are very practical. I saw one the other day, Groombridge, that fetched £192, no less. But this collection of handwriting of yours wouldn't sell for the price of a puff of smoke from a cigarette."

"You think so, sir?" The clerk's voice betrayed that his feelings had been touched. "But some manuscripts have a way of being valuable, haven't they? Wills, and contracts, and so forth, sir? And an expert opinion about them might be of some use in a suit, surely—more valuable even than a postage-stamp."

James Corwen disdained to indicate the obvious slip in Groombridge's argument. He took the paper which the clerk held out.

"What's this?"

"A note written by Mrs. Fenton, sir. The contents are of no importance, and the date's two years back. I don't want to photograph it as a whole, sir; merely to make a microphotograph of one or two letters in it."

James Corwen handed the sheet of paper back to Groombridge.

"She's dead now, in any case," he commented. "There seems to be no reason why you shouldn't photograph a word or two here and there in it, if you want to. There's no breach of confidence involved in that. Add them to your collection if you like. And, Groombridge"—he stopped the clerk on his way to the door—"send Mr. Seaforth to me at once."

When Seaforth presented himself, a few moments later, James Corwen pointed to a seat near his desk, without opening his lips. He had a firm belief that one learned something by forcing the other man to start the conversation; and he acted on this hypothesis when it was convenient. In the present circumstances, it was convenient, because the inquest on Mrs. Fenton had just been closed, and he wished to gauge the effect of the verdict upon Seaforth. The opening remark would give the key, he hoped.

Seaforth took the chair which James Corwen indicated, and by sitting down in it he brought his face full into the light, whilst Corwen's back was turned to the window. The solicitor was something of a psychologist; and it was not by accident that he had chosen for his clients a low comfortable armchair whilst he himself sat on a higher level.

Seaforth did not keep him waiting long.

"What about this inquest, sir?" he demanded in an anxious tone. "I don't like the look of things. Miss Hazlemere's quite upset about it. She thinks everyone imagines she did it."

James Corwen refused to be drawn so easily as that. There was something which he meant to elicit, if possible; and in order to get at the truth it was essential to put Seaforth off his guard. The interview would have to be spun out until this was achieved; so the solicitor made no direct reply to the query. He contented himself with a dubious shake of the head which might have meant anything.

"People are beasts!" Seaforth exclaimed violently. This mood hardly suited James Corwen's purpose, and he took immediate steps to change it.

"I distrust general statements," he said, drily. "And another thing, Seaforth: vehemence is out of place in legal questions."

"But if you saw how it's affecting Miss Hazlemere, sir!" Seaforth protested. "She's nearly at the end of her nerves."

"All the more reason why you should keep your head," Corwen pointed out, coldly. "May one ask what definite ideas have been evolved out of this brain-storm of yours? Anything helpful?"

"Helpful? How do you mean, helpful? Of course I've done all I could to hearten her up and tell her she's exaggerating the thing in her own mind."

"H'm! We're evidently thinking of different aspects of the case. I don't see much advantage in holding a girl's hand while someone else is fitting a noose round her neck. I'm speaking metaphorically of course."

Groombridge entered the room, deposited a packet of papers on the desk, and withdrew again without a word.

"Doesn't it occur to you," the solicitor said, as the door closed behind Groombridge, "that the most urgent thing is to prepare Miss Hazlemere's defence? That's how I should look at the matter myself, in the circumstances."

Seaforth's face furnished an interesting study in expression, as he heard this blunt statement.

"Her defence?" he demanded. "You don't think it'll go that length, surely? There's no evidence against her. It's all hints and suspicions—putting two and two together and making five out of them. There's nothing solid in the whole affair."

"Perhaps not," Corwen assented indifferently. "It may never come into court. But in any case, she's bound to be questioned very sharply. Did you notice a big clean-shaven man who sat near the jury at the inquest? He was wearing grey and had a grey felt hat beside him. He gives the impression of a kindly, free-and-easy fellow who'd get on well with most people. Sometimes he tilted his chair back and seemed bored by the whole affair. He's Superintendent Ross, sent over from the County Headquarters to take up the case. I know Ross."

Seaforth recalled a recent case in which Ross had brought a man to the gallows by piecing very fragmentary evidence into a convincing fabric; and the thought of Joyce falling into the hands of this formidable Superintendent perturbed him deeply. Corwen's next words added to his trepidation.

"The prosecutor will have to satisfy a jury on at least three points: first, that Miss Hazlemere had an opportunity of killing Mrs. Fenton that night; second, that she had a motive for killing her; and, third, how she killed her. These are the three main lines of attack which will have to be blocked if possible."

Seaforth's hands tightened on the arms of the chair as he heard this tranquil exposition of the matter. There was a bluntness about it which made a far deeper impression on him than anything else had done. Corwen took so calmly for granted that their business would be to get Joyce safely out of the dock; and the final "if possible" put the case at its blackest.

"You talk as if she might be guilty," Seaforth said, hotly. "That's a strange attitude to take."

James Corwen's gesture suggested that he had no time to enter into side-issues.

"As her legal adviser, it's no affair of mine whether she's guilty or not. That's the business of the jury. Our business is to prevent the prosecutor from establishing his case—nothing else."

Seaforth nodded a gloomy assent to this view.

"The first point's gone by the board already," he confessed grudgingly. "Miss Hazlemere was alone with Mrs. Fenton between the time I put her ashore and the moment when I came back in answer to her calling me. We can't deny that without landing ourselves in a mess."

James Corwen accepted this obvious reasoning so readily that Seaforth's courage ebbed a shade further.

"That leaves two possible lines of defence still available," the solicitor observed dispassionately. "There's the question of motive, first of all. Was there anything that a prosecutor could use to convince a jury on that point?"

James Corwen already had very clear ideas on this subject; but he preferred to learn what Seaforth thought about the matter. There was always the chance that a fresh mind might have seen something which he himself had overlooked.

"Oh, there's enough to impress a jury," Seaforth admitted with something that sounded almost like a groan. "You know she and I are engaged. We can't get married—no money. She doesn't come into her money till she's twenty-five. I mean, if Mrs. Fenton had lived, Miss Hazlemere wouldn't have got control of her own money for some years yet; but now, under the will of her father, she's come into all he left. Besides, the maid let out enough at the inquest to show anyone how things stood at The Cedars. An unscrupulous prosecutor could twist all that into a motive, without actually having to misstate the facts. That's the motive that'll be faked up, if any one is. Certain to be. And I don't see how one's going to get round the plain facts."

James Corwen nodded as though he shared Seaforth's views.

"The facts will impress the jury, unless we can find some other interpretation to put on them," he said, driving Seaforth's hopes still lower by his acquiescence. "That leaves us with a third line of defence, provided we can prove that the method of killing excludes Miss Hazlemere from suspicion."

"I don't see how it's to be done," Seaforth said in a tone of despair.

James Corwen gave him little encouragement.

"Obviously the police are at work; and they will have persuaded the coroner to limit the evidence given in public as much as possible, so as to leave them a free hand. That is one difficulty in the affair; we don't know what they may keep up their sleeve. And yet it won't do for us to wait with our hands folded while they are putting their case together. We shall have to forecast, if it's possible, the line they are most likely to take in the prosecution. Then we shall have to fix up the rough outlines of a defence and make up our minds what we are going to say. That will enable us to settle what evidence we need in support of our case and give us some chance of collecting it."

He picked up a scribbling-pad from his desk, drew his fountain-pen from his pocket, and turned towards Seaforth again.

"If I were put in charge of the prosecution," he said, with a tacit assumption which jarred on Seaforth, so plainly did it indicate Corwen's belief that a criminal case was a foregone conclusion, "if I were put in charge of the prosecution, I should be inclined to work along the following lines."

He made a jotting or two on his pad to remind himself of the order in which he meant to handle the facts.

"In the first place, I would fix the jury's attention on the fact that two years ago, Mrs. Fenton was perfectly well. There's the best evidence for that. She passed an insurance doctor. Then I'd be inclined to describe the state of affairs produced by the late Mr. Hazlemere's will: the fact that Miss Hazlemere was dependent on her aunt for pocket-money, that she was bound to live with Mrs. Fenton, and that she could not get control of her own money till she was twenty-five, come what might.

"The next stage would be to picture to the jury the state of affairs at The Cedars and the friction between Mrs. Fenton and Miss Hazlemere. As we know, that has been almost constant for a long time; and it will be easy enough to bring evidence about it. Miss Hazlemere has said imprudent things more than once—it's common knowledge.

"Eighteen months ago, you appear on the scene, shortly after Miss Hazlemere comes to The Cedars. You and Miss Hazlemere get engaged. It's a question whether you will be represented as a fortune-hunter or not. In any case, your income isn't enough to allow you to marry. Obviously, the removal of Mrs. Fenton would be a happy solution of your difficulty.

"Fifteen months ago—three months after the engagement—Mrs. Fenton begins to have heart-attacks, a new state of affairs for which her previous history affords no explanation. These attacks are intermittent: sometimes she is free from them, at other times she suffers from them. Digitalis would produce the pathological conditions. Digitalis was found by the analyst in the bottle of Paronax. She used Paronax only when she had a cold or a cough, which would account for the intermittency in the heart troubles. The Crown case will be that all through the last fifteen months Miss Hazlemere has been putting digitalis into Mrs. Fenton's Paronax bottles in the hope that sooner or later a fatal dose would be taken.

"But, the prosecutor will say, this scheme failed. Mrs. Fenton never happened to take enough of her cough-remedy to poison herself, only enough to bring on these intermittent heart-attacks. For fifteen months, Miss Hazlemere is disappointed by the failure of her plan. Meanwhile, conditions at The Cedars grow, if anything, worse. She feels that she cannot afford to wait for three years more, when she will be free from her aunt's control. She wants to get married at once. Everything combines to make her desperate and reckless.

"She decides to brisk up matters and clear Mrs. Fenton out of her way at a stroke. An act of folly, naturally; but murder is always an act of folly, and yet that has not deterred murderers in the past. Because murder appears like a fatal blunder to a person in cold blood, one must not suppose that it looks quite the same to someone suffering under grievances and unnerved by constant friction. In such circumstances, it may well happen that the normal perspective is distorted and murder appears merely a simple solution of the situation.

"Further, a girl like Miss Hazlemere has no conception of the methods of criminal investigation. Quite possibly, she might not realise how accurate are the methods which would be employed by the police. She might under-rate the risks. All convicted poisoners have made that very mistake. It is no defence to say that none of us would take that risk in cold blood; for we know that some people have actually done so.

"The Crown case will be that Miss Hazlemere took this decision. Opportunity to carry the decision into action was the only thing needed. The Crown will not contend that she manufactured the opportunity. The facts suggest quite the opposite. If she had planned the affair, she would obviously have chosen a time when

Mrs. Fenton's system had worked off the latest dose of digitalis, so that no suspicion would have arisen with regard to that peculiar factor in the case.

"The prosecutor's contention will be simple. On the night of Mrs. Fenton's death, Miss Hazlemere dined with her aunt as usual and then went off with you in your canoe. After she had gone, Mrs. Fenton took a dose of veronal. A normal dose of that drug induces a deep sleep in about half an hour—at least I remember my doctor prescribed it to me once or twice and that is my recollection of its effects.

"Shortly after midnight, while Mrs. Fenton is still asleep in the drawing-room, Miss Hazlemere returns with you, disembarks, leaves you behind, and enters the house alone. In the drawing-room, she finds her aunt asleep, helpless, at the mercy of this girl who has already done her best to rid herself of this incubus. This is an opportunity so good that it is hardly likely to recur. Her predetermination comes to the front of her mind, and she seizes the chance thus flung in her way. Her victim can make no struggle, being stupefied. There will be no need for any violent exertions, any heavy pressure which might leave marks. Miss Hazlemere is no anatomist. Intending to stop her aunt's breathing, she hits by pure accident on the position of the vagus nerves and the arteries which supply the brain. She presses her fingers lightly on her victim's neck and, probably to her surprise, very slight pressure accomplishes her object. Mrs. Fenton dies.

"There are no marks on the neck. There are no signs of any struggle, which might arouse suspicion. Miss Hazlemere hurries out and recalls you before you have gone far away. Less than five minutes would be enough to carry the whole thing through.

"You come back with her and ring up the doctor. The earlier heart-attacks seem sufficient to explain this sudden collapse. Everything would have been plain sailing. But Dr. Platt refuses to give a death-certificate. After the body has lain for some hours, the marks of pressure on the neck make their appearance. Suspicion is aroused. And so the whole damning chain of evidence comes to light.

"That's how the prosecutor, most likely, will present the case. There may be variations in detail, but I should expect him to work along those lines."

James Corwen stopped abruptly and examined Seaforth's face. It did not seem to have struck him that he was not consulting a colleague but was dealing with the person who, next to Joyce herself, was most concerned in the affair. Seaforth's expression appeared to remind the solicitor of this aspect of the interview.

"Now, plainly," he demanded abruptly, "do you think she's guilty? Out with it!"

The brutal unexpectedness of the question seemed to jar Seaforth's nerves like an electric shock. For a moment or two he seemed too staggered to make any answer. Then, with an effort, he recovered his self-control, lifted himself in his chair, and steadied his voice with an obvious effort.

"That's a funny question to ask, sir. Of course she's innocent."

"Of course," James Corwen acquiesced at once. "It was a stupid question. But when a case looks black, it's a comfort occasionally to get some definite statement on the other side. It gives one confidence in one's own views."

But that movement of Seaforth's was what James Corwen had been leading up to throughout the interview. Not for nothing was Admiral Hall's book on his library shelves; nor was it by mere chance that his clients' chair was one with a low seat and a sloping back. Again and again he had occasion to confirm the Admiral's observation that when a man in such a chair starts to lie, he instinctively pulls himself upright in order to meet his interlocutor on a level instead of looking upward. It was the very movement that Seaforth had made when he proclaimed his belief in Joyce's innocence.

"So he thinks she did it, after all," James Corwen reflected. "And he's probably the crucial witness on her side. That's going to be awkward, if he lets the jury get a glimpse of his mind by accident."

For a moment or two he occupied himself with making a few jottings on his pad, merely with the object of allowing the effect of his question to die down in Seaforth's mind. When he spoke again, he chose an entirely fresh aspect of the subject.

"Suppose the case against Miss Hazlemere were presented as I sketched out, how would you meet it?"

"Fasten on the weak points," Seaforth said eagerly. "Far too many loose links in that chain for a conviction."

"There seems to be a fair chance, certainly," Corwen admitted, "provided they don't find anything further and keep it up their sleeves. Now what do you select as the weak points?"

Seaforth had already settled that question in his mind; and he gave his opinion immediately:

"The digitalis first of all. As they proved, it's a scheduled poison and can't be procured without the purchaser being identified. The defence could demand proof that Miss Hazlemere bought digitalis, or even had it in her possession in any shape or form. Snag waiting for them there, I think."

"Possibly," James Corwen conceded, though with some unwillingness which he did not trouble to disguise. "But you must remember that the police have a knack of unearthing most out-of-the-way facts."

"You're not suggesting that Miss Hazlemere actually committed a murder?" Seaforth demanded hotly.

"I'm not suggesting anything," Corwen answered coldly. "I'm trying to find a real line of defence. Miss Hazlemere wasn't asked at the inquest whether she ever had digitalis in her possession. She may have had, for all I know. Not being questioned, she said nothing on the subject—which leaves us in the dark at present. I didn't suggest that she was lying, if that's what you're excited about, Seaforth. You must keep cooler if you're to be any use at all."

Seaforth nodded sullenly in answer to the rebuke.

"What would she be doing with digitalis? The thing's ridiculous," he said impatiently.

James Corwen seemed still unsatisfied.

"You've never had digitalis in your own possession, I suppose?" he asked incuriously.

"Of course not."

"Well, then, what is your next weak link in the chain?" the solicitor questioned, dismissing the digitalis affair as though he had secured all the information he wanted.

"The fact that Mrs. Fenton was killed in a peculiar way. The chance against anyone hitting on the right spot on the throat—on both sides—was hundreds to one if it was a mere accident. Miss Hazlemere has no knowledge of anatomy or physiology. She'd never guess anything about the vagi. I didn't know about them myself till it came out at the inquest."

James Corwen tapped his pen on his pad unconsciously and then examined the point of the nib as though he feared he had damaged it.

"There's a Public Library in Stanningmore," he pointed out. "I daresay information about the heart and its action could be obtained there, by anyone who chose to take out a book or two. Miss Hazlemere reads in the Public Library. I've seen her there once or twice."

Seaforth's face had grown darker during the last stages of the conversation.

"It seems to me," he said, with more than a touch of suspicion in his voice, "that you're more interested in proving Miss Hazlemere guilty than you are in defending her. Everything you've suggested has been something pointing that way. If you don't feel you can act for the defence, wouldn't it be fairer to let her get a new adviser at once?"

James Corwen seemed more contemptuous than annoyed by this.

"My business—and your business—is to put things at the worst and then see if we can't upset the other side's arguments. It would be futile to leave out of account any argument the prosecution may think of bringing forward. That's why I am looking on the black side of things, as anyone ought to know. Now, what's your next weak link in the chain?"

Seaforth tapped his finger on the arm of his chair for a moment or two, and his face showed that he was thinking hard. But in the end, evidently, he failed to discover anything.

"These seem to be all the weak spots, so far as I can see," he admitted, gloomily. "Unless you take the time into account. She wasn't out of my sight for more than five minutes."

James Corwen was completely unimpressed by this suggestion.

"The prosecution will trip you up there without the least difficulty. First of all, five minutes were quite enough to put the business through. Secondly, the prosecutor will ask you if you are a good judge of time—if you can estimate, say, an interval of two minutes accurately. You'll have to say yes to that. Then he'll pull out his watch, ask the jury to note the time, and tell you to say "Now!" when you think the two minutes span is up. You'll underestimate for a certainty in these conditions. Most likely you'll call "Now!" at the end of ninety seconds or so, unless you count your pulse. Then the prosecutor will call the jury's attention to how far out you were in your guess—and after that your value as a witness to lapse of time will be exactly nil. I've seen it done. Once you've made your mistake, the jury will simply discredit your evidence, and agree with the prosecutor if he suggests that you really spent eight or nine minutes instead of five. Naturally, he won't point out that in the test you *under*-estimated the time."

"I suppose you're right, sir," Seaforth admitted, rather disconcerted by the solicitor's certainty on the point.

James Corwen seemed slightly placated by this complete submission.

"The real weak point is the digitalis. If you can establish that Miss Hazlemere had access to digitalis, they've got a very strong case: motive, attempted murder by poison, opportunity, murder by physical violence, it all hangs together. That would take a lot of shaking; and we might not convince the jury in the end. No. I don't like that line of defence except as a sort of forward zone. The real defence will need to be elsewhere."

"Elsewhere? I don't see what you mean, sir."

"Aren't they putting up a theory to account for the facts?" Corwen demanded. "Well, if we can put up a theory—an alternative one—which accounts for even a single extra fact, we might be able to pull the jury round to our view. Juries don't like condemning women on the capital charge if they can honestly find some matter of doubt to save themselves with."

"You mean we'll have to get the real story of the affair and make the jury believe it?" Seaforth's voice had a new tinge of hope in it as he began, but that died away again as he added: "But how can we do that? Your theory accounted for everything—I mean the theory you said the prosecution might put up."

James Corwen's heavy features showed the first smile he had given during the interview.

"Everything except the dose of veronal," he pointed out. "You ought to have seen that, Seaforth. It stares you in the face."

CHAPTER V
SUPERINTENDENT ROSS

SUPERINTENDENT ROSS HELD FIRMLY that "if you want reliable evidence, you'd better collect it yourself." Information, he had learned long ago, always suffered a process of clipping and trimming as it passed from mind to mind. Some witnesses were unable to observe efficiently; others, who had the faculty of observing, lacked the power of expressing clearly what they had noted mentally. Unless one handled a witness personally, factors like these were apt to be lost in transmission and thus a totally false view of the real value of the evidence was set afloat.

In its early stages, the affair at The Cedars had not attracted special interest from the police. Their attention was first aroused when the results of Keymer's post-mortem examination came to their knowledge; and as none of the local men had any experience of a complex murder case, Superintendent Ross was despatched to Stanningmore from the County Headquarters, nominally to give his assistance but actually to take over the whole investigation.

He had attended the inquest, partly in order to hear the evidence, but mainly to see the chief witnesses and gauge for himself beforehand the credibility of some people whom he meant to question later on. He came away satisfied with the maid at The Cedars. She seemed to be reliable in her statements, though obviously biased in favour of Miss Hazlemere. Dr. Platt made a poor impression on account of his tendency to emphasise some details unduly. As to Seaforth and his fiancée, the Superintendent kept an open mind.

Their evidence was unsupported, but that did not necessarily mean anything, one way or another.

Superintendent Ross knew that in one respect he was badly handicapped. If the case had cropped up in his own district, he would have had a certain amount of floating information, easily accessible, with regard to the chief actors in the drama. In Stanningmore, which he knew only slightly, all this material would have to be sought out and pieced together as best he could, before he had much chance of picking up even the main threads of the case. And that meant time wasted in inquiries, most of which would lead to nothing important.

A methodical worker, Ross had a habit of drawing rough diagrams to indicate relationships between the characters in his cases; but he had to admit to himself that the affair at The Cedars had, so far, furnished a very meagre scheme. All that his notebook contained, after the inquest, was this:

```
Miss Hazlemere——>Mrs. Fenton<——Mr. Fenton
        ↑                ↑
Mr. Seaforth        Dr. Platt
```

He was not discouraged by the paucity of names on his sketch. These things had a knack of growing more complex as a case proceeded. New relationships generally appeared, bit by bit, when one was able to fill in the outline.

He had been in no hurry to begin his personal examination of the witnesses. Joyce Hazlemere was obviously the most important of them; and in normal circumstances he would have gone straight to her. But he knew James Corwen, and he guessed that Joyce would be well protected. He would be given no chance to put awkward questions and take her unawares. That being so, there was no need for haste; and before paying a visit to The Cedars he took time to reconsider the evidence in all its bearings and draft the main lines of his inquiry. The authorities, he knew, had taken steps to preserve absolutely undisturbed the drawing-room in which Mrs. Fenton's body had been found.

He rang the bell at The Cedars, produced his card, and asked to see Joyce Hazlemere. His reception had evidently been rehearsed; for the maid showed him into a morning-room overlooking the garden, retreated with his card, and was absent for some minutes, during which he heard the sound of a conversation at the telephone. Ross smiled a trifle wryly at this confirmation of his forecast.

"So she's ringing up Corwen's office," he reflected. "I thought so."

While waiting for the maid's return, he glanced round the room, and on a half-moon table he noticed a book on gardening which showed signs of frequent use. Superintendent Ross was not an enthusiastic gardener; his knowledge of flowers did not extend much further than that of the average man. But at the sight of the well-worn volume his face lighted up, and he opened the book at the index. It was still in his hand when the maid returned.

"Miss Hazlemere says she's sorry she's engaged just now; but if you can wait for a quarter of an hour, she'll be glad to answer any questions you want to ask."

Superintendent Ross put down the book and acknowledged the message with a pleasant smile.

"There's no hurry," he said reassuringly. "I can easily wait."

Then, as though merely making a casual remark, he turned to the window, and detained the maid with an innocent question.

"Nice garden you have out there. Who looks after it?"

The maid, slightly flattered by the Superintendent's manner, lost some of her nervousness.

"Our gardener comes twice a week to look after it," she explained. "The rest of his time he goes to Mr. Marton across the road, and to another house further along."

"Only two days a week!" The Superintendent seemed surprised. "He must be a bit of a worker, to keep that size of garden so nice if he only comes twice in the week. Perhaps he's got a boy to help him, or something?"

"No, he does it all on his own. Of course, Miss Hazlemere, she's keen on gardening. She does quite a lot. But the man does all the heavy work, the hedge-cutting, and rolling the lawn, and that sort of thing. He's very keen on his work; he likes it."

The Superintendent had established the friendly atmosphere he needed; and now he slid across the dangerous ground as carefully as he could.

"It's a nice old garden." He gazed out of the window as he spoke. "I wish I had something of that sort myself, with the river there at the foot of it. It's the sort of place one could take an interest in. I suppose Mrs. Fenton was quite keen on the garden?"

The maid shook her head.

"Not a bit. She'd no interest in it. Miss Hazlemere, she looked after everything, gave the gardener his orders, ordered plants, cut flowers for the house, and arranged them. I never saw Mrs. Fenton as much as look at a flower—I mean look at it as if it *was* something."

"Well well!" The Superintendent was duly impressed. "It's funny how some people have one taste and some another, isn't it? Miss Hazlemere and her aunt don't seem to have been alike in that, at any rate."

"No, nor in much else, either," the maid commented. "It often puzzled me how they came to be related at all, they was so different. Oil and water, you might say. Miss Hazlemere's a real young lady. Mrs. Fenton wasn't what *I*—"

She broke off, suddenly realising that she was attacking a dead woman. Ross hastened to break in before she had time to reflect.

"I guessed from one thing and another that they didn't quite hit it off, somehow," he confessed. "Faults on both sides, I imagined; but the way you put it seems to throw a fresh light on things."

"It wasn't Miss Hazlemere's fault at all, not a bit of it. You couldn't get anyone nicer or kinder than Miss Hazlemere, not if you went through the whole town. She's always got a pleasant word for one and she never finds fault, even when it *is* your fault. But nobody could have got on with Mrs. Fenton, and that's just the plain truth and nothing more."

"Quarreled, did they?"

"Well, if you was to call it quarrelling when all the nastiness is on one side, then it would be quarrelling. No human being could have stood it without saying something for herself, no matter if she was a saint," the maid explained heatedly and confusedly. "Sometimes it was all I could do to keep from putting in my own word when Mrs. Fenton was going for Miss Hazlemere and sneering at her over Mr. Seaforth."

Superintendent Ross had got his second transition without even having to build towards it. Seaforth's name was the next on his mental list.

"Mr. Seaforth?" he inquired, as though the name was not quite familiar to him. "Mr. Seaforth? Let's see. Oh, yes, he's engaged to Miss Hazlemere, isn't he?"

"That's him."

The maid's voice did not sound altogether cordial, the Superintendent fancied.

"Perhaps he and Mrs. Fenton didn't hit it off well?" he asked. "Sometimes an engagement makes a bit of a change in things and people don't settle down very well to it."

"She was afraid of him, I shouldn't wonder," the maid asserted with a certain emphasis. "He's one of the growly kind, and his bite would be worse than his growl, to my way of thinking. He was always there in the background, you see? And Mrs. Fenton, she was always afraid he might find some way to get Miss Hazlemere's money out of her clutches. I could see that from the way she talked. She'd no decency, Mrs. Fenton. She used to talk in front of me at dinner when I was waiting at table. Made me ashamed, for her, it did. And poor Miss Hazlemere having to sit there through it all—her private affairs dragged out for my benefit. It wasn't right to go on so. No real lady would have done it."

The Superintendent saw that there was little of value to be found in this field, so he changed the subject slightly.

"Maybe she was jealous of Miss Hazlemere," he suggested. "A woman of forty-odd, now, might feel that way, mightn't she? when she saw a pretty girl like Miss Hazlemere with a young man dangling after her. It often takes 'em that way," he added philosophically.

The maid rose to the bait at once.

"Jealous? What would she be jealous about? She'd got a husband of her own somewhere, hadn't she? And wasn't Dr. Hyndford about the house all the time—far more than ever Mr. Seaforth was? She'd no call to be jealous that way."

The Superintendent allowed a flicker of expression to pass over his face as though the hinted scandal had attracted him more than the rest of the conversation.

"A husband, was there?" he asked, with just the right note of mean eagerness in his tone. "That's interesting, right enough. And I suppose they were living separately, eh? He didn't stay here?"

"Not he. He's never been here since I came to the place and that's nearly two years ago now."

"Perhaps the cook knows him, then?"

"Not she. She came here a year after me. No, neither of us ever saw him cross the door. But I saw him just the other day; a gentleman friend of mine pointed him out to me in town because he knew I'd be interested-like. A nice-looking gentleman, Mr. Fenton. I didn't wonder a bit at his leaving her. No one could stand her tantrums unless they had to, like Miss Hazlemere."

Superintendent Ross twisted his good-natured face to an equivocal expression, as though he were hot on the track of some rakish idea.

"H'm!" he said, "sometimes there's more in it than that, when a man clears off and leaves his wife. Might be another woman in the case, perhaps? There usually is."

He found, to his satisfaction, that he had hooked his fish.

"I've heard something of the sort," the maid confided. "They say he's tied up with some girl or other and wants to get married to her, if only he could have cut loose from his wife. That's what people say. I don't know, myself. And they say that Mrs. Fenton wouldn't have a divorce, just out of spite. She was just that sort, spiteful to a degree. I expect she was jealous of the other woman and meant to take it out of the pair of them that way since she couldn't manage it any other way."

The Superintendent's expression still suggested that he loved nosing into a scandal.

"But what about this other man you were talking about?" he demanded with an air of knowingness. "If she was so friendly with him, why didn't she go for a divorce and get her own hands free? Then she could have married this Dr.— what d'you call him?"

"Dr. Hyndford?" the maid filled in the name. "Well, you see, it takes two to make a marriage, doesn't it? And what supposing Dr. Hyndford wasn't the marrying sort? Much good her divorce would do her in that case!"

Superintendent Ross's leer was an excellent effort.

"Aha!" he exclaimed, as though enlightened. "So that's how the land lay, eh? I hadn't thought of that side of the case. That would explain it, of course. Very likely you're right. By the way, where does this Dr. Hyndford live?"

The maid pointed across the river to a house on the opposite bank.

"That's his house yonder, the one with the red tiles on the roof and the creeper half across this side. Very handy, you can see for yourself. He was always popping over here in his canoe at all times of the day. He and Mrs. Fenton both did a lot of betting and he had always that excuse for coming across, to talk about the latest odds, you know."

"And what sort a person is he—to look at, I mean?"

"Oh, a big man with one of those grim-looking faces and a pair of eyes that seemed to bore into you when he looked at you. Nice-looking, some people would say, I suppose, but not a bit the sort of thing I'd want in a man. He always made you feel as if you were just a worm or something that was of no importance at all. Not rude, you understand, but just the kind of impression he gave you, somehow."

Superintendent Ross nodded understandingly.

"Yes . . . I know the sort of thing you mean. One meets them at times. . . . He's not married, you say?"

The maid shook her head decisively.

"No, nor likely to be, I should say."

The Superintendent did not ask her reason. Instead, he made a pretence of suppressing a slight sigh.

"Lives alone, does he? It's a lonely sort of life for a man in his forties."

"He wouldn't feel lonely, so don't you worry. Besides, he doesn't live alone. He shares that house with his brother now, Mr. Richard."

"Two cross old bachelors, eh?"

The maid seemed to object to his sweeping classification.

"Oh, no! Mr. Richard Hyndford isn't a bit like that doctor. He's very nice, a rather nervous sort of gentleman compared with his brother. A very pleasant kind of way with him, always smiling. Says good-day to you when you open the door to him, instead of stalking past you as if you was a bit of machinery, the way the doctor does."

"In business here?" the Superintendent inquired.

The maid shook her head.

"No, he just potters about the garden. They say he made enough money in Japan to keep him going for the rest of his life. He was out there for a long time, so I'm told."

The Superintendent glanced furtively at his wristwatch.

"By the way," he said, dropping the subject of the Hyndford brothers, "did Mrs. Fenton suffer much from colds? I mean was she worse than most people in that way?"

"No, not that I noticed. She had a pretty bad one a day or two before . . . you know."

Evidently she preferred euphemism when the actual death of her late mistress was in question, however frank she might be about Mrs. Fenton's affairs in general.

"And about this stuff Paronax," the Superintendent pursued. "You're quite sure she always had it by her in case of these colds?"

"Oh, I'm quite sure about that. She kept it in a medicine case usually, and I saw it when I was dusting. When a cold came on, she kept the bottle handy on the dressing-table."

"So anyone could have got at it if they'd wanted?"

"Oh, yes. But no one else used it. It just stood there."

"H'm!" The Superintendent dropped the subject abruptly. "Now about this French window in the drawing-room. In this hot weather we've been having lately, was it kept open or shut as a general thing? You would be going in there with tea or something in the evening, I suppose, so you may have some idea of what was done."

"Well, generally it was left open; but of course it was shut before the last person went up to bed. It was always shut in the mornings, that I can remember."

"So you'd have expected it to be open that night?"

"Most likely it would have been, unless someone had shut it on purpose. But I don't really know."

"No, of course not," the Superintendent agreed. "It's not the kind of thing one does notice, is it? And now, what about that night? You knew nothing about it all until Miss Hazlemere waked you up, of course. What did she look like when she went up to your room?"

"She was terribly upset, all shivering, and then she seemed sort of stunned, as if she'd nothing to say. Of course, that's just what one might expect, isn't it? I was all shook up myself at the thought of that dead body lying down there in the drawing-room. Kind of unnatural-like, it seemed to me. Not like an ordinary death-bed, you know what I mean? It made the house sort of eerie, and I didn't like to go downstairs by myself. If it wasn't that I liked Miss Hazlemere so much, I'd have left the place at once, the very next day. It gives me the jumps to see that drawing-room locked, and anything might be behind it—"

She broke off suddenly.

"That's Miss Hazlemere calling me. I've got to go."

Superintendent Ross made no objection. He had secured more information than he expected; and he saw that his diagram would require a certain amount of filling-in as a result of this interview. As the maid left the room, he turned again to the window and examined the garden with renewed interest. Then, for a moment or two, he consulted the gardening book and memorised some of the names on one page. This done, he laid the book back on the half-moon table and waited without impatience for the arrival of James Corwen. By this time, he had a pretty fair idea of a source of one of the drugs which formed a central factor in the case.

CHAPTER VI
DIGITALIS PURPUREA

When James Corwen entered the morning-room alone, the Superintendent was not surprised. He knew the solicitor's reputation for caution; and he had half-expected that there would be some preliminaries to get through before Joyce Hazlemere appeared.

Corwen wasted no time in polite formalities.

"H'm!" he said, looking Ross in the eye, "before I produce my client, I want to know exactly what the present position is. Your mental attitude in this case governs your powers in making inquiries. You know that?"

The Superintendent nodded. All trace of the gossiper had vanished from his manner and he had become merely an official carrying out a piece of work.

"The Judges' Rules, you mean?" he asked.

"I want to know exactly where you stand, Superintendent. Just let's hear your application of the Rules to the present state of affairs."

Superintendent Ross had the Rules by heart.

"Very well," he said. "Rule One. When a police officer is trying to find the author of a crime, there's no objection to his putting questions in respect thereof to anyone, whether he suspects them or not, if he thinks he can obtain useful information in that way. Rule Two. When a police official has decided to charge a person with a crime, he must first caution such person before asking any questions. My position is the one stated in the First Rule. My mind's quite open. I've no case against anyone, so far. Therefore I'm entitled to ask any questions I choose."

"That is correct," James Corwen admitted. "Then I take it that you are not at present bringing any charge against my client; and that if you imagine you have grounds for a charge later on, you will interpose a caution before going on with your questioning?"

"You can take that as agreed," the Superintendent confirmed. "I make notes of any answers I get, and Miss Hazlemere signs the document after she's read it over. That's in Rule Nine."

"There is no objection to that," James Corwen assented. "Just wait a moment while I fetch my client."

There was something more than a mere insistence on punctilio here, as both of them understood quite well. The solicitor was fencing for position, and he had chosen his ground skillfully. If the Superintendent managed to elicit any evidence which he considered to be crucial, he would have to show his hand then, either by cautioning Joyce or by desisting from further questioning; and the exact point where this danger-signal appeared would give James Corwen a fair indication of what facts had most impressed Ross. That would be a considerable gain to the defence, since it would give a clue to the main lines on which the prosecution might proceed. The weak spot in the plan lay in the possibility that the Superintendent might ignore the agreement. He could safely do that if he chose, since no one but himself could tell when he actually made up his mind. But Ross had the reputation of playing fair. He had sufficient trust in his own capacity to get at the truth eventually, and he could afford to keep within the four corners of the restrictions laid down in the Judges' Rules.

When Joyce was ushered into the room by James Corwen, the Superintendent's manner underwent yet another chameleonic readjustment to the environment. The dry official vanished and was replaced by a friendly person whose sole desire, apparently, was to get through a distasteful task as smoothly as possible.

"I'm very sorry to trouble you at all, Miss Hazlemere," he explained, briskly, "and I shan't worry you with more than a question or two. But, you see, you're the only person who can tell me certain things. That's my excuse."

He ended with a pleasant smile, as though anxious to put the girl entirely at ease. Joyce glanced at the solicitor before replying.

"I'll be glad to answer any question that Mr. Corwen allows me to answer," she said, guardedly. "I've nothing to conceal, of course; but I'm in my adviser's hands, you know."

The Superintendent guessed that these words had been put into her mouth. Obviously there was going to be very little chance of trapping her into making uncalculated admissions. He made up his mind to try a test question.

"I understand, Miss Hazlemere, that your aunt had control of your income up to the time of her death, but that now you have come into possession of your private fortune?"

Again a glance passed between Joyce and Corwen. The solicitor intervened bluntly.

"I think I understand the legal position better than Miss Hazlemere does," he pointed out. "If you want the facts, the best thing will be for you to come to my office and go through the papers with me."

Superintendent Ross recognised the adroitness of this interjection. What he wanted was the exact extent of Joyce's knowledge regarding the financial position. What Corwen was offering him was the legal position in its entirety—a completely different thing. If Joyce were the murderess, the motive must lie in her knowledge of the contents of her father's will and her appreciation of the effect of removing Mrs. Fenton. Corwen's intervention was a plain hint to Ross that he need not trouble to ask any further questions on that subject, and it was couched in terms which covered the denial of evidence with a deceptive show of frankness. Ross accepted the inevitable. There was no point in asking questions which Corwen would simply refuse to allow Joyce to answer. Instead, he tried a fresh line.

"Mrs. Fenton was rather difficult to get on with?" he asked in a sympathetic tone.

Corwen shook his head definitely.

"You can't expect my client to answer that sort of question," he said. "You've had other people's evidence on the subject at the inquest. Miss Hazlemere doesn't need to strengthen it."

"You think so?" the Superintendent said, with an air of giving in to superior wisdom. "Very well. We won't press the matter. Now what about this stuff Paronax? I understand the bottle was in Mrs. Fenton's room. Could anyone get access to it? For instance, could the maid have laid hands on it at any time?"

"Oh, yes," Joyce admitted, before Corwen could say anything. "It wasn't locked up, if that's what you mean."

"You never used it yourself, did you?"

Joyce shook her head.

"I never use patent medicines. Besides, I never happened to have a really bad cold."

"Really? I wish I could say as much myself. Now about the veronal. Have you ever used veronal, Miss Hazlemere?"

"Dr. Platt once—"

"I shouldn't answer that question," Corwen broke in, too late.

The Superintendent shrugged his shoulders as though amused.

"I think you're putting unnecessary difficulties in the way, Mr. Corwen," he suggested. "I can get the information from Dr. Platt myself if necessary. He'll know what he prescribed. Miss Hazlemere will save me a little trouble if she answers now—that's all there is in it."

Corwen evidently recognised this for he allowed Joyce to continue.

"Dr. Platt prescribed it for me once, about a year ago."

Superintendent Ross seemed to attach no great importance to the point. His next question was in a fresh field.

"This maid of yours—the one who opened the front door to me—how long has she been with you?"

"She came here shortly after I came back from France—about eighteen months ago," Joyce explained, since Corwen seemed to have no objection to the question.

"Before your engagement to Mr. Seaforth, then? . . . Quite so. And you've had no trouble with her, I suppose?"

"None whatever," Joyce assured him. "In fact, once or twice she wanted to give up her situation and I persuaded her to stay on. I hate changing maids."

"Really? Well, I don't wonder. New faces are always a fresh factor in a house. Now I'd just like to ask a question or two about your neighbours. There's a Mr. Marton across the road, isn't there? Was he a friend of Mrs. Fenton's?"

Joyce shook her head.

"Not a bit. He was never in the house. Mrs. Fenton knew him just as a neighbour—a casual acquaintance, nothing more."

"Then there's a Dr. Hyndford, isn't there? Lives across the river? He knew Mrs. Fenton, didn't he?"

"I'd rather you asked Dr. Hyndford himself," Joyce said, coldly. "I really know very little about him. He came about the house a good deal, but it was Aunt Evelyn whom he came to see. He had no interest in me, and I had no interest in him."

"You know his brother, perhaps?"

"Mr. Hyndford? Yes, I know him much better than the doctor."

The Superintendent did not pursue the subject of the Hyndfords. Once again he changed ground.

"Now, if it wouldn't be too much trouble, Miss Hazlemere, I'd like you to take me into the garden and show me one or two things. I'm not quite sure about the geography of the place, and I'd be glad if you'd help me to get it clear in my mind."

Joyce consulted Corwen with a glance and apparently received permission. Without answering the Superintendent directly, she led the way out of the house.

"I'd like to see where you landed from the canoe that night," Ross suggested.

As they walked down toward the river, the Superintendent displayed more than his usual languid interest in gardening, for he lingered here and there as some choice display of flowers caught his attention.

"Your violas make a fine mass of colour, there," he observed, pointing to them as he passed. "What are they? Edinas?"

Joyce shook her head.

"No, they're Acmes."

"I've found that Blue Rocks do very well in my little garden," the Superintendent confided, artlessly.

A few yards further on, a fresh bed attracted his notice.

"You seem to have more luck with verbenas than I ever have," he confessed. "That's a wonderful show yonder. They never seem to do well with me, something wrong with the soil, perhaps. These are Miss Willmotts, aren't they?"

This time Joyce nodded without speaking. The Superintendent's effort to bring matters on to a more friendly footing did not seem very successful. James Corwen was growing obviously restive at what he regarded as a mere waste of his time; and by his manner he succeeded in dragging the unwilling Superintendent past the remainder of the display. They emerged on the river-bank.

"This is where I got ashore from Mr. Seaforth's canoe," Joyce explained, going forward to point out the exact spot.

The Superintendent went to her side and then turned round to face the house.

"You could see the French window from here, I notice," he said. "You'd see the light was on in the drawing-room when you came ashore?"

Joyce considered for a moment or two.

"If you mean I noticed it specially, then I didn't. It was on, of course, but that had no particular importance so far as I was concerned."

"It was on, that's all I wanted," the Superintendent explained. "And I suppose, since it was on, you decided to go into the house through the French window?"

"Well, I usually go in that way from here, if the window's open. It saves walking round the house to the front door."

"Exactly. And you were surprised to find the window closed?"

"I expected it to be open, of course, on a warm night like that, since my aunt hadn't gone up to bed. I guessed that, since the light was left on."

"Of course. And you went straight up from here to the house? You could see your way all right?"

"Yes, it was a brilliant moonlight night. Every thing was as clear as day."

"I remember; that came out in the evidence, somewhere or other. Now, Miss Hazlemere, you said at the inquest that it took you five minutes to go up to the house, make your discovery, and come back here again. That's the best estimate you can give? It wasn't, say, seven minutes or eight minutes?"

"I should say it was about five minutes," Joyce confirmed, after a pause for consideration. "I can't time it to a second, of course; but at any rate it wasn't ten minutes. You understand what I mean, don't you?"

The Superintendent made a gesture of comprehension.

"To be sure! It's always hard to gauge time without a watch beside you. And you came back again to this point, didn't you, when you called Mr. Seaforth in again?"

"Yes. At least I called to him before I actually got to the bank."

Superintendent Ross seemed to have lost interest in details.

"Shall we go back to the house again?" he suggested. "I'd like to have a look at that French window."

As they were passing along one of the paths, the Superintendent paused in such a way as to detain his companions.

"That's a nice bed," he said, admiringly. "Perennials, aren't they? You don't change them often, I suppose?"

"They were there when I came here first, so they've been in for a couple of years at least," Joyce explained, rather impatiently. "They may have been there for longer, but I can't say."

Superintendent Ross nodded thoughtfully. His next question was directed to James Corwen, but it was Joyce's face that he watched while he was putting it into words:

"Perhaps you can tell me, Mr. Corwen. Is this *Digitalis grandiflora* or *Digitalis purpurea?*"

"How should I know?" Corwen growled. "I'm not a botanist."

He had some reason for his vexation. By this unexpected method of attack, the Superintendent had over-reached him. Though the question was, in words, addressed to the solicitor, it was evidently in Joyce's face that Ross hoped to read the response to the unspoken demand: "Do you know that digitalis can be extracted from this plant in your garden?" And the deliberately indirect method of attack left it uncertain whether this was the crucial piece of evidence or whether Ross had already seen something which had decided him to press home a charge against Joyce at a later stage. Corwen was left in doubt as to the Superintendent's outlook, the very thing which he most wished to ascertain.

What was even more irritating to a man like James Corwen, the Superintendent had evidently proved himself the sharper of the two. While the solicitor was preparing to base one of the most important parts of the defence upon the fact that digitalis was a scheduled poison, hedged about with all sorts of restrictions, Ross had outflanked the whole argument and had discovered what Corwen himself had failed to note—a possible source of the digitalin which figured so ominously at the inquest, a source outside all the restraints of the Pharmacy Act. With less than ten words, the Superintendent had knocked away what seemed to be one of the strongest props in the case for the defence.

James Corwen's eyes followed those of the Superintendent and he watched Joyce's face to see the effect of Ross's thrust. Effect there was, certainly. No one could have missed Joyce's start of dismay as the Superintendent pronounced the ill-omened "*Digitalis.*" But here Corwen had grudgingly to admit the cleverness of the attack. He himself failed to determine whether the change in Joyce's expression implied one or other of two things. It might have indicated a guilty knowledge of the plant's properties; or, equally well, it might merely have been dismay at the realisation of the sinister interpretation which could be placed upon a wholly irrelevant fact—the presence of the digitalis in the garden of The Cedars.

"Hardly fair, that, Superintendent," the solicitor said between his teeth.

Ross seemed not to hear the low-voiced censure. He turned away and examined plants more carefully. At last he broke off one or two flowers and some leaves, as though to study them comfortably in his hand.

"I'm not sure, but it looks like *Digitalis purpurea*," he decided at last.

James Corwen was in danger of forgetting his own advice to Seaforth about keeping temper out of legal affairs. He had seen Joyce's face—just as Ross had done—under the shock of that grim hint so neatly conveyed; but that was of no help to him in guessing the inference Ross had drawn from the girl's behaviour. Had it convinced him of her guilt? James Corwen wanted to know that very much indeed. If the Superintendent continued to question Joyce, that would settle the matter for the present. He would have to abide by the Judges' Rules and show his hand by cautioning the person he suspected. But if he put no further inquiries it might mean either that he meant to bring a charge later on or else merely that he had already secured all the information he could get from this particular witness.

"I don't think I need trouble you any further, Miss Hazlemere," the Superintendent volunteered. "I shall have to look over the drawing-room now, but I'm sure you won't want to go there."

As he spoke he slipped the leaves and flowers he had gathered into his pocket; but the gesture was so mechanical that it looked as if he were merely stowing them away to avoid littering the paths with the debris. Joyce accepted her dismissal with obvious relief. She was still visibly perturbed by the Superintendent's last stab and seemed only too glad to get away. James Corwen was about to follow her when Ross restrained him.

"I think you'd better come with me," he suggested. "Perhaps it would be as well if you saw things with your own eyes."

The turn of this phrase seemed to give the solicitor some food for thought as he accompanied the Superintendent through the garden to the house. Taken at its face value, it suggested either a complete exculpation of his client in the detective's mind, or else a case against her so strong that Ross felt he could play with all his cards on the table.

The Superintendent led the way to the French window of the drawing-room, which had been left closed as it was on the night of the tragedy. Ross examined the little terrace in front of it in a very cursory fashion and then, stepping forward, he inspected the lever catches of the double window through the glass.

"H'm!" he said, half to himself. "The usual horn-shaped handles with a small knob at the point of the horn. I thought as much. There's nothing in it."

He did not trouble to divulge what "it" was, rather to Corwen's annoyance; and before the solicitor could make up his mind whether he could venture a question on the point, Ross turned away from the window and led the way round the house to the front door.

At the entrance to the drawing-room, the Superintendent paused to break some seals which secured the door; then, standing aside, he ushered the solicitor in. A glance assured James Corwen that the place had been left completely undisturbed since the night of the tragedy; and his eye was caught by further seals on the inner side of the windows. Ross saw the look and smiled rather sardonically.

"My colleagues seem to have done their best to make the place burglar-proof," he said in explanation. "They had orders to leave everything exactly as it was until I came across; so they had to make sure there was no unauthorised tampering."

"Burglar-proof!" James Corwen grunted contemptuously. "You don't imagine anyone who really wanted to get in would be stopped by a yard or two of tape and a few bits of sealing-wax, do you?"

Superintendent Ross's smile broadened slightly, but he offered no defence. It was his business to tell the solicitor that the police were keeping a day-and-night watch on the house. He was not the person to leave important evidence at the mercy of anyone who chose to break in at night; and he was not above setting a trap with the evidence as a bait, even though he regarded the chance of a catch as practically negligible.

"Let's see," he said, crossing the room to a small side-table. "Yes, that's all right—two tumblers along with the decanter and the bottles of soda—Grattan's brand with screw stoppers."

James Corwen came up to his side and looked down at the tray, on which stood the articles the Superintendent had mentioned.

"They all look a bit dusty," he commented.

"Our men have been looking for finger-prints, dusting the things over and then photographing anything that appeared," Ross explained casually.

"Did you find anything interesting?" the solicitor inquired in a tentative tone.

The Superintendent seemed to have no objections to giving information on this point.

"Nothing in the way of finger-prints on the empty sodas. Mrs. Fenton's own prints on the tumbler and on the decanter. An unidentified set of prints turned up on the second tumbler."

James Corwen immediately saw the inference which could be drawn from this to help his client.

"So Mrs. Fenton had a guest that night apparently. Miss Hazlemere doesn't drink whiskey and soda." He stopped and sniffed unavailingly at the mouth of the second tumbler. "I suppose there was whiskey in both of them?"

"There was," the Superintendent admitted frankly.

He did not seem inclined to waste any further time over the tray. Though he did not think it necessary to tell Corwen so, he had photographs of the finger-prints on an enlarged scale in his pocket; and all he had wanted was to see the tray itself in case it might suggest anything to his mind. But nothing out of the common met his eye, so he turned elsewhere.

"You knew Mrs. Fenton's handwriting, of course," he said, directing Corwen's attention to a small escritoire. "I've got to go through the papers in that thing—they tell me there are some letters and so forth in it which will probably pass into your hands later on, since you're her lawyer. I expect you have some idea of the people she corresponded with and it'll be a help to me if you can tell me something about them. They'd be mere names to me if I looked through the papers alone. And you'll be able to pick out any stuff in her own writing much quicker than I could do."

James Corwen made no objection to this obviously reasonable suggestion; and the Superintendent, after a glance at the top of the escritoire, opened the first drawer. The huddled mass of papers in it betrayed the character of its late owner; and Ross groaned inwardly at the thought of having to wade through the confusion. One sheet of manuscript, carelessly thrown in on top of the rest, attracted his attention first; and he lifted it gingerly so as to leave as few finger-prints as possible on it.

"That's some of Mrs. Fenton's writing," Corwen volunteered as the Superintendent held up the paper.

"Well, we may begin with it—"

Ross broke off his sentence with an inarticulate expression of surprise. James Corwen leaned over and read the document. It was evidently the draft of a letter which the dead woman had written on the day of her death, as the date showed.

> "Sir,—I see no reason for changing my mind. This morning I told you plainly that I expected you to pay the money before the end of this week, and you must do so without any further putting off. I have been put off again and again, and now this must stop. You have collected the rents on my property long ago and you have no right to make all this delay in paying over the cash to me and I am surprised at your even suggesting it now after all the delay. If I do not get your cheque by return post I shall consult my solicitor and make you pay without more ado. He will go into your accounts and square up the whole business, as I shall now, of course, take my affairs out of your hands. I am keeping a copy of this letter.
>
> "Yours faithfully,
>
> "E. Fenton."
>
> "Mr. H. Watchet."

The Superintendent read the letter over twice before saying anything.

"Who's Mr. H. Watchet?" he asked at length.

"He is the estate agent who looked after some house-property that Mrs. Fenton owned," Corwen explained. "His office is a few doors away from mine on the same side of the street."

"Did she write to you on this matter?" Ross inquired.

Corwen shook his head.

"No, we got no letter bearing on that point."

"H'm! She saw this fellow on the morning of her death. This letter was probably written in the afternoon or evening. Before her time-limit for his cheque was up, she was dead; so she didn't need to write to you about it. I expect that's it."

James Corwen had drawn an obvious inference from the state of affairs revealed by the document.

"That's a new thread in your case for you, Superintendent," he commented with a certain relief in his tone. "Mrs. Fenton's death seems to have come very conveniently for Mr. Watchet."

"That's one way of looking at it, certainly," said the Superintendent, evasively.

He put the draft letter aside, and began to go through the rest of the papers as systematically as was possible in view of their confusion. From time to time he referred to the solicitor for information about the persons whose names cropped up; but by the time he had completed his search, nothing of any apparent importance had come to light.

"That seems to be the lot," the Superintendent said as he put down the last document. "Barring that draft letter, there's nothing here that's of any importance to me. I suppose there's no question that it's in her own handwriting?"

"None whatever."

Superintendent Ross closed the drawer on which his hand was resting and turned away from the escritoire. He made a brief examination of the handles of the French window, but seemed to find nothing fresh in them. With an apology to Corwen for keeping him waiting, he made a rapid search of the room; but so far as the solicitor could see this produced no new evidence.

"I just want to ask that maid a couple of questions before I go," Ross explained as he abandoned his perquisition. "Where's the bell? Oh, it's here."

He rang for the maid, but before she arrived he had ushered the solicitor out of the drawing-room and closed the door.

"I wonder if you can tell me something," he said when the girl appeared. "I want to find out if Mrs. Fenton posted a letter either in the afternoon or the early evening, that night she died. Perhaps you saw her go out with an envelope in her hand?"

"Oh, I can tell you that. I posted one for her myself in the afternoon. I remember it because she left it to the last minute, and then told me to run for the post at the pillar along the road."

"You don't remember the address on it?"

The maid shook her head.

"No, I didn't look at it. Why should I?"

"No reason at all. I just thought your eye might have dropped on it as you were posting it, or something like that."

"Well, I don't remember anything about it."

Ross had hardly expected more than this. He turned to a fresh subject.

"You answer the front door, don't you? On that night, had Mrs. Fenton a visitor? Did you let anyone in?"

The maid shook her head positively.

"No, nobody called that night that I know of. I mean I let nobody in by the front door."

"What about the cook? She didn't open the front door to someone, by any chance?"

"It was the cook's night out. There was nobody but me to answer the front-door bell."

"What made me ask was because there were two tumblers in the drawing-room. Did Mrs. Fenton not ring for an extra tumbler at any time? She'd need only one for herself."

"Mrs. Fenton always had the tray brought in with two tumblers and two half-bottles of soda, whether there was anyone expected or not. She didn't like ringing the bell when she had a visitor."

"You mean that you left the tray with the decanter and so forth in the room after dinner, before Mrs. Fenton went in?"

"Yes."

"Now I see," said the Superintendent gratefully. "There's another point. I suppose there might have been a visitor all the same, that night. Someone might have come in through the French window of the drawing-room. Would you have seen that if it had happened? Any of the windows of the kitchen look out on the garden?"

"No. All our windows face the road. Only the reception rooms and the bedrooms face the garden."

"Suppose anyone *had* come in, and later on went out by the front door, would you have heard anything?"

The maid shook her head definitely.

"No, the kitchen's ever so far away from the front door. Anyhow, I didn't hear anyone going out, if that's what you mean."

The Superintendent had no further questions to ask, so he dismissed the maid.

"Just a moment, Mr. Corwen," he added, when she had gone. "I want to refix these seals on the door."

He pulled some sealing-wax from his pocket, replaced the tapes, and settled things to his satisfaction.

"Now, if you're walking back into town, I'll go along with you," he suggested. "But perhaps you want to talk to Miss Hazlemere?"

James Corwen seemed to hesitate for a moment before replying. Evidently he came to the conclusion that there was a chance of learning something from the Superintendent, even at this stage; for after a moment he fell in with the proposal.

"Then if Miss Hazlemere wouldn't mind putting her signature to these notes of mine," Ross suggested, "we might push along."

The solicitor went in search of Joyce and brought her to the morning-room into which he had directed the Superintendent. Ross glanced critically at the girl's face as she came in. She was even less confident than she had been when he first encountered her; and he noticed that she seemed to rely more on her solicitor than before.

"I'll just read over my notes, Miss Hazlemere, and then if you find them correct, you can sign them and put things in order," he suggested.

James Corwen intervened.

"I think it would be more correct if Miss Hazlemere read them herself. Or perhaps I could read them over aloud to her?"

"Just as you please," the Superintendent conceded, handing over his notebook open at the proper page.

Joyce listened apathetically to the jottings which Ross had put down. Quite obviously she was depending upon James Corwen to object to any errors if he found them. The solicitor read out the statements deliberately, pausing for consideration after each clause; but as he drew near the end, he unconsciously began to hurry a little. What he specially wanted to see was how the Superintendent worded the part of the notes dealing with the digitalis. But when he reached that point in the notebook, he found that all reference to the incident was omitted. For a moment he paused, as though considering whether to challenge the correctness of the report; but almost immediately he seemed to make up his mind to let sleeping dogs lie. Technically, the Superintendent was quite within his rights in leaving out the topic.

"That seems correct," he said, as he finished his reading. "Miss Hazlemere will sign it for you."

The detective offered his fountain-pen and Joyce put a shaky signature at the end of the notes.

"That finishes the matter," Ross said briskly, as he put the notebook back into his pocket. "Thanks for your patience, Miss Hazlemere. I hate worrying people."

He turned to the solicitor.

"I think we'd better be getting along back to town," he suggested. "But perhaps you'd like to have a word or two with Miss Hazlemere before you leave? I'll walk on slowly and you can overtake me."

When he had left the room and closed the door behind him, Joyce turned eagerly to James Corwen.

"What does he think?" she demanded in a quivering voice. "Does he think I did it? Has he found out anything?"

James Corwen considered for a moment before answering. After all, he was under no pledge of secrecy with regard to Ross's discovery.

"He's found something that might point to someone else," he assured her, cautiously.

"Not to Leslie?"

"No, someone quite different," James Corwen reassured her. "But if I were you," he added, "I think I should be very careful about mentioning names like that. It might casily be twisted into a suggestion that you suspect Mr. Seaforth yourself."

CHAPTER VII
THE MAN WITH THE ALIASES

THE SUPERINTENDENT had lingered intentionally, and James Corwen overtook him only a hundred yards from the gate of The Cedars. When they fell into step, side by side, the solicitor pursued his usual policy of forcing the other man to speak first; and for a short time they walked in silence. The Superintendent, however, had not waited for James Corwen merely in order to have his company; he wanted information from him; consequently he was driven into making the first move.

"The difficulty in this case," he said, half-apologetically, "is that most of the people in it are nothing more than names so far as I'm concerned. The result is, one's tempted to concentrate one's attention on the persons that one's seen; and that means a wrong perspective of the whole business."

James Corwen was sufficiently acute to see the bait thrown out to him. In effect, the Superintendent had said: "My attention's been mainly devoted to your client because I know most about her. If you gave me some facts about other people, it might incline me to look further afield and trouble my head less about Miss Hazlemere." The solicitor was too wary to reveal that he perceived the underlying meaning.

"I'm not the editor of a 'Who's Who in Stanningmore,'" he said, gruffly. "You'd better try Dorrington. He sub-edits the local rag, and rather prides himself on knowing most things that go on in the place. You've seen him: foreman of the jury at the inquest."

"I know something about him," the Superintendent admitted cautiously. "But I'd rather trust your information than his."

James Corwen was not specially amenable to flattery. He merely grunted in response to this feeler, and the Superintendent was driven to more direct methods.

"I'll save you the bother of speculating," he said. "The line of argument's simple enough and I've no objection to putting my cards on the table. Two glasses used that night in the drawing-room: a visitor. Whiskey in both glasses: a male visitor, most likely. Male visitor hasn't volunteered his evidence: suspicious, perhaps. Mrs. Fenton had various male friends: which of 'em was it? I've no suspicions of anyone in particular. My mind's quite open on that point. But I must have some information about these people if I'm to get any further forward. You have information, therefore I come to you for it."

James Corwen discounted the apparent frankness of the Superintendent. Ross had told him nothing that an average intelligence would have failed to see.

"Well, ask your questions," he said, grudgingly. "But you needn't expect much. There's a law against slander."

The Superintendent seemed in a mood to be grateful for even small mercies.

"So far, I've only come up against five names of men who had anything to do with Mrs. Fenton. That's excluding yourself, of course: you were her lawyer. The ones I mean are Mr. Fenton, Mr. Seaforth, Dr. Hyndford, Mr. Hyndford, and this estate agent—what's his name?—Watchet, isn't it? I want to know as much as I can about these five to start with."

"Ask your questions," James Corwen repeated, impatiently.

He had hoped that Ross would betray something by inquiring first about the man of whom he was most suspicious; but the Superintendent had avoided this pitfall by offering the names in a perfectly logical order beginning with the husband and going down through grades of intimacy until he ended up with the estate agent.

"I'm just going to," Ross answered. "Can you tell me anything about Mr. Fenton?"

"No. He's one of my clients."

"Ah! indeed! Then that finishes us with him," the Superintendent admitted with no sign of chagrin. "Then what about Mr. Seaforth?"

"He's an employee of mine."

The Superintendent seemed slightly taken aback by this second rebuff.

"You're not proving exactly a mine of information, Mr. Corwen," he commented rather ruefully. "Perhaps you can do something more for me in the case of the two Hyndford brothers? What sort of people are they?"

James Corwen relaxed slightly. Now that the line of inquiry was passing away from the girl whose defence he was preparing, he seemed more inclined to be communicative; but his natural caution restrained him from too blunt expressions of his opinions. He took refuge in an illustrative anecdote.

"I used to know the Hyndfords fairly well when they were boys," he began, somewhat to the surprise of the Superintendent who had not expected to dive so far into ancient history. "Simon—that's the doctor—was one of these athletic fellows, in those days: good at football and gymnastics and not much else."

"More brawn than brains, you mean?" the Superintendent interjected.

"He hadn't a first-rate intellect by any means," James Corwen confirmed. "But he had a certain subtlety somewhere in his character and he was a bit of a bully, as I remember him. He liked to domineer over smaller boys, order them about, and thrash them if they didn't do as they were told. But I never saw him try it on with anyone near his own size."

The contempt in James Corwen's voice was perfectly perceptible to the Superintendent. Ross began to see why the solicitor preferred to deal with ancient history rather than to give his opinion of Dr. Hyndford at the present day. Reminiscences of one's boyhood may be illustrative, but they are hardly slanderous.

"It has always seemed to me curious that one finds such contrasts between members of the same family," James Corwen went on in a reflective tone. "Take the Hyndfords as an example. Dickie was almost the complement of his brother in every way. If you could have taken the good qualities out of each of them, you might have made quite a decent creature with what you got. Dickie was a miserable little brute, physically: thin, small-boned, no muscular development of any sort, hopeless at games. It was only on the intellectual side that he scored over Simon, for he had twice as good a brain as his brother if he could only be persuaded to use it."

The solicitor gave the impression that he had drifted away on a tide of reminiscence; but Superintendent Ross had more than suspicion that there was something definite behind all this. He refrained from interrupting, so as to let Corwen choose his own line.

"Dickie Hyndford was cursed with another characteristic," the lawyer went on. "On the surface, he gave the impression of being the most easily discouraged creature you could well imagine. He never tackled a thing without looking on the black side of the prospect. Everything he took up was a sort of forlorn hope, if you believed all he had to say about it. And yet, somewhere in him there was a streak of the most damnable tenacity that pulled him through in the end, generally. The result was that he got very little credit for anything he achieved. He had made such a show of being disheartened that people put the final success down to a stroke of luck and discounted it accordingly. But my own impression of him always was that he took the long view and would see a thing through if he once took it up."

He paused for a moment as though wondering whether to go on or not. At last he seemed to make up his mind.

"One doesn't need to be much of a psychologist to see what would happen in a family like that," he continued. "Simon had it all his own way. I saw a good deal of it, and there must have been a lot behind that no one knew except the two of them. You can guess what it means when a small boy falls into the hands of a bullying brother; the moral effect is thoroughly bad, not so much on account of the bullying as because it affects the child's whole outlook. It's a case of fighting a losing battle the whole time, and knowing that the decision's settled before the thing has even begun. There isn't even a chance of winning."

The Superintendent was something of a psychologist himself, and he began to find Corwen's narrative amusing.

"Why didn't the youngster give the show away?" he demanded. "That seems an obvious way out."

The solicitor shook his head.

"I confess it's almost incredible that he didn't. But you have to take into account that subtlety in Simon's character that I mentioned to you. He didn't depend altogether on physical force. Dickie was a sensitive youngster and very fond of his father. Simon played on that string—very cleverly too. Amongst his other qualities, he had a certain turn for low spying; and naturally he was soon able to detect Dickie in a lot of little peccadillos. That was the weapon Simon wanted. He had enough cunning to play on Dickie's sensitive imagination and persuade him that if these things came out, their father would be furious. Nonsense, of course; but a child's perspective is very different from ours. A shilling picked up off his father's desk may loom as big to him as the embezzlement of £50,000 to a grown man. And Dickie wasn't by any means a plaster angel in those days. He supplied Simon with plenty of ammunition."

James Corwen glanced at the Superintendent's face as though to determine if he was bored. Apparently what he saw was sufficient to encourage him.

"Perhaps I have not laid enough stress on Simon's ingenuity in this persecution. He really was rather subtle in his methods. Dickie was little better than a slave to his brother, after a fair course of this treatment. He had to do exactly as he was ordered, or else—!"

"A form of blackmailing, eh?" the Superintendent epitomised. "Blackmailers are about the lowest grade of criminals, to my mind. But surely," he went on, "a game of that sort would be bound to be spotted, sooner or later."

"I think you underrate Simon's subtlety, Superintendent. I can't have stressed it enough. Here's an example of it. Suppose you were in Simon's place and you wanted to give orders to the youngster under his father's nose. Perhaps, feeling a bit more courageous than usual, the boy refuses to do as you tell him. Remember, the orders had to take the form of mere suggestions in these circumstances. How would you have applied an extra touch of the spur?"

"Oh, I expect a scowl or a wink or something of that sort would have served the purpose."

"And their father might have seen the scowl? Simon was more ingenious than that. So far as the rest of the family knew, he and Dickie were on perfectly good terms. Half Simon's amusement came from that, I believe. He liked to be able to flourish the whip right in front of his father, knowing that only Dickie could see the lash. You see, he wasn't depending on a single peccadillo of Dickie's. He had quite a list of them. What he did was to invent a series of . . . well, cues, one might call them. One of Dickie's misdeeds had to do with a broken fishing-rod. The catchword for that was Izaak Walton. If Dickie showed any signs of rebelling when his father was there, Simon would drag Izaak into the talk as a gentle hint."

"The psychology of that's sound enough," the Superintendent admitted. "You mean that he could suggest a concrete example of what he could tell, just by an apparently innocent word or two; and he could select the particular example that he thought would tell most in these special circumstances?"

"Something like that," James Corwen agreed. "Simon had a general gale warning as well. It was even more ingenious, I believe. Sometimes it might be inadvisable to talk inconsequently about Guy Fawkes or Izaak Walton. In that case, Simon fell back on one of the airs out of *San Toy*. It was new in those days. Perhaps you remember it?"

James Corwen hummed a couple of lines which the Superintendent recognised:

> "Kowtow! Kowtow to the great Yen How!
> And wish him the longest of lives. . . ."

"For Yen How, read Simon; and the application's obvious," the solicitor pointed out. "And there's nothing very suspicious in a boy's humming 'Kowtow, kowtow . . .' under his breath."

"That's pretty ingenious for a youngster," Ross admitted, with no great admiration in his tone. "But you seem to know a lot about it. Did you never think of stepping in yourself?"

"I only heard the whole story long afterwards. Mr. Hyndford told most of it to me himself after he came back from Japan. It came up somehow to illustrate some point we were talking about. Something to do with lack of self-confidence produced by early influences."

"You don't paint a very attractive picture of Dr. Hyndford, I must say," the Superintendent pointed out.

"I wasn't talking about Dr. Hyndford as he is," James Corwen declared with a grim smile. "I was merely indulging in a few reminiscences of a couple of schoolboys."

"I understand that," Ross returned with a perfectly grave face. "But isn't it rather surprising that they're living in the same house nowadays? I'd have thought, with a history like that, the younger brother would have dropped his senior like a hot potato as soon as he could. Most people would."

"Oh, I suppose one gets broadminded as time goes on. After all, why should one keep these things alive? I see no sign of any ill-feeling between them. In fact, if they have a difference of opinion, the doctor always gets his way without any fuss, which would hardly be the case if his brother cherished a grievance. They've no other relations, which perhaps makes a difference."

The Superintendent asked no further questions about the Hyndford brothers. James Corwen had made it clear enough that he would give no information about their present doings; and Ross had no intention of courting a direct rebuff. He turned to the last name on his list.

"What about this fellow Watchet?" he asked. "There seems to be hankey-pankey in the affair somewhere, to judge from that letter you saw. Do you know anything about him?"

The solicitor was not encouraging.

"Mrs. Fenton looked after that part of her affairs herself. My firm had nothing to do with it. I never spoke to Watchet in my life."

"A blank end, there, then," Ross admitted. "I'll need to try elsewhere for information."

By this time they had reached the streets of the town, and James Corwen obviously had no desire to discuss confidential matters where they might be overheard. The Superintendent forestalled an impending attempt to shake him off by halting and taking his leave.

"I go up this way," he said, indicating a side-street. "I suppose you're going back to your office?"

The solicitor nodded and they parted. For a moment or two Ross watched his late companion's figure threading its way through the traffic on the pavement.

"Sly old fox!" he commented inwardly. "I wonder what he's really after. Was he merely trying to attract my attention away from that client of his or had he something else in his mind? He certainly didn't lay himself out to give me a good impression of the doctor, and that's a fact."

Musing over this problem, he walked slowly along the street, when suddenly he heard someone calling after him.

"Superintendent Ross! Just wait a minute, will you?"

He swung round and confronted a sandy-haired little man with an eager face which somehow reminded him of a friendly terrier.

"You don't know me, Superintendent . . ."

Ross's mobile face assumed an ominously solemn expression.

"You're mistaken," he said, seriously. "I do know you. In fact I know all the suspicious characters in town."

The little man was plainly taken aback. "Suspicious characters?" he demanded. "What's suspicious about me, eh?"

"I'm always suspicious of a man who passes under an alias," the Superintendent explained, gravely. "And when it runs to half-a-dozen aliases, it makes me seriously perturbed."

"Aliases? What're you talking about?"

"Aliases," said Ross patiently. "On Mondays, when you're writing the 'Garden Notes,' you call yourself Spademan; on Thursdays, you're Lady Maisie, who gives 'Household Hints'; on Saturdays, you go completely over the score, for you pose as A.C.F. when you're doing the 'Talks with Mothers' column, and as Wayfarer when you write 'From an Armchair' in a religious vein. I've more than a suspicion that you may be Singleton of the Bridge Article, and Hook-up who turns out the stuff on wireless once a week. And, finally, you're Mr. William Dorrington at your home address. A man with all these aliases must have some dark secret in his life—or lives, as the case may be. Shortness of staff is what I'm inclined to suspect."

The Superintendent had gauged his man accurately.

"Keep it dark," the journalist begged in mock terror. "I'm nominally a sub-editor and I'd hate anyone to know I did any writing with anything except a blue pencil. I'll own up and come quietly if you'll keep my guilty secret. I do write about half the *Gazette* myself, if the truth must come out. The office-boy helps us with the rest, and the printer does the poetry for us."

"And just now, I suppose, you're Thorndyke Holmes, the Crime Expert of the *Stanningmore Gazette*, hot on the trail?"

"Something of the sort. Come along to the office and have a drink, will you? I want to talk to you."

"You mean you want me to talk to you?" corrected Ross. "No drinks then, thank you. The charm of your company's enough attraction in itself. And since you've so obviously got no ulterior motives, I'll give you a bit of exclusive information. The police have a clue."

"They always have a clue," the journalist exclaimed disgustedly. "That's no use to me. Not interesting enough."

"Well, then," the Superintendent suggested soothingly, "you can say the police have several clues. That'll make it ever so much more exciting for your readers. Several times as interesting, in fact."

"Is that all the length you've got?" Dorrington demanded. "Why, I thought that by this time you'd have found arsenic in the weed-killer and a new cement floor in the cellar. These are the very first things to look for in any case nowadays. You don't seem to read the newspapers at all, in the Force."

He halted at a door which bore the name of *The Stanningmore Gazette*.

"Here we are! We'll go upstairs."

By the time that Superintendent Ross was ensconced in an easy-chair in the sub-editor's room, he had established his relations with Dorrington on an easy footing, and it was time to turn to serious business.

"I'll be quite frank with you, Mr. Dorrington," he said in a tone from which all flippancy had vanished. "When you came across me in the street, I was actually on my road here to see you. There's no use in beating about the bush. I want you to work the Press for me."

Dorrington pricked up his ears. This looked as though *The Gazette* might make a scoop after all.

"That's talking," he said. "Let's hear what you want, and I'll see if it can be done."

Superintendent Ross considered for a moment.

"I'll put my cards on the table," he said slowly. "I know enough about you to rely on your discretion, Mr. Dorrington. The fact is, Mrs. Fenton had at least one visitor that night—someone who got in and out of the house without being seen. What I don't know, and what I very much want to know, is the identity of that visitor. I'm not without a suspicion or two, but I want something definite."

"I see," said Dorrington, reflectively. "You want us to put a paragraph into *The Gazette* hinting that you know a bit more than you really do, and suggesting how suspicious it is that this visitor hasn't volunteered evidence?"

"Something of the sort," Ross confirmed. "But be diplomatic over it. Don't get all four feet in the trough at once."

"I'll see that's done for you."

The sub-editor made a jotting on a pad.

"Anything else?" he inquired.

"Another thing, but you won't be able to use it in the paper. Not immediately, at any rate," Ross added, as he saw Dorrington's face fall at the qualification. "You're a bit of a botanist. It breaks out here and there in your Garden Notes. I want an expert opinion."

"I only know some of the commoner things—"

Dorrington began doubtfully.

"This is one of them," the Superintendent interrupted.

He put his hand into his pocket and extracted some of the leaves and flowers which he had secured at The Cedars.

"What do you make of these?" he asked, holding them out in the palm of his hand. "Which is it: *Digitalis grandiflora* or *Digitalis purpurea?*"

The ill-omened name had its immediate effect on the journalist.

"By Gad," he exclaimed. "That's smart! I take back what I said about weed-killers and cement floors. This is a winner! I could kick myself for not having thought of it myself. So damned simple when you see it in front of you: a poison factory in the garden, what?"

He examined the debris on the Superintendent's palm.

"*Digitalis purpurea*," he pronounced.

"So I thought," Ross answered. "By the way, have you an envelope?"

Dorrington passed one across to him, and the Superintendent sealed up the leaves and petals, putting the packet into his pocket when he had done so.

"Where did you get 'em?" Dorrington demanded.

"In a garden," answered the Superintendent with a grin. "We needn't mention names, need we? And we certainly won't print anything about it in our Garden News, I take it?"

"Well, if you say so, of course " the journalist conceded reluctantly. "You'll give us the first rake-off, though, when the time comes to turn on the publicity-tap?"

"That's understood," Ross agreed readily. "Well, I've given you a paragraph; I've entrusted you with a State Secret; and now it's about time you did something for me, by way of a change. I want some odds and ends of information about various people."

"The sort of thing we don't print, I suppose?" the sub-editor questioned in a doubtful voice. "I might be had up for slander."

"I've trusted you; now you trust me," the Superintendent pointed out.

"I've heard something like that before," Dorrington said in a derisive tone. "And to think I believed that the confidence trick was dead! One lives and learns, apparently, even in journalism. Well, what do you want me to tell you?"

"Are you a friend of Dr. Hyndford's?" Ross inquired.

"Not particularly. I nod to him in the street."

"I don't know him as intimately as that," Ross explained. "Your description of him makes me feel I'd like to hear more. Can you give me a character sketch of him—just a few salient points?"

Dorrington considered for a moment or two before answering.

"This is the best I can do," he began. "Professional standing: he's a good average G.P. and would never be anything better. Social position: not unpopular, but he consorts mostly with people just a shade lower than himself socially. Mrs. Fenton was an exception. Literary tastes: he reads nothing but the football and racing news, and *Ruff's Guide*. If you ask him a date, he says: 'That was the year of Sansovino's Derby,' or 'It was the summer that Pogrom won the Oaks.' Financial status: not usually very flush, unless he happens to have picked a winner. Matrimonial intentions: strictly dishonourable, according to gossip; they say he leans towards polygamy with a complete disregard for ceremony."

"That doesn't help very much," the Superintendent commented, as Dorrington paused after delivering his summary.

"Well, strictly between ourselves," the journalist added, "the impression I get of him is that he's an unscrupulous devil. Mind, I've no evidence to back it. It's just what one feels about him. There's a sort of mean streak somewhere, though I couldn't put my finger on it exactly."

"'I do not like thee, Dr. Fell'?"

"Exactly."

The Superintendent changed the subject.

"I believe Mrs. Fenton dabbled in betting too?"

"So they say. She and the doctor had that taste in common."

"It's quite certain, isn't it?" Superintendent Ross asked. "What puzzles me about it is that we haven't found a trace of any betting-books amongst her belongings. Now if she really went in for betting, you'd think she'd have kept some notes; but we can't lay our hands on anything of the sort."

He stared at the journalist and then added hastily:

"That's confidential, of course. I don't want any little paragraphs about the matter."

"It seems a bit rum," Dorrington admitted thoughtfully. "She had the name of being pretty keen on the dibs; but she spent a lot on herself—dress and so forth—so probably there wasn't much to splash about after all. Haven't you found any account-books that might give a clue?"

Ross shook his head.

"She kept no accounts, it seems."

Again he changed the subject.

"This niece of hers, Miss Hazlemere, what about her?"

"I don't know her," the journalist admitted. "Nice girl, though, from all one hears."

"And young Seaforth?"

"Can't help you much with him either."

"Well, what about the doctor's brother?" Ross inquired.

"Hyndford? Oh, I do know a little about him. Nervous little beggar. The sort of man who starts all his sentences with: 'What I mean is . . .' instead of getting to his subject direct. He gives me the impression of being a bit under the shadow of his brother, somehow. Always gives in at once if there's any argument between them, and that sort of thing. At least, I only saw them together once or twice, and it rather struck me; so it must be fairly obvious."

"What does he do to fill in the time? I understand he's given up business."

"Oh, yes, lucky devil! He made some money in Japan—not a fortune, but enough to exist on. He does nothing that I know of. Potters around the garden and takes the dog for a walk. He's the sort of man who always gets interrupted when he begins to talk with three or four people there. Before he's got his little 'I mean to say . . .' off his chest, someone else has cut in and Hyndford subsides. He gives you the impression of a suppressed individuality, somehow, especially when his brother's about."

"Was he friendly with Mrs. Fenton?"

"Not particularly, so far as I know. She liked the doctor's type—the big, assertive brand. The younger brother wasn't her sort, I should imagine. But remember, I never knew them well enough to give an opinion; I'm just passing on some impressions I picked up here and there."

"Anything more about him?"

"Oh, yes, your speaking about Mrs. Fenton reminds me that Hyndford used to know Mr. Fenton. I shouldn't say they were anything in the Damon and Pythias line; but they had one or two things in common. Must have been a bit awkward for Hyndford when his brother got mixed up with Mrs. Fenton. Luckily Fenton doesn't live in town now."

Ross showed his comprehension with a nod, and the journalist did not pursue the subject.

"There's another man I want to know about," the Superintendent went on. "I believe Mrs. Fenton had some house-property run by an agent called Watling or Watchet or some such name. Know anything about him?"

The journalist's sharp eyes scanned Ross's face keenly. Evidently the introduction of Watchet's name had taken him by surprise.

"Watchet, you mean?" he said, after a moment. "Well, if it's strictly between ourselves, there's a good deal of talk going round about Watchet's affairs. The general impression seems to be that he's got his business into rather a muddle; and that he may have to go bankrupt. I can't guarantee it's more than a rumour, of course; and I'm giving it to you as such."

He looked up vexedly as the opening of the door interrupted him.

"Well, what is it?" he demanded, as the office-boy appeared on the threshold.

"There's a man downstairs, Mr. Dorrington. Wants to see you particularly, he says. I asked him what it was about, but he wouldn't tell me. So I got him to write it down and give it to me in an envelope."

He extended the missive as he spoke. Dorrington tore open the flap, glanced at the contents, and passed the sheet over to Ross with a warning glance.

> "Dere Sir,—I have some valuble infermation about the afair at the cedars. It will be a great sensasion for your paper and worth a lot of monney to you.
>
> "Nathan Sturry."

Dorrington turned to the office-boy.

"Who is this beggar? D'you know him?"

"He's one of the gardeners up at the Struan Museum," the boy explained, evidently delighted to show his knowledge. "I've seen him working there in the gardens often. He's in his best clothes now."

The sub-editor nodded.

"Well, tell him I'm busy just now with one of my reporters," he directed, giving the Superintendent an ironical side-glance as he spoke. "Ask him to wait for a minute or two; and then I'll be free to attend to him. You can bring him up here when I ring the bell."

As the office-boy closed the door behind him, Dorrington swung round in his swivel chair and faced Ross.

"I might have made a scoop over this—whatever it is," he pointed out, "but I'd rather work along with you than against you, if you'll deal fair with us. You won't let us down?"

The Superintendent made no reply in words, but his nod was reassuring.

"All right, then," said Dorrington. "You'd better sit over yonder at that table and make a noise like a reporter. A sort of Busy Bee sound, if you know what I mean. I'll dig into the informer's innards and bring the truth to light. By the way," he added, maliciously, "you'd better travel incognito. I'll call you—let's see—Hildebrand Robinson. It'll be a new experience for you, Superintendent, to have a fine alias like that. You can start suspecting yourself, now. Won't that be nice?"

As the Superintendent moved over to the table, Dorrington had a fresh idea.

"You'd better pretend to be doing something," he suggested. "An idle reporter would spoil the tone of the picture—an unheard-of phenomenon. Take a bit of paper and write: 'There-is-a-tide-in-the-affairs-of-men-which-taken-at-the-flood-leads-on-to-fortune' twenty or thirty times over and then start afresh. That'll help in the illusion."

"I think I can find something to occupy me," Ross retorted, pulling out his notebook. "I'm not so used to these time-wasting tricks as you are. You've got so much leisure in journalism that you're up to them all, I expect. In the police, it's different. Ring away. I'm ready."

He spread his notebook open on the desk and began to draw up a revised form of his diagram. As he sketched it out, it now assumed the following shape:

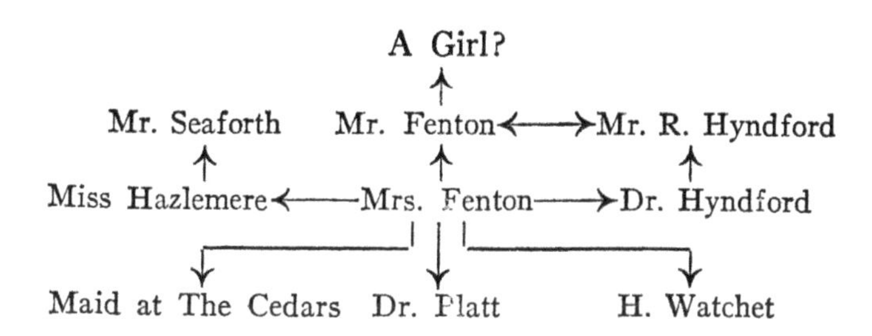

When the door opened, the Superintendent glanced up from his work with a frown, as though irked by the interruption. At first sight, the newcomer made no favourable impression. Greed and slyness were written large on the dull face; and his manner, as he entered the room, was a combination of self-importance and suspicion. Just the sort of man who tries to get the better of everyone, the Superintendent reflected. And the sort of man, too, who seldom brings it off.

"Well, what is it?" Dorrington demanded, testily. "We're busy just now."

The Superintendent gave the journalist a good mark for his method of attack. At one stroke he had cut away the self-importance of the gardener and reduced him to the state of someone receiving a favour instead of conferring one.

"My name's Nathan Sturry. . . ."

"I know that."

"I'm second gardener up at the Museum. . . ."

"I know that. What do you want?"

The gardener cast a suspicious glance in the Superintendent's direction.

"I asked for to see you private-like," he said, sullenly.

"About the business at The Cedars? I know that. This gentleman is working up the case; he'll be able to check what you say. That's why he's here. Go on."

The gardener seemed slightly reassured by this, though still suspicious.

"He'll be right smart if he can check this," he declared. "For why? Nobody knows it but me and two other people, and you can take your oath *they* won't split about it. Not much!"

"If it's important why don't you go to the police with it?"

"The police isn't offering any money," said Sturry frankly. "What would there be in it for me, if I went to the police. Just sweet damn all. That would be about it. But you, see? you would be paying for a bit of news, they say. And this *is* news, see? It ought to be worth a bit of money to you. What would you think of paying, I wonder?"

"Nothing for a pig in a poke."

The gardener seemed rather dashed by this.

"But if I was to tell you about it, then where'd I be?" he pointed out. "Some pigs is worth nothing, once they're out of the poke. This is one of them kind of pigs. If I was to tell you what I know, then you'd know it too; and you wouldn't likely give me anything for my pains. You don't catch Nathan Sturry like that, mister."

The journalist's bright eyes fastened themselves on the face of the gardener for a moment as though in an attempt to gauge his price.

"Ten bob down, then, and more later if your stuff's worth it," he snapped.

Apparently he had estimated correctly.

"Ten bob's not much," said Sturry complainingly. "It ought to be more nor that. What about a pound?"

But his tone showed that he was prepared to accept the original offer.

"Here's your ten bob," said Dorrington, passing a note across. "Now get on with it! I've no time to waste,"

Sturry examined the note carefully before stowing it away in his pocket. Then a fresh thought seemed to strike him, and his little piggish eyes showed a gleam of animation.

"Here's your ten bob's worth, then," he said, insolently. "Just before that there murder at The Cedars, a young fellow and his girl came up to see the Museum. By-and-by, they came outside and began to potter round about the gardens and at last they sat down on one of the seats and fell to talking. I was behind a hedge, near-by, and they didn't notice me. They thought they was all alone, see? I was sort of interested-like in their talk. They sounded at first as if they was quarrelling, and it was that attracted my attention and made me listen. I didn't pay no particular attention at the time to what they said; but afterwards things looked a bit different, once I'd heard some talk about the inquest. What them two talked about would be a titbit for that paper of yours, you can take my word. It'd put the blame on the right shoulders, see?"

He halted for a moment as though trying to see what effect he had produced.

"And I reckon that's all you get for your ten bob, mister," he added. "You'll have to fork out some more for the rest of the story."

He glanced slyly at the journalist, evidently feeling that he had out-manoeuvred him.

Dorrington swung round in his swivel chair and made a gesture to Ross.

"You'd better take it in hand now," he suggested, ignoring the gardener completely.

Sturry was evidently all at sea. Just when he thought he had gained his point, the game had become incomprehensible to him; and the expression on his face changed first to bewilderment and then to faint trepidation.

"I'm Superintendent Ross," the detective said, rising to his feet and coming across the room to confront Sturry.

There was something menacing in his attitude as he came to a halt in front of the gardener; and Sturry lost his air of truculence as a cold eye looked him up and down.

"I'm in charge of this case," Ross went on. "You've confessed that you've been suppressing evidence which ought to have been given to the police long ago. Got yourself into a tight corner, my man. Ever hear of being an accessory *ex post facto* or of committing misprision of felony? Pretty serious offences, both of them."

Sturry was too dumfounded to reply. All his self-assurance was gone, and he merely stared apprehensively at the Superintendent, without making any effort to defend himself.

"You'd better make a clean breast of it, Sturry," Ross advised him authoritatively. "I'm not inclined to stand any nonsense. The only thing left for you to do is to cough it all up. If you don't—"

The journalist suppressed a grin by a violent effort. He appreciated both the art and the meaning of that vague ending to the Superintendent's speech.

Sturry's standpoint was quite different. He had no knowledge of the law, and he had a very considerable fear of consequences. His attempt to make a little money out of his information had not been quite so successful as he had hoped. Still, he had that ten-bob note in his pocket; and most probably they'd forget about it and let him keep it. That would always be something. He made up his mind to take the Superintendent's advice.

"I didn't know there was any harm in it," he protested. "I hadn't a notion of that, see? I'll tell you anything you want for to know."

"Very well," said the Superintendent acidly. "Go ahead with your story. And this time, see you bring the whole pig out of the poke—every bristle of him."

Sturry nodded rather disconsolately.

"It was this way," he began. "Young Mr. Seaforth—him that's Secretary to the Struan Trust—he brought his girl up to the Museum that day. I'd never seen her before but I took notice of her, for she's a nice-looking piece and worth looking at. Him I knew, of course; known him for years.

"They sat down on a seat, like as I told you before; and I was near enough for to hear what they said. First of all the girl talked a lot about some aunt of hers and how she hated her. Then Mr. Seaforth he took a turn and talked a lot about somebody's will. I wasn't paying much attention to that, so I can't tell you exactly what they said. I know they seemed down-in-the-mouth, more than a bit, but that's all.

"Then, all of a sudden, the girl got angry over something or other, and I got interested. I thought it was a row they were having or something like that, you see? She was fair raging, I can tell you; and she said something or other was 'the last straw.' There was something about her aunt beating her, but I can't rightly remember just what it was. Anyways, the girl began to cry and she said something about being 'at the end of her tether.' I remember that plain enough because it struck me when she said it—the tone of her voice, I mean.

"Then Mr. Seaforth, he said something about it being a good thing for the world if someone would poison this aunt of hers. Now, you might say that in a joking sort of way, meaning no offence, you understand? But he said it as if he meant it, like as if he'd have been quite glad to take a hand in it. And he said something about its being 'a bit risky.'

"They was talking fast, by then, and I didn't catch every word they said; but it was all against this aunt of hers and wondering if there wasn't any way of getting rid of her. And at last the girl she says: 'Suppose I lost my temper and struck back? And suppose that heart of hers failed when I hit her? It would just be an accident, wouldn't it? They couldn't do anything to me, could they?'

"And at that, Mr. Seaforth began to look around him as if he thought there might be somebody about; so I shifted my pitch and went off a bit out of earshot. He might have given me the push, if he'd thought I'd been overhearing all this kind of thing, see? And that's the gospel truth of the whole thing. I'll kiss the Book on it, if you like."

The Superintendent exchanged a glance with Dorrington at the close of the gardener's recital. While Sturry was giving his evidence, Ross had been taking notes; and he now made the informant sign them, after reading them over to him. When this had been done, he passed the notebook to Dorrington for him to initial as a witness.

"That's all you have to tell, Sturry?"

"That's every bit of it that I can remember."

"I'll think over it," said the Superintendent, in no very cordial tone. "You may not be out of the wood yet, my friend. And there's just one thing! Don't you breathe a word of all this to anyone. That's a bit of good advice for you, even if it costs you nothing. You bear it well in mind, my man."

And with that he dismissed Sturry, who was glad to get out of his clutches. As he descended the stairs, the gardener comforted himself as best he could by feeling the ten-shilling note in his trousers pocket. After all, he had made something out of the business.

When the sound of his steps on the stairs died away, the journalist turned to Ross and allowed his suppressed grin to appear.

"*Was* it misprision of felony?" he demanded ironically.

"I didn't say it was," the Superintendent retorted with an answering smile. "I said misprision of felony was a serious offence. So it is. No harm in stating the fact, is there? I like people to learn a little about the law."

"Ah," said Dorrington flippantly, "Latin's a wonderful language. He sat up like a startled rabbit when you rolled out 'accessory *ex post facto*.' The terror of the unknown, I suppose. And yet if I were to say *suggestio falsi*, I don't suppose you'd so much as blench, Superintendent? Education's a marvelous thing, I always feel."

He paused for a moment, and then went on: "Like to wash your hands?"

Ross seemed puzzled for a moment; then he laughed.

"I see what you mean. He was rather a dirty tool to handle, wasn't he? But I'm paid for handling that kind of instrument and I've got used to it, Mr. Dorrington. I even find it interesting at times."

"You surprise me," the journalist retorted, unabashed.

Then, in a more serious tone, he demanded: "What do you think about this story that he gave us?"

"No use making up one's mind until one's got all the facts," Ross answered, evasively. "I expect he told us something like the truth; he could hardly have made it all up. But the importance of any fact generally lies in its relation to other facts; and I don't pretend to have got enough facts yet."

"You don't want me to use the stuff, I take it?"

"I don't see how you could, without being libelous," the Superintendent pointed out cheerfully.

"I suppose that's so," Dorrington confessed. "Now, is there anything else you want to know? I hate to draw comparisons, but I'm a fairly busy man, with very little time on my hands."

Ross ignored the insinuation.

"I'd like to know something about Mrs. Fenton's husband," he answered. "You mentioned him in passing, didn't you? Have you anything more about him in stock?"

The journalist looked thoughtful and paused for a moment or two before replying.

"Well, it's more or less common talk, so there's no harm in saying it, since you'll pick it up elsewhere if you go looking for it. But we're speaking in confidence, remember. You're not to quote me as an authority."

The Superintendent gave a confirmatory nod, and Dorrington went on.

"It's pretty well an open scandal in the place," he exclaimed. "Things had been going from bad to worse in the Fenton ménage for a good while; but the final burst-up came about two years ago. I suppose Fenton had stood her as long as he could; and the last straw was when a girl turned up, staying here for a visit. Fenton got to know her somehow. Apparently they got keen on each other. I gather that she's one of the younger generation that looks on sex affairs more or less in the way that you or I might look on a good dinner—sort of thing that's nice while it lasts but certainly isn't worth worrying about once it's over. Tastes the same, whether you say a blessing to start with or not. You know the sort of thing—there are plenty of 'em about."

"They used to call them privateers in my young days," the Superintendent interjected. "I know what you mean."

"Well, Fenton and this girl—Nancy March, her name is—seem to have dispensed with the blessing and tucked into their dinner; and that didn't tend to smooth matters in the Fenton household, naturally. In fact, before very long, there was a bit of an explosion; and Fenton cleared out."

The journalist seemed doubtful whether to go on or not, but the Superintendent's silent persuasion overcame his diffidence.

"That's more or less established on the face of things," Dorrington went on. "The rest of it's partly guess-work; but the general impression seems to be that Fenton and the girl have really fallen in love with each other, and that's made a bit of a difference. The girl's living with her people, you see, and they can only meet on the sly. So apparently they've come round to the notion that it would be a sound plan to say grace after meat, so to speak, and regularise things so that they could set up house together openly. The girl's fond of her people and they're a bit old-fashioned by her standards. They don't know anything about her little game. Everything would have been O.K., if Fenton could have got a divorce; but that wife of his wouldn't take proceedings. Too spiteful, or something, I expect. That's how the land lay, if one believes what one hears. Now, of course, it's plain sailing, since Fenton's a widower."

"Very interesting," the Superintendent commented.

He refrained from betraying the fact that only part of the story was new to him.

"I expect you're busy," he said, rising to his feet. "I'd like to drop in some other time and hear what you make of the whole business. You had special advantages, being on that jury and seeing the witnesses give their evidence. If anything turns up that can be used by the *Gazette*, I'll let you know about it at once. In the meantime, you won't forget that paragraph about the mysterious visitor? Thanks."

CHAPTER VIII
NINE TO ELEVEN P.M.

AT THE BREAKFAST-TABLE next morning, Superintendent Ross opened his copy of the *Stanningmore Gazette* and turned at once to the column headed: THE CEDARS MYSTERY. He was not disappointed. Dorrington had carried out his suggestion; and an expression of approval flitted across the detective's face as he read the paragraph.

"That ought to draw the badger," he reflected contentedly as he poured out his tea. "If he doesn't appear immediately, it'll be dashed awkward for him when he's dug out in the end. This leaves him no excuse for concealing himself any longer."

Even yet, however, the Superintendent was by no means sure of the identity of his "badger." Three names suggested themselves as possible: Mr. Fenton, Dr. Hyndford, and the estate agent Watchet. If the newspaper paragraph failed to do its work, he would have to find out where each of these people had been on the night of the murder. There would be no great difficulty in that, probably; but it would save trouble if the mysterious visitor disclosed himself instead of having to be sought out; and Ross, after re-reading the ingeniously worded paragraph, felt grateful to Dorrington.

So confident was he of immediate results that he spent the morning at the Stanningmore police headquarters, so as to keep in touch with the telephone.

About midday, there came a message making an appointment for him at Dr. Hyndford's house that afternoon. The badger had been drawn, as he hoped. The next problem was how to tackle him now that he had come into the open.

But Ross was in no hurry to draw conclusions from such evidence as he had. Even if Dr. Hyndford was the man who had visited Mrs. Fenton on the night of the murder, that did not necessarily connect him directly with the crime itself. It was perhaps curious that he had not come forward and volunteered his evidence; but there might be some perfectly reasonable explanation for this; and Ross restrained himself from any prejudging of the case. At the present stage, information was what he wanted: inferences could wait.

"I expect I'd better be rather dull, this afternoon," he decided at last. "From all I've gathered about that doctor, he's not simple, even if his name's Simon. One can meet that type best by playing the stupid fellow, if one doesn't overdo the acting."

At three o'clock he was ushered into the doctor's study, prepared to play the part he had assigned to himself. When he entered, Dr. Hyndford rose from an easy-chair: a big slow-moving man whose creased grey flannel suit hardly suggested the successful practitioner. As he came forward, the Superintendent had to admit to himself that Dr. Hyndford possessed the mysterious quality which enables even stupid men to impose themselves on their fellows. Ross's glance took in the massive features, the big heavy-bridged nose, the square jaw, the sullen and sardonic lips; then his own eyes were fixed by the direct and rather contemptuous gaze from the doctor's pale-blue ones.

After a conventional greeting to the Superintendent, Dr. Hyndford made a gesture introducing a second person:

"My brother," he explained concisely.

Mr. Richard Hyndford proved to be not unlike Ross's preconceived picture of him. A shade below normal height, he had none of the formidable appearance of his brother; and his quick nervous movements were in strong contrast to the doctor's deliberateness. When he came forward, at his brother's introduction, the Superintendent noticed that his eyes had that faint touch of vagueness which comes from incipient short-sightedness.

"Hot day for walking up here," said the doctor, as though to put matters on a friendly footing. "Have a drink, Superintendent?"

He indicated a try with a decanter and soda on a table near the window. Superintendent Ross shook his head.

"You won't? Sure? Well, if it's not bad manners, I'll take one myself."

He turned to his brother.

"What about you, Dickie?"

"Well . . ." Richard Hyndford hesitated for a moment. "A small one for me, then. Don't make it more than two fingers, Simon, please; and fill up with the soda."

Dr. Hyndford went across to the tray and picked up one of the soda-water bottles which he wrapped in his handkerchief before opening it. Seeing the Superintendent's astonishment at this unusual procedure, the doctor laughed.

"I'd rather look fussy than run risks," he explained, holding out his hand for the detective to examine. "One of these things once cracked at the neck when I was opening it. You can see the scar there where it cut me. Since then, I've been on the careful side where soda's concerned. They had to put five stitches into the gash."

He gave his brother one tumbler and returned with the other to his easy-chair. The homely series of manoeuvres had established a more normal atmosphere.

"You wanted to see me about something or other?" the Superintendent suggested tentatively, as though anxious to get to business as soon as possible.

Dr. Hyndford took a long pull at his whiskey and gave a faint sigh of satisfaction as he put down his tumbler again.

"I see from this morning's *Gazette* that you want to get in touch with the visitor Mrs. Fenton had on the night she died," he said unhesitatingly. "Well, I was that visitor. If you've any questions to ask, then ask them. I'll give you all the help I can."

The Superintendent had hardly expected such bluntness; and he had little difficulty in letting the doctor see that he was taken aback.

"You were the visitor?" he exclaimed with carefully calculated astonishment in his tune. "Then why didn't you give some evidence at the inquest?"

"Nobody asked me, sir . . ." Dr. Hyndford retorted. "Look here! I'm not so deaf that I can't hear talk behind my back at times. You must know as well as I do that there was a damned lot of scandal talked about Mrs. Fenton and me. We were supposed to be pretty thick. I don't admit it. I don't deny it. It's a side-issue. Now suppose I'd rushed in and volunteered my evidence at the inquest. I had nothing to tell. I went across after dinner and I left her, alive, at about eleven o'clock. An inquest's held merely to discover the cause of a death. I've no sympathy with this modern notion of using it to drag all sorts of irrelevant private affairs into the limelight. My evidence wouldn't have thrown any light on the cause of her death. What would have happened would have been a damned lot of gossip and whispering about Mrs. Fenton and me. 'What was he doing in her house, eh?' and nods and winks. No need to let that sort of thing loose, was there? It would have been different if my evidence had been any use. It wouldn't. But it would have been used as a handle to dig up a lot of things that are best left alone. *De mortuis* . . . and all that sort of thing, that seems to me sound policy in this case. So I didn't volunteer evidence."

There had been an increasing twang of irritation in his voice throughout his explanation, and when he stopped, his lips set in a hard expression which betrayed his feelings just as clearly.

"There's something in that," the Superintendent admitted, frankly. "It's a fresh way of looking at it, certainly. I hadn't thought of it in that light before."

Dr. Hyndford's lips relaxed a trifle.

"Well, I'm glad you see it," he said, in a not too conciliatory tone. "I thought no one knew I'd paid her that visit on the night of her death. It had nothing to do with the case. So naturally the best thing to do was to keep my mouth shut about it and not give people a chance to gossip, damn their eyes! Of course, as soon as I saw that paragraph this morning, I knew someone had spotted that I'd been there. It was no good lying low any longer—might have looked suspicious, in fact. So I rang you up as soon as I could. Now if you've any questions to ask, I'll tell you all you want to know."

The Superintendent nodded thoughtfully in reply to this and pulled out a loose-leaf notebook.

"I'll have to take notes of what you say," he pointed out, "and I shall want you to sign them afterwards. It's the usual procedure, I suppose you know."

Dr. Hyndford's curt nod gave his agreement to this condition.

"I think," said Ross, "it would save time, probably, if you simply told me your own story of what happened that evening—I mean your movements, and so on. We'd get on quicker, that way."

Dr. Hyndford again nodded brusquely.

"Very well," he said. "My brother and I dined here at 7.30 as usual. After dinner, say about 8.15 or a shade later, I sat out in the garden for half an hour or so. My brother was with me. That's so, Dickie?"

Mr. Hyndford seemed a shade taken aback by being brought into the matter at this point.

"Yes, quite true," he confirmed. "I was busy with one of the beds just then. What I mean is, I was clearing out some stuff that seemed to me to need thinning."

The doctor continued:

"Just about that time, I saw young Seaforth come down the river in his canoe; and Miss Hazlemere walked across the lawn of The Cedars to join him. She got into the canoe and they went off together downstream. I can't give you the exact time of that; and it's not important so far as I can see. I merely happened to notice it. A little later, I went down and got out my own canoe to go over to The Cedars—"

"You've missed something, Simon, haven't you?" Mr. Hyndford interjected. "What I mean to say is: wasn't it just about then that I happened to mention to you I was expecting Fenton to drop in? I think it was about that time when I told you about it."

The doctor threw a rather unpleasant look at his brother, and Mr. Hyndford seemed to shrink a little under the baleful glance.

"If you start interrupting, Dickie, I'll be apt to lose the thread; and I want to have this thing quite clear."

"Oh, very well," Mr. Hyndford agreed, nervously. "You tell your story. I mean I won't interrupt again. That's all right."

The doctor turned back towards the Superintendent and continued:

"After dinner, Mrs. Fenton usually sat in the drawing-room of The Cedars—the room with the French window. I went over in my canoe, walked up to the house, went in through the French window, and found her there, as I expected."

"Just a moment," interrupted the Superintendent. "You're a medical man. Did you notice anything abnormal about her when you saw her then, anything you think suggestive?"

Dr. Hyndford's cold eyes regarded the Superintendent with some slight surprise, not unmingled with contempt.

"Abnormal?" he demanded. "What exactly do you mean by abnormal? I saw nothing unusual in her. She wasn't throwing herself about or going into hysterics, so far as I remember."

Then a thought seemed to strike him.

"She wasn't drunk," he added, brutally. "I suppose that's what you're after. No, she was quite sober."

The Superintendent made no comment, and after a moment the doctor continued:

"We talked about various things—bets she was thinking of making; some trouble she'd had with her agent, a man Watchet; her niece, I think. Nothing of any importance that I can remember."

"Did she offer you anything to drink? Whiskey and soda?" the Superintendent inquired.

"No. There was some whiskey and soda on a tray—there usually was. But we didn't take any."

The Superintendent hoped that he had succeeded in controlling his face sufficiently to suggest that the matter was of little importance; but Dr. Hyndford had seen what was behind the question.

"I see," he commented. "It's the used tumblers you're after. I remember that in the evidence at the inquest. Probably she had a drink or two herself after I'd gone. They weren't used while I was there, so far as I remember."

He paused, as though thinking over the point; but he was evidently satisfied in his own mind, for when he spoke again it was to continue his narrative.

"About eleven o'clock, I got up to go. I can't give you the exact time, but it must have been round about eleven."

"It was about five to eleven," Mr. Hyndford interrupted. "At least, what I mean to say is that I remember hearing the clock chime the quarter just as Fenton left me at the garden gate; and it was ten minutes or so after that that you came in again, Simon."

"All right," the doctor agreed impatiently. "Call it five to eleven if you like. I came into the house and rang for a drink, so it can't have been much later than eleven or the maid would have been in bed. My brother and I sat talking for a while—I forget what about."

"It was about the green-fly on the roses, part of the time," Mr. Hyndford put in timidly. "I was telling you about the new stuff I'd been trying to cure it with."

"Some rot or other, anyhow," the doctor said, rudely. "I can't remember exactly what it was. After that, I went up to bed. I remember that all right, because I slipped on the stair and came down on all-fours with the devil's own thump. One of the maids—damned little idiot!—poked her head out of her room and wanted to know if it was burglars. As if any burglar would come sneaking into a house with all the electric lights on!"

"That's a very clear account, doctor," the Superintendent said with a fatuous expression, when he saw that Dr. Hyndford had finished. "I wish all witnesses would put things as plainly as you've done. There's just one point I'm not quite clear about. You went in by the French window of The Cedars. So it was open then. Did you come out by it? Was it open when you left the house?"

Dr. Hyndford seemed to reconsider.

"It was open all the evening," he said at last, "but if I remember rightly, the curtains were drawn across it. And I'd forgotten something else. Just as I was going away, Mrs. Fenton found she wanted something from her room upstairs and I went out with her into the hall. When I got there, the shortest way out of the house was by the front door; so I went out that way. When I got on to the doorstep, I saw Mr. Marton in the garden over the way with his telescope. He evidently saw me—it was bright moonlight—for he called over and asked me to go across. I said I was in a hurry—if you know Mr. Marton, you may guess why I said that—and I walked round the house and down to my canoe again."

The Superintendent displayed no particular interest in this emendation of the narrative. He would have the means of checking it later on.

"Just another point, doctor," he said. "You mentioned some talk about betting. Did Mrs. Fenton keep a betting-book or anything of that sort?"

"Of course she did," answered the doctor, in a tone of slight astonishment. "How else could she have kept track of her bets?"

"Where did she usually keep it?"

"In the writing-desk in the drawing-room, I think," Dr. Hyndford answered, after thinking for a moment or two.

"She didn't keep her old betting-books, did she?"

"How should I know?" the doctor demanded.

The Superintendent tried a new line.

"I suppose you know what scale she betted on? I mean, was it a question of a tenner now and again, or did she really bet heavily?"

"I know she plunged, now and again; but really I've no clear ideas about the general run of her bets. Once or twice she had a thousand on. I know that. But I don't think she went in for it on that scale as a rule."

"I suppose you don't know the name of her bookmaker?"

Dr. Hyndford shook his head.

"No. In some ways she was rather a secretive person. And I'd no interest in the matter. No business of mine."

The Superintendent seemed to have come to the end of his questions. He detached the loose leaves of his notes from the notebook and handed them across to the doctor, with a request for his signature. Dr. Hyndford read over the jottings, pulled out his fountain-pen, scrawled his name at the foot, and handed the sheets back to Ross.

"That's all that's official," the Superintendent pointed out, as he closed his notebook. "But I'd like your views on one or two points. The plain truth is, doctor," he admitted ingenuously, "I'm completely stuck in this case. It seems to have no head or tail to it. Now you knew Mrs. Fenton well. You must have some suspicions. A thing that means nothing to me, might mean a lot to you. Who do you think did it? You can give me a pointer, perhaps?"

The doctor's cold eyes met those of the Superintendent squarely.

"No," he said with the utmost concision, in a tone which would have prevented most people from pursuing the subject.

The Superintendent, however, showed no sign of appreciating the atmosphere. Defeated in his frontal attack, he made a clumsy attempt to get round the doctor's flank by putting a further question.

"What do you think about her death? Could it have been accidental?"

"Accidental? What are you talking about?" the doctor demanded, making no effort to conceal his contempt at the question. "How could it be accidental? People don't get finger-marks on their necks by accident."

"You don't see what I mean," the Superintendent protested in the tone of a schoolboy excusing himself. "There's a difference between murder and manslaughter; and to tell you the honest truth, I'm not sure which of them it was. If I were to take a person by the throat, I might just hit by accident on the right spot, and the person might die without my having meant to go that length; but if you took someone by the throat, you've got anatomical knowledge that I haven't got, and you might be able to put your fingers intentionally on the right place. In my case it would be manslaughter; in your case it would be murder. You see it now?"

Rather to the Superintendent's discomfiture, the doctor burst into a peal of laughter, which was obviously due to genuine amusement.

"I see," he said, when he had recovered his control. "This is your line of reasoning. Somebody killed in a certain way. A medical would know about that way. Therefore a medical did it. Where is the medical in the case? Dr. Hyndford. Therefore Dr. Hyndford did it. I'm sorry, Superintendent. You'll have to guess again. I didn't do it. Try another medical—say Platt. Oh, I bear no malice; don't worry. I've no doubt you're doing your best."

The Superintendent winced visibly under the contempt in the doctor's tone.

"Oh, now you're putting words into my mouth, doctor," he expostulated, feebly. "That wasn't what I said at all."

"No," said Dr. Hyndford cuttingly, "but it was what you insinuated, wasn't it? I'm not obtuse, Superintendent. It's just as well, perhaps, that I can put a stop to this before it goes any further. Luckily for me, as it happens, I was called up that night before I'd got into-bed; and I had to go out. My patient was Mr. Mundford, of 10 Pollen Grove; and I was with him until 1 a.m., long after Mrs. Fenton was dead. If you check that, you'll find it O.K."

Superintendent Ross looked obviously confused by this fresh piece of evidence.

"You've taken me up quite wrong," he protested. "I meant just what I said—not what you've twisted it into, doctor."

"Well, let it go at that," Dr. Hyndford rejoined in a tone which suggested that he would not forget the incident in a hurry. "Now, is that all you want?"

"I'd just like to ask Mr. Hyndford a question or two," the Superintendent explained with a crestfallen air.

Dr. Hyndford leaned back in his chair, as though retiring from the business.

"Go on, Dickie," he said, rather like an employer ordering a subordinate to attend to a customer.

"I'd just like to get one or two points clear in my mind," the Superintendent explained slowly, turning to his fresh witness, and opening his notebook again. "You and Dr. Hyndford were out in the garden here till about a quarter to nine, I gather. That's your recollection of the time?"

Mr. Hyndford rubbed the back of his head in a perplexed manner. Evidently he was doing his best to tax his memory.

"I should think it would be just about that," he said at last. "What I mean to say is, it's a while back, now; and I'd really no reason for taking a note of the time, so it's a bit difficult to be exact. You understand what I mean? That's the best of my recollection; but if you asked me to swear to it within ten minutes, I shouldn't care to do it. Somewhere about a quarter to nine."

The purely professional side of the Superintendent's mind made the involuntary comment that Mr. Hyndford would be a nuisance as a witness if he were ever called. He was evidently of the type which, by striving after exactitude in detail, succeeds almost invariably in fogging the clearness of any statement.

"A quarter to nine, then, roughly," Ross noted down. "And just before that, you saw Miss Hazlemere and Mr. Seaforth go off together in a canoe. Then Dr. Hyndford took his canoe over to The Cedars?"

"Yes. I happened to look up once, and I saw my brother tying it up on the other bank, at the foot of The Cedars' garden."

"And after that?" prompted the Superintendent.

"After that? Oh, I don't remember anything much until Mr. Fenton came in. I'd met him down town that afternoon, quite by chance; and I asked him up here in the evening. I hadn't seen him for quite a while, you know; he's not living here nowadays."

"When did he come in, Mr. Hyndford?"

"Oh, about a quarter past nine. I asked him to drop in any time after nine; and I remember looking at my watch before he came, to see how time was getting on. It was ten past nine, then; and he turned up soon after that—a few minutes later."

"And then?"

"We had a whiskey and soda, and a talk. Nothing worth repeating in the talk. I mean it was just odds and ends, nothing in particular that I remember."

"And he stayed till a quarter to eleven, you said?"

"Yes, the clock struck the quarter while we were standing at the gate; and he went away just after that, a few minutes later at the most, probably less."

"And Dr. Hyndford came back almost at once?"

"Yes, I noticed that particularly," Mr. Hyndford pointed out, with a nervous glance at his brother. "You see, I'd been rather worried for fear my brother came in when Fenton was here. It would have been a bit awkward, perhaps. . . ."

He broke off and threw a nervous glance at his brother.

"Fenton and I are not particularly sweet on each other," Dr. Hyndford interjected, cynically. "Your suggestive mind will supply you with a reason for that state of affairs, I've no doubt."

The Superintendent ignored both the hint and the sarcasm.

"And after your brother came in, Mr. Hyndford, you talked for a while before he went to bed. How long did you talk?"

"Oh, perhaps ten minutes or so, not more."

"Then what *did* you do?"

"I went out into the garden; it was a bright moonlight night, you know."

There was something just a shade shame-faced in Mr. Hyndford's manner as he said this; and the Superintendent, rather puzzled, pushed his inquiry harder.

"What did you do in the garden?"

Mr. Hyndford became rather confused.

"Well, you see," he confessed at last, turning rather red, "when I'd been out there for a good while—it was a hot night, you may remember, and I liked the cool air—I happened to look across at The Cedars; and, quite by accident, I saw a man's figure in the garden. I couldn't see him very well; but I was a bit curious, if you understand. There was a burglary not very far off here not long ago. So, naturally, I was a bit inquisitive about this fellow."

"What time was that?" the Superintendent demanded.

"Well, it must have been getting on for twelve o'clock, I should think. After half-past eleven, anyhow; I'm fairly sure of that."

"And what did you do when you saw this man?"

"Well, naturally, I was a bit suspicious. You see what I mean? I think anyone would have been, if they'd seen a man lurking about in a neighbour's garden at that time of night. So I came into the house here and picked up a pair of glasses."

He halted again and turned red.

"Anything else?" demanded the Superintendent, feeling that Mr. Hyndford was concealing something.

Mr. Hyndford glanced sheepishly at his brother as he answered.

"I took an old revolver out of a drawer. It's a very old thing, but it would be useful enough at short range. What I mean to say is, it's one of those old things with a leaden bullet, a good man-stopper. You see," he added, with a certain unconscious pathos, "I've never been a rap of good in a scrap, Superintendent. I'm not like you in physique. So I thought I'd take the revolver, just in case I needed to hold the fellow up."

The doctor's sneering chuckle underlined his brother's rather pitiful confession of physical impotence. Mr. Hyndford winced.

"Then I went out again," he continued hurriedly, as though to cover up the matter. "I really needn't have bothered; for when I put up my glasses, the fellow was just creeping away out of the garden. I watched him off the premises and then I came back into the house."

"You didn't think of telephoning to the police about it?" asked the Superintendent. "We might have laid hands on the fellow."

"No," Mr. Hyndford said, with a marked hesitation. "What I mean to say is, he'd gone away by then. . . . I didn't really think . . . I mean, he'd gone off the premises. . . ."

He shot a glance at his brother, who was examining him with a sort of contemptuous curiosity.

"You're not making much of it, Dickie. Why not give the show away and be done with it?"

"I think I see what you mean, Mr. Hyndford," the Superintendent interrupted. "Perhaps you recognised this man and thought he had a right on the premises say, like Mr. Seaforth?"

"Out with it, Dickie," the doctor advised. "You're simply making a mess of things, and you'll have to spit it out sooner or later. You're only raising a lot of suspicions in the fertile mind of our friend here."

Quite obviously the doctor had not forgiven the earlier episode.

"Well, you see," Mr. Hyndford explained lamely. "I *did* recognise him; and he *had* a right to be there. So, of course, I didn't think of telephoning to the police. You understand what I mean, don't you?"

"Oh, you needn't beat about the bush, Dickie," the doctor interrupted with what seemed an undercurrent of malicious glee in his voice. "It was Fenton, of course, sneaking about the place. Just the low-down sort of thing he would do."

This explained Mr. Hyndford's reluctance to give away the true state of affairs. And he made the position rather worse by attempting to gloze over the matter.

"Well, you see, Superintendent, you don't know Fenton as I do, and I expect you'll begin suspecting him next. That's really why I didn't want to say anything. What I mean is, there's no possibility that Fenton had anything to do with the affair. He's not that kind of man, if you see what I'm after. I really shouldn't have said anything about him at all, but you rather got it out of me without my intending it. There's nothing in it."

He broke off rather hopelessly, evidently realising that he had managed to do a good deal of harm by his admissions. The Superintendent was not blind to this side of the affair, but he forebore to push the matter further. He had enough to go on for the present.

"I think that's all I need for the present," he said, as he detached his notes from his book and handed them across to Mr. Hyndford. "If you'll just read these over and sign them, it'll be all right."

Mr. Hyndford complied, and the Superintendent prepared to take his leave.

"Have a drink before you go, Superintendent?" the doctor inquired as he heaved his bulk out of his easy-chair. "Just to show there's no ill-feeling," he added in a rather grim tone which belied his word.

"No, thanks," Ross replied. "There's no ill-feeling so far as I'm concerned, doctor. And that reminds me"—he seemed struck by an after-thought—"you haven't any digitalis tincture you could show me, have you? I'd like to see the stuff. You've got some in your dispensary, perhaps?"

The doctor apparently guessed what might lie behind these inconsequent inquiries.

"No, Superintendent, I haven't any in stock," he said with a sardonic smile. "There isn't a heart case amongst my patients, so I've no need of it. And there's no use keeping the tincture on the off-chance of requiring it. It deteriorates too much if you keep it. You draw blank there, I'm afraid. And if you're thinking of pushing your inquiries, the druggist I deal with is Rilston in Main Street. He'll be able to tell you I haven't bought digitalis for ages. Satisfied?"

"Completely," the Superintendent assured him, covering his defeat as best he could.

And with that he took his leave.

The house of the amateur astronomer was his next port of call: and there he was lucky enough to find Marton at home. But here the Superintendent was doomed to another disappointment. He had hoped to score a point against the doctor; but very few questions sufficed to confirm Dr. Hyndford's story even more completely than might have been expected.

As it chanced, Marton had just completed a drawing of Jupiter when the doctor appeared at The Cedars' front door that night. Marton produced the drawing for the Superintendent's inspection, and pointed out that, following the usual custom of astronomers, he had not only dated it, but had added the exact hour and minute at which it was begun and completed. He was thus able to establish definitely that Dr. Hyndford had left the Cedars at 10.47 p.m.

An even more important contribution by Marton was the fact that when the door of The Cedars opened, he had caught a glimpse of Mrs. Fenton in the hall, talking to the doctor. That was definite confirmation of the doctor's statement that he had left Mrs. Fenton alive when he went home.

Superintendent Ross was very thoughtful as he betook himself to the police headquarters after leaving the astronomer. Dr. Hyndford had left a bad impression by his needless discourtesy; but the detective had to admit that perhaps this was merely the doctor's way. He had never been described to Ross as an amiable character; and a man of his type, in a perfectly safe position, might possibly find it amusing to be rude to the police. A guilty man would be more circumspect in his treatment of a detective, in all probability.

The Superintendent had one last shot in his locker. The business of detaching the loose leaves of notes from their cover and handing them separately to each of the brothers had not been done without forethought. The finger-prints on the glass in Mrs. Fenton's drawing-room were among the few definite clues in the case; and Ross meant to identify them if possible, without exciting suspicions by actually asking anyone to make a print of his own fingers. On the notes in his pocket, he now had the prints of both the doctor and his brother; and when he reached headquarters he proceeded to develop the prints in the usual manner. When he had brought them up, he compared them in turn with the enlarged photograph of the prints on the tumbler.

"Damnation!" said the Superintendent, as he glanced from one set to the other, "all three are different. Another blank end!"

CHAPTER IX
MRS. FENTON'S HUSBAND

"IN A CRIMINAL CASE, you've got to leave personal feelings out of account, and stick to reason, pure and simple," was one of Superintendent Ross's favourite dicta. Another was: "Nothing ever surprises me nowadays."

But as he re-examined the finger-prints, he found both these aphorisms doubtful. On the face of things his reason told him that Dr. Hyndford's story held water wherever it could be tested; but the doctor's sneering manner had roused some antagonism in the mind of the Superintendent, and that antagonism persisted in suggesting suspicions with which reason had nothing to do. Personal feelings were creeping in, despite all his principles. And there was no getting away from it: he had been surprised to find no correspondence between the three sets of prints. That latent distrust of Dr. Hyndford had led him almost unconsciously to expect something different from the real results.

Putting the various papers in a place of safety, he summoned a constable.

"Ring up that man Watchet—the estate agent—and make an appointment with him for me tonight, any time after nine o'clock," he directed. "I'll be in here later on. Leave a message for me."

A glance at his watch assured him that he had still a chance of catching James Corwen before his office closed; so, picking up his hat, he made his way to the solicitor's premises, which were only a couple of hundred yards up the street.

"You probably have Mr. Fenton's address," he explained when he was shown into James Corwen's private room. "The place where he's staying in Stanningmore at present, I mean. I want to see him, if possible."

"He's at Hollingworth's Hotel," the solicitor answered.

"May I use your 'phone? . . . Thanks."

Superintendent Ross hunted up the number in the directory and got his connection. By a stroke of luck, Fenton was in the hotel, and Ross was able to speak to him.

"I'd like some information, Mr. Fenton. I'll come to the hotel, if you like; but perhaps it would cause less talk if you dropped into the headquarters in Main Street. It's more private there. . . . Thanks. In half an hour, then."

Ross put down the telephone and found James Corwen regarding him with a certain veiled interest; but, true to his policy, the solicitor made no comment and waited for the Superintendent to begin.

"While I'm here, I'd like to ask a question or two, Mr. Corwen. You have the information all at hand. I suppose you're settling up Mrs. Fenton's money affairs: finding out what debts she had, and so forth?"

"We haven't got probate yet," the solicitor pointed out, "but we're looking into things."

"Have you any notion about the extent of her betting transactions?"

"We haven't troubled much about them," James Corwen pointed out. "They're not legal transactions, strictly speaking."

"No, of course not. You've no idea on what scale they were?"

"I really don't know," the solicitor said, impatiently. "My impression is that she didn't gamble in thousands, because she hadn't thousands to gamble with."

He halted, as though something had struck him, then continued in a less decided tone:

"Of course, now and again she may have plunged, if she was able to raise money for it in some quarter or other."

"Does Miss Hazlemere come into anything under Mrs. Fenton's will?" the Superintendent demanded.

James Corwen's eyes twinkled with a faint malice.

"Not a penny!" he said with emphasis.

He glanced at the Superintendent's face and added:

"If you'll take my advice, Superintendent, you won't push this case of yours against Miss Hazlemere. You haven't enough evidence to hang a cat on."

"You think so?" said Ross placably. "It's quite possible. I've never had any experience of hanging cats—*as yet*."

James Corwen evidently thought it inadvisable to probe into the possible meaning of this cryptic remark.

"Anything else you want to know?"

"What's the value of Mrs. Fenton's estate?"

James Corwen's gesture implied that it amounted to very little.

"Her private income came from money that her husband placed with trustees at the time of their marriage. As there were no children, that money goes back to him, under one of the provisions of the settlement deed."

"H'm! That's an interesting point," the Superintendent admitted. "How much is it?"

"About £10,000."

The Superintendent did not put into words his reflection that Fenton had an obvious interest in his wife's decease. Instead, he asked a fresh question. "Will anyone be better off, so far as her ordinary estate's concerned?"

The lawyer shook his head.

"It'll barely cover her debts. In fact, some people will be left out in the cold—Dr. Hyndford, for one."

"How's that?" the Superintendent inquired, pricking up his ears at the doctor's name.

"He holds some I.O.U.'s of hers for fairly big figures. They're no better than waste paper now. If she had lived, she might have repaid the money; but the estate will be far too small to cover them."

The Superintendent seemed to grow thoughtful, all of a sudden. He had been struck by the doctor's complete lack of sympathy over Mrs. Fenton's death; but if the man were a heavy loser, financially, it might account for his feelings.

"Could you get hold of these I.O.U.'s?" Ross asked. "I'd like to see them."

"I daresay I could make some excuse to handle them," James Corwen answered, doubtfully. "Hyndford knows they're no better than trash, so he will hardly want to cling to them."

"Oh, he knows the state of affairs, does he?"

"Yes. He mentioned the I.O.U.'s to me after her death and I told him very plainly how the land lay. My impression is that in any case he might have had some difficulty in getting the money. It's quite clear that he advanced it to her so that she might use it for betting; and I would like to know counsel's opinion as to how that sort of loan stands in respect to the Gaming Acts of 1710 and 1835. It might make a pretty case," the solicitor ended, in a professional tone.

"You think she used it for betting?"

"Well, it was about £10,000. There's no trace of her having spent anything like that sum on solid things. Obviously she gambled it away."

The Superintendent nodded, as though this reasoning satisfied him.

"What about this insurance policy she took out? It was mentioned at the inquest. What company was it?"

"The Canterbury and Mercantile United. It was only for £500. I suspect she used it occasionally to secure a bank overdraft when she had run things too fine."

"It's quite on the cards," the Superintendent agreed in an indifferent tone. "Well, that's all I wanted, thanks. I must go off and see about the hanging of this cat you were talking about."

And, leaving this parting shot to rankle in James Corwen's mind, the made his way back to the police station.

The constable to whom he had given instructions about Watchet appeared as Superintendent Ross entered the station. He had not been able to get hold of the estate agent. Watchet had made three appointments with clients for that day, according to the office-boy; but he had kept none of them; and inquiries revealed that Watchet had left Stanningmore the previous night. He had given no address to which letters might be sent on; and apparently no one knew when he meant to come back.

"Cut his stick, has he?" the Superintendent mused. "I'll need to think this out before acting drastically. By the way, when Mr. Fenton calls, send him in to me at once."

He had not long to wait. Mr. Fenton proved to be a fair-haired, slightly built man, with good teeth which showed when he smiled. The Superintendent, judging by male standards, thought him good-looking, but rather ordinary on the whole. As he came into the room, it was evident that he was striving to conceal a certain nervousness.

Ross, noticing this, went straight to the point before his visitor had time to accustom himself to his surroundings.

"I have some information about you, Mr. Fenton," he said bluntly. "Why didn't you come forward and give your evidence at the inquest on Mrs. Fenton? You must have known perfectly well that you should have stated frankly that you were at The Cedars that night."

Fenton was taken completely aback and showed it clearly.

"How do you know I was there?" he demanded, his face whitening under its tan.

"That's my business," Ross answered curtly. "I know you were there. In fact, I know a good deal more than you evidently think I do. My advice to you, sir, is to tell the whole truth. You can see for yourself that you've done no good by this attempt to conceal things."

Fenton's face showed that he felt he was caught in a trap. Quite obviously, when he was summoned to the police-station, he had not expected to find the Superintendent so sure of his ground; and he had no story ready.

"You know I was at The Cedars?" he said, slowly, as though fighting for time in which to think. "Well, suppose I was? What else do you know?"

"I know quite enough to check any statements you make, Mr. Fenton."

"Are you bringing a charge against me?"

"No," said the Superintendent. "But if you don't tell your own version of the story, it'll look very suspicious. What's to hinder you from making a statement? All I want to know is your account of what you did on the evening of your wife's death."

Fenton thought for a moment or two before answering.

"That evening's a while back," he pointed out. "I can't guarantee to remember exactly every detail just as it happened. Suppose I make a slip somewhere, quite honestly; I may quite well do that, since it's not a matter of yesterday. Then you'll probably think I'm lying. I really can't remember everything."

"Tell me what you do remember," said the Superintendent, pulling his notebook in front of him on the desk. "Start at dinner-time, say."

"I had dinner at my hotel," Fenton began. "The waiter knows me and he could corroborate that. Then after dinner I went into the lounge and had some coffee. I remember the waiter who brought me it, and perhaps he'd be able to recall seeing me. I think on that night I spoke to another man staying at the hotel for a few minutes; but he's gone away now."

He paused, as though expecting some comment, but the Superintendent merely waited with his pen ready to write.

"I had arranged to look up Mr. Hyndford about nine o'clock," Fenton continued, moistening his lips nervously as he spoke. "I sat in the lounge for a while, and then I left the hotel. That must have been somewhere about ten to nine. I remember going over to the hotel desk and looking at the letter-rack to see if anything had come for me. I don't think I gave up my key; at least, I can't remember doing it. Usually I don't, when I go out. It's only a nuisance doing it."

"When did you reach Mr. Hyndford's house?" the Superintendent demanded.

"That would be shortly after nine, I expect. I don't really know to a minute. It must have been after nine, because one doesn't usually drop in on a man just on the tick of the time when one makes an engagement of that sort."

"You found Mr. Hyndford at home?"

"Of course. We talked for a while about one thing and another—I really forget what we did talk about. Japan, I think, and the Customs examination at Victoria, and a play or two that's on in town, and some other things of that sort. Just the usual things one does talk about when one's a bit at a loose end, you understand. And then we had a drink. And then we talked for a while longer. And by and by I began to feel I'd stayed long enough; so I cleared out. Hyndford came out to the gate with me, I remember, and we remarked on what a fine night it was. And—I'd nearly forgotten that—the clock near by struck three-quarters while we were still talking at the gate: that was 10.45, I know. And I didn't stay more than a minute or two after that."

He glanced at Ross's face as though trying to discover how much of all this the Superintendent knew already; but Ross had too much experience to betray things of that sort.

"After that," Fenton went on, "I walked back towards town. It was a nice night, so I turned down towards the bridge, and I stood on it for a while watching the moonlight on the river. I should think that would be somewhere round about ten or a quarter past eleven most likely. And as I was standing there, it occurred to me that I might go along and take a look at The Cedars."

"One moment," interrupted the Superintendent. "When you were at Mr. Hyndford's, did you know that Dr. Hyndford was out?"

"Yes, I did," Fenton admitted. "His brother told me he was."

"Then may I take it that your decision to visit The Cedars had some connection with Dr. Hyndford's absence from his own house?"

Fenton flushed as he grasped the underlying meaning of the Superintendent's query.

"You may if you like," he said, with an attempt at carelessness. "I'm telling you what I did, just as you asked me. I went along the road to The Cedars. Naturally, I took some trouble to get into the garden without being seen. There's a little lane runs down by the house, before you come to the gate: and I turned into it. I saw Marton fooling about with his telescope in his garden opposite, but I managed to keep out of his sight. Then, from the lane, I slipped over into the garden."

"What time was that?" Ross asked.

"I don't know," Fenton answered. "I really don't. It might have been round about half-past eleven, more or less. I really can't put a figure on it with any certainty. I didn't look at my watch."

The Superintendent nodded without saying anything.

"When I got into the garden," Fenton continued, "I saw a light in the drawing-room. The curtains were drawn close, so I couldn't see into the room, you understand? So I went along one of the paths and sneaked up to the window. I'd seen that it was closed. Sounds rather a low trick, of course; but I'd a right to do as I liked in my own garden, hadn't I? So I went up quietly to the French window and I tried to get a look through the curtains, just to see who was inside."

His nervousness seemed to return in full strength at this stage in his narrative. Whether because he disliked telling of his spying on his wife, or for some other cause, he seemed to find difficulty with his story.

"There was only one place where the curtains were not properly drawn together," he went on, "and I tried to see into the room through the hole between them. All I could see was the end of the settee, with a woman's feet and ankles. I looked for a while, but she didn't move; and I could hear no sound of talking in the room. That wasn't what I'd come to see; and there seemed to be no good waiting. She was alone, evidently. So as soon as I'd made up my mind about that, I slipped off the terrace, made my way through the garden, and got back into the little lane again.

"Naturally I took good care that Marton didn't see me as I came out of the little lane. He was busy mucking about with that telescope of his, so I don't think he saw me. I wasn't exactly anxious to meet anyone, just then; I was feeling rather low-down, somehow; though I'd been doing nothing I hadn't a perfect right to do, you understand? So I put my best foot foremost, and came round by the bridge again, and so back to my hotel. The night-porter might be able to tell you when I got in that night; I didn't look at my watch."

"When you were in the garden," the Superintendent asked, "did you notice anything—anything at all—that might help to fix the time? It may be important."

Fenton rubbed his chin in perplexity.

"I don't remember anything," he said at last. "You see, one doesn't bother about the time much, does one? Oh, yes! I do remember one thing: there was a light in the Struan Museum up above. I just happened to notice it, and wondered what they could be about at that time of night. But that's all I can call to mind," he concluded, in a rather despondent tone. "Not much good, is it?"

Superintendent Ross detached his notes from the loose-leaf cover.

"You saw nothing of Dr. Hyndford that evening, then?" he asked.

"Nothing. I never came across him. In fact, I haven't seen him since I came back to Stanningmore this time."

"There's just one thing I want to know," said the Superintendent abruptly. "You tell me you saw into the drawing-room at some time round about half-past eleven. Knowing what you know now, do you believe Mrs. Fenton was alive or dead at the time you saw her?"

Fenton looked extremely confused when this question was shot at him.

"Well, really," he said hesitatingly, "I don't . . . I couldn't tell you; honestly, I can't say. I only saw her feet and ankles, just as I described; and I suppose that she'd fallen asleep when I looked in at the window. That may have been it; or she may have been dead by that time. If I'd seen her face, of course, I'd have realized—"

He broke off, evidently deciding that he would make things no better by continuing.

"Now just a couple of further questions," said the Superintendent. "Do you know anything about the relations between Miss Hazlemere and her aunt? Were they friendly or did they not get on together?"

"I really can't say much about that—from personal knowledge, at any rate," Fenton answered dubiously. "You see, I separated from my wife almost as soon as her niece came to stay here. I hardly saw them together at all. One picks up a lot of tittle-tattle, without particularly wanting to hear it; and I make no bones about it: my sympathy was entirely with Miss Hazlemere, if there was any disagreement between them. But I've no direct information on the point. Naturally, any time I did run across Miss Hazlemere, we didn't discuss my wife; it was a subject both of us rather avoided, and I think it was what one might expect, wasn't it?"

"You had some suspicions about Dr. Hyndford, perhaps?"

"Well—" Again Fenton showed some hesitation. "People do talk, don't they? And I may as well be frank with you: if I'd been able to get hold of anything definite, I'd have used it without scruple. I wanted to get rid of my wife, everyone knew that. But that doesn't mean I've any grudge against Hyndford now, you understand? I wasn't jealous of him in the very slightest."

"You don't seem to be much cut up over the affair," said Ross in a dry tone.

"Well, why should I be?" Fenton demanded, with a revealing flash of brutality. "My wife was just a drag on me—nothing more. She and I had parted for good, long ago. She drank, and she had the temper of a fiend. I'm not much of a hypocrite, really; and I see no need to cry into a pocket-handkerchief just because she's gone."

He studied the Superintendent's face for a moment, and then added:

"If you want the plain truth, there it is, whether you like it or not."

Superintendent Ross made no pretence of offended virtue.

"I'm not adding these points to my notes," he said, as though the subject had no interest for him. "Here are the sheets I've written on. You might read them over, and if you find they're correct, just put your signature at the foot."

He handed over his notes, and Fenton read through them carefully.

"That seems correct," he admitted, putting his name to the documents.

"You'll leave your address if you go away from Stanningmore," the Superintendent cautioned him. "I may want to see you again."

Fenton agreed to this, and the Superintendent let him go. As soon as he was out of the office, Ross powdered the papers and brought up his visitor's finger-prints on them.

Fenton's finger-prints were identical with those on the tumbler which had stood in the drawing-room of The Cedars on the night of the murder.

"Well, somebody's doing a hell of a lot of hard lying in this case," reflected the Superintendent, whose mental imagery was often more vivid than his *viva voce* expression of it.

He put away the leaves of notes bearing Fenton's incriminating finger-prints, and then sat down at his table to wrestle with the whole problem. Taking a sheet of paper, he jotted down the following to help him in his speculation.

> 1. The intermittent administration of digitalis would provide the false suggestion that Mrs. Fenton's heart was deranged.
>
> 2. Veronal would put her to sleep, and thus make it possible to assault her without leaving traces of a struggle.
>
> 3. Pressure on the vagi would cause death by what would, at a casual examination, appear to be failure of the heart's action, following naturally on the earlier symptoms of derangement.

He read over this thoughtfully after he had written it down. It seemed to point convincingly to a single thread of purpose connecting the main points of the case together. Satisfied with that, he turned next to a list of the various possible culprits; and under each name he set down the pros and cons which occurred to him, thus:

Joyce Hazlemere.—She had digitalis plants in her garden.

She could have made an extract from them simply enough.

She had easy access to the bottles of Paronax.

She once had a dose of veronal in her possession and might have preserved it instead of using it.

She *might* have succeeded in administering veronal to Mrs. Fenton at dinner-time, say in whiskey and soda.

She had ample time to kill Mrs. Fenton when she found her, probably asleep, in the drawing-room on her return at midnight.

She had a fairly good motive.

But: She would hardly know about the vagus nerve unless she had read up about it or had consulted an expert.

Seaforth.—He could only have worked in conjunction with Joyce Hazlemere. If he did, then all that fits her case will apply equally to his.

Fenton.—He suppressed the fact that he was near the house that night, until it was dragged out of him.

The finger-prints on the tumbler will not fit his story. He had a very strong motive for wishing to be rid of his wife.

But: He could not have administered the digitalis unless by collusion with someone who had ready access to the Paronax bottles.

He could not have administered the veronal in time for it to take effect before the crime was committed, *unless* he was in The Cedars, unknown to anyone, before Dr. Hyndford came over at about 8.45.

His story, such as it is, was partly corroborated by R. Hyndford's evidence.

DR. HYNDFORD.—He might have administered the digitalis *if* he had access to the Paronax bottles—i.e. if he was able to get into Mrs. Fenton's bedroom.

He has the technical knowledge about the vagus nerve.

He *might*, after leaving by the front door, have walked round the house, entered by the French window, and killed Mrs. Fenton. By Marton's evidence, he left the house at 10.47. By R. Hyndford's evidence the doctor got home at 10.55 approximately. It leaves very little time, but it might *just* have been possible.

But: His story is completely confirmed by both his brother and Marton, whose times agree as well as can be expected.

Mrs. Fenton was awake when he left the house, for Marton saw her. She could not have been killed without a struggle at that time, even if Dr. Hyndford had reentered the house.

He actually stands to lose money by her death—a considerable sum.

WATCHET.—No access to the Paronax bottles. No chance of administering veronal.

Unlikely to have expert knowledge of the vagus nerves.

No really strong motive for murder, since he seems to have been embezzling all round and it would come to light even if he silenced Mrs. Fenton.

THE MAID AT THE CEDARS.—She had the same chances as Miss Hazlemere so far as the digitalis plants, the Paronax bottles, and the veronal were concerned.

But: She could hardly have had the special knowledge required to use these opportunities, much less an acquaintance with the vagus nerves and their function.

She had no motive which would be strong enough to cause her to commit the murder.

Superintendent Ross considered for a time after writing down these notes, then he added three fresh jottings:

1. Dr. Hyndford's story excludes any chance that he administered the veronal.

2. The soda-water had been opened, but there were no finger-prints on the glass of the bottles.

3. Why was the French window closed? And when was it closed?

The Superintendent went back to the beginning and conned over what he had written.

CHAPTER X
I.O.U.

Superintendent Ross had assumed that there would not be much expedition in James Corwen's procedure; and it was therefore a pleasant surprise when the lawyer rang up in the late forenoon of the following day with the news that he had obtained Mrs. Fenton's I.O.U.'s from Dr. Hyndford.

When the detective entered the solicitor's private room, James Corwen glanced up at him with an inscrutable expression; invited him with a gesture to take the client's chair; and then, putting down his pen, waited for his visitor to make the first move.

"You've got these papers?" the Superintendent asked, perfunctorily.

"I have. I made some sort of excuse about them, and gave him a receipt for them temporarily."

James Corwen paused for a moment; then turning square on his guest, he demanded:

"Have you still got my client on your list of possible culprits?"

A faint sardonic tinge in the lawyer's tone caught the ear of the Superintendent and made him all alert.

"I've brought no charge against her yet," he observed rather stiffly.

"Not enough evidence to hang a cat, was how I estimated it," James Corwen reminded him. "But perhaps I was wrong. I forgot there are tom-cats as well as tabby-cats."

He leaned back in his chair, evidently taking a cynical pleasure in the Superintendent's bewilderment at this turn in the conversation.

“You couldn’t say it in plain English, I suppose?” the detective suggested crossly.

“No. This conversation isn’t privileged,” the solicitor pointed out blandly. “I’m not inclined to run the risk of slander, even in a good cause. But I think I can promise to divert your attention into a fresh channel for all that, Superintendent.”

He rang the bell and, evidently by pre-arrangement, his clerk Groombridge came into the room, followed by Seaforth. James Corwen opened a drawer in his desk and took out four papers, which he spread out before him.

“These are the I.O.U.’s which Dr. Hyndford gave me this morning,” he explained. “When he handed them to me, I glanced at them casually. They seemed to me perfectly in order. When the doctor had gone, I happened to ring for my clerk here. He takes an interest in handwriting; and, just as a joke, I showed him these documents. He takes that sort of thing seriously; and as it chances, he has made a study of Mrs. Fenton’s writing.”

A fresh light was dawning in the Superintendent’s mind.

“And there’s a screw loose?” he demanded.

“I think we’ll leave cats and screws aside just now,” James Corwen said decidedly. “Groombridge will tell you what he noticed. That is a matter of fact. Any inferences you may draw from his statement will be a matter for yourself. I wish it to be quite clear that I am making no insinuations. I am simply calling your attention to certain . . . well, shall I say, peculiarities which may interest you. Now, Groombridge.”

The clerk took his cue and came forward rather nervously.

“This is how it is, Superintendent,” he explained. “I’ve always taken an interest in handwriting. It’s been a hobby of mine for years. And in this office, of course, I get a lot of manuscript material through my hands, written by all sorts of different people. Now, Mrs. Fenton’s handwriting’s always interested me specially. It’s got some characteristics that don’t occur in normal script at all. You know she—” He glanced rather apprehensively at his employer. “Well, she wasn’t strictly temperate, if I may put it that way.”

"She drank like a fish at times," Seaforth growled, with evident impatience. "You needn't make any bones about it to Superintendent Ross, Groombridge."

Groombridge was rather taken aback by this blunt description.

"She was very intemperate," he paraphrased, finally. "Now, Superintendent, anything of that sort leaves its mark on a person's handwriting. For instance, there's writer's cramp. I've had that myself, once or twice. Now when I get writer's cramp, my handwriting changes. It takes on an irregular character. There's a sort of angularity in it and I don't form my letters well. Naturally that leads me to retouch what I've written, to make it clear. Then there's exophthalmic goiter. That leads to a very characteristic trembling in the writing, very fine, very regular, and quite continuous. And so on, you see. Each type of nervous disease has its own sign-manual, if you understand me."

He picked up a paper from the desk.

"Now, here's one of these documents. You see it's quite short. 'I.O.U. the sum of three thousand pounds. Evelyn Fenton.' It's exactly like her writing. If I hadn't paid special attention to her script at one time and another, I don't suppose I'd have seen anything wrong with it. But I know her writing like a book, you see? I've used her script as a study in chronic alcoholism's effects. That I.O.U. was never written by her, Superintendent. If you've got a minute or two to spare, I'll prove it to you so that you won't have a doubt left, not one."

"I'm open to conviction," the Superintendent admitted, though there was scepticism in his tone. Groombridge turned to James Corwen.

"May I bring my microscope and one or two other things?" he asked, with the air of a small boy begging a favour.

The solicitor nodded, and the monk-like face of Groombridge crinkled in a smile of relief. Evidently it was a pleasant experience to find his hobby treated with anything except contempt by his master. In a few seconds, the clerk returned with a small microscope and a bundle of papers which he arranged on the desk. His manner was compounded of a modest pride in his hobby and a very distinct fear of ridicule from his employer.

"Now, Superintendent," he began, when he had fixed things to his satisfaction, "this document here is a letter written to the firm by Mrs. Fenton. Look at it, and you'll see it bears a date close to the one on the I.O.U. for £3,000. Now, do you see any marked difference between the two scripts?"

Superintendent Ross examined the letter, and compared it with the I.O.U.

"They seem much the same to me," was his comment as he handed them back. "I'm certainly no expert."

Groombridge spread out the two documents side by side on the desk.

"Now, would you just look carefully at the relative sizes of the letters as you read through each script from start to finish," he suggested. "I mean, just see if a letter A at the start of the script is the same size as a letter A at the end of the writing in each case."

Superintendent Ross pored over the two papers for quite a long time.

"So far as I can see, there's a slight diminution in the size of the letters in the one case; and can't detect it in the other. But it might be mere imagination or accident, for all I can see."

Groombridge was gaining confidence, and his head-shake was that of a master disapproving of a pupil's exercise.

"To the trained eye," he declared, "there's not the least doubt about it. The small letters in the I.O.U. are all uniform in height; in the other document they diminish steadily from start to finish. I've measured them under the microscope. It's absolutely beyond dispute. I'd swear to it in the witness-box."

"That doesn't seem much to go on," the Superintendent said, with a hint of disparagement in his tone. "For all I know, I may vary the size of my letters myself when I write."

Groombridge seemed in no way dashed by this criticism. He put his finger on the letter.

"Now, Superintendent, please have a good look at the ends of her words here."

"She seems to have slurred them in most cases, so far as I can see," Ross reported, after scanning the document. "But there's the same slurring at the ends of 'three' and 'pounds' in the I.O.U."

"But not in 'thousand,' although it's a longer word," the clerk pointed out. "Now, will you look at how Mrs. Fenton wrote 'and' in her letter."

"She writes it with an ampersand [&] instead of 'and,'" Ross said, after reading through the letter.

"Yes," Groombridge pointed out. "If a forger wanted to get the termination 'and' for the word 'thousand' he'd have some difficulty in finding a model to copy, since she used the ampersand in her writing and 'and' isn't a common termination in ordinary English words—words one uses currently, I mean. That's just a point in passing. Now I think we'll take the microscope."

He adjusted the instrument, inserted a part of the letter in the field, and invited the Superintendent to focus the microscope to suit his own eye.

"Now look at the actual formation of the lines of the letters," he directed. "You see there's a continuous vertical trembling. That's characteristic of chronic alcoholism. See, I'll shift the paper through the field bit by bit, and you can see for yourself that her pen's been vibrating continuously as she wrote."

He did as he suggested, and Ross had to admit that the description was correct.

"Now I'll take the I.O.U.," Groombridge said, removing the letter and replacing it by the second paper. "Look for the trembling in this."

The Superintendent studied the I.O.U minutely, shifting the paper gradually through the field until he had completed his survey. What he saw evidently impressed him more than the earlier evidence.

"There's quite a marked trembling at the start," he said, lifting his eye from the microscope eyepiece and looking across at Groombridge. "Then it fades out and begins again. In fact, it's clearest on the upstrokes and near the joins between the letters; elsewhere it seems to recur only now and again. I'm quite prepared to admit that the two scripts do differ in that."

Groombridge smiled with the satisfaction of a man who is making a convert.

"The upstroke is a difficult one for a forger, so he's apt to hesitate there and take more pains. On the downstroke his pen runs naturally, and he forgets to put in peculiarities. And as he goes on with his work, he gets engrossed and forgets the finer details, just as you see there. I mean that he thinks more of copying the broad character of the lettering and omits the finer detail like the shake of the pen. Then, after a moment or two, he remembers the quivering of the pen, puts it in for a bit, and then forgets about it again. That's what the I.O.U. looks like, doesn't it?"

"You're quite right, so far as that goes," Ross conceded. "But you haven't proved your case yet, to my mind. These things might be accidental."

"Then it's no use showing you the points where the pen was lifted by the two writers," Groombridge declared. "It just happens that in alcoholism you get frequent pen-lifting in the middle of writing, and that approximates to the way in which the forger lifts his pen often as he goes along, so as to get an idea of what his work looks like. But now there's another point. You see how Mrs. Fenton's occasionally retouched her words—she wrote them, and then went back over them and gave a touch here and a touch there. So does the forger in the I.O.U. Just compare them, will you? and see if you make anything out of that."

Superintendent Ross studied the two texts minutely for a time.

"I see what you mean," he said at last. "When Mrs. Fenton touched up her writing, she did it to make it more legible; and her retouching is bold and obvious. In the I.O.U., these afterthoughts are concealed as far as possible. They're not meant to improve legibility. They're put in to improve the resemblance between the forgery and Mrs. Fenton's real writing. Is that what you're after?"

"That's it," said Groombridge, with an obvious air of giving a good mark to a promising pupil. "Now you'll admit that there's something there? Here's the final proof. It's quite conclusive, to my mind. Look at Mrs. Fenton's way of writing a capital I. She makes it like a Roman numeral I, doesn't she? Not like the usual capital I in writing."

"Well, it's the same in the I.O.U., isn't it?" Ross demanded. "What's wrong with that?"

Groombridge pushed forward a sheet of paper. "Just write a capital I in that way, will you?" he asked. "Don't think about it. Put it down quick."

The Superintendent took out his pen and made the character.

"Now," said Groombridge, "I'll make a copy of that as well as I can."

He took up a pen and made the three necessary strokes on the paper, below the Superintendent's letter.

"We'll let this dry naturally," he said. "Now, Superintendent, did you see any difference between our ways of writing?"

Superintendent Ross shook his head.

"Can't say I did," Ross admitted. "It's just three strokes."

Groombridge made no comment on this, but turned to something fresh.

"Here's a capital O in Mrs. Fenton's letter—here, at the word 'On.' You see she makes a *closed* oval. That's how it appears in the I.O.U. as well, naturally, since the forger copied her writing. Now will you write an O of that sort, Superintendent, and I'll do the same."

Rather mystified, Ross did as he was requested; and Groombridge made a careful copy of the detective's O.

"Now we've got what we need," the clerk announced. "Just have a look at the capital I, Superintendent. You began it by making the top horizontal stroke first; then you drew in the vertical; and you finished off with the lower horizontal. That's the way Mrs. Fenton used to make her I's—top stroke, vertical, lowest stroke: in that order. Now as it happens, when I write the letter, I start with the vertical stroke, then I fill in the top stroke, and I finish up with the lowest horizontal. That's the way the forger makes his I's."

"That's very neat," the Superintendent admitted in a dubious tone. "You've got a winner there—if you can prove it."

"There's nothing easier," said Groombridge, confidently. "See, I'll put the letter under the microscope for you. Here's an I written by Mrs. Fenton. Look at the crossing of the top horizontal stroke and the vertical. Do you, see, very faintly but still quite distinctly, two thin dark streaks of ink like this | |, running vertically and cutting right across the horizontal ink line? They're clear enough. You could see them with a magnifying glass."

"I see something of the sort," the Superintendent admitted.

"Well, then, when one ink line—written fairly boldly like the ones in this I—crosses another earlier ink line, the last-written line generally has these two bars marking its limits on either side. They show up better if the writing has been blotted after the first line is written and before the second one is put on; but you can see them even when the thing has been written straight on without blotting. You see it?"

"I think so," the Superintendent said, with increased interest in his tone. "What you mean is this. Suppose a vertical line and a horizontal line cross. You look for these two tiny parallel lines at the crossing. If they lie like this | | then the vertical stroke was written after the horizontal one. But if the two parallel hair-lines lie like this =, then the vertical line was written first and the horizontal line was written afterwards. The later line is the one that has these two little parallels showing its course across the original line."

"That's it," Groombridge confirmed. "Luckily in this case the hair-lines are clear enough for anyone to see. Sometimes they're so feeble that you need to be pretty expert to spot them. Now here's Mrs. Fenton's way of making her I. Have a look at it under the microscope. You can see that where the top bar joins the vertical, the thread-lines are like this | |. That shows she wrote the top horizontal before the vertical line. Now look down below at the second crossing of the I. See there, the thread-lines are like this =. That means the lower horizontal was written after the vertical. So her order was: top line, vertical, lower line. That's quite clear. Now try the I.O.U. The vertical's over-laid by the two horizontals. Both the hair-lines lie like this =. So the forger wrote his vertical line first and then put in the two horizontals—quite different from Mrs. Fenton's way of doing it."

"Very neat," said the Superintendent admiringly. "And if you can prove that Mrs. Fenton invariably made her I's that way, I think it would weigh heavily with a jury."

"There's more yet," Groombridge pointed out, with a faint trace of exultation showing in his emaciated face. "There's this O. Look at your own O. It's a closed oval, but you can see the join clear enough. I'll put it under the microscope for you. See? Your join is at the summit of the O. You started with your pen at the very top and began with a full downstroke, so that the join is right at the summit of the character. Now my O—here it is—was started-half-way down on the left side, and I finished on a downstroke; so the join in my case is about the middle of the left-hand line instead of being at the top, like yours. Mrs. Fenton's joins are all at the tops of her O's. The forger's join is on the left side, like mine. That's conclusive, I think, isn't it?"

The Superintendent lifted his eye from the microscope and caught James Corwen eyeing him with a certain sardonic amusement, as though he were enjoying a double jest which included Ross and the clerk's graphology in a comprehensive contempt.

"Damn that man," the Superintendent reflected, crossly. "He doesn't believe a bit in all this, but he sees he can use it to extricate that girl from the mess. That's all he cares about."

To avoid the solicitor's derisive glance, Ross turned to Groombridge.

"You'd better take good care of these things," he cautioned. "And of course all this is strictly confidential. You mustn't go talking about it outside. If it's needed in court, it'll be quite time enough to use it then."

Groombridge's lean face lighted up at the last sentence. His inward vision conjured up a picture of himself in the witness-box, holding an audience intent upon his exposition of the peculiarities of the documents. What a chance of fame for that unpublished work: *Some Minor Characteristics of Handwriting*, by Benjamin

Groombridge, Notary Public. "Who's Groombridge?" "Oh, that fellow who gave the crucial evidence in the Fenton murder case, you remember? Very smart man." That would be a reward for all these years spent in poring over manuscripts. And James Corwen would be impressed then, in spite of himself. Groombridge, for some reason which he could not even have formulated to himself, was deeply desirous of gaining his employer's esteem. Surely, now that his expert knowledge had opened up an unlooked-for line in this murder case, James Corwen would have to take him more seriously. Graphology would be justified in spite of all the sneers.

The lawyer's harsh voice awakened him abruptly from his daydream:

"That's all we need you for, Groombridge. And clear all this rubbish off my desk, will you?"

No impression, then, in spite of it all. His work was just "rubbish" in Corwen's opinion: merely something one could use to throw dust in the eyes of that sharp Superintendent and put him off the scent of the firm's client. Rather mournfully, Groombridge collected his papers, picked up his little microscope, and made his way out of the room. Two sentences had been enough to knock him off his tiny pedestal and turn him back into a mere clerk again.

When the door had closed behind him, James Corwen turned to the Superintendent with a glance of interrogation.

"Very ingenious," said Ross, in a judicial tone. "It's a complex case."

If the solicitor could restrain himself, Seaforth could not.

"That knocks the bottom out of any case against Miss Hazlemere, anyhow," he broke in triumphantly.

Superintendent Ross seemed amazed by this point of view.

"I don't see that it has anything to do with Miss Hazlemere," he explained patiently. "You're going too fast for me, Mr. Seaforth. First, I've brought no charge against Miss Hazlemere. Second, even if this I.O.U. is forged, I've seen no proof yet that the forgery has benefited anybody. In fact, Mrs. Fenton's death has apparently cut clean across that part of the business since her assets are next door to nil. There's a good deal to be done yet, I'm afraid."

He picked up the remaining I.O.U.'s which Groombridge had left on the desk and scrutinised them carefully.

"H'm! If she got through all that in such a hurry, she must have been plunging heavily."

He opened his notebook and jotted down the dates and the values of the I.O.U.'s:—

10th May, 1926	£1,500
25th May, 1926	£3,000
17th June, 1926	£2,000
9th July, 1926	£2,500

Closing his notebook, he resumed his study of the papers.

"I suppose Groombridge certifies that these are forgeries as well—the whole lot, I mean?" he asked.

"So he told me,"' James Corwen confirmed. "You can ask him yourself as you go out."

The Superintendent seemed to have passed to a fresh line of thought.

"Let's see," he said in an almost absent-minded tone, "I think you said Mrs. Fenton took out a £500 insurance with the Canterbury and Mercantile United. What date was that, can you remember?"

"It was 10th August, 1926."

"A month after the date of the latest I.O.U.," said Ross in a reflective tone. "And I suppose the cash from that insurance forms part of her estate now?"

James Corwen nodded. He seemed to have lost interest in the Superintendent, now that he had sprung his mine with the forgeries; and he turned to his desk with the air of a man who has work to do.

"Hadn't you better get on with your cat-hanging, Superintendent?" he suggested gruffly. "I've given you all the help I can, for the present."

Ross could not ignore the plain dismissal.

"I'll see what I can do," he retorted, without betraying any vexation at the lawyer's manner. "Groombridge is outside? I'll just ask him about these other three I.O.U.'s as I go out."

Superintendent Ross, after leaving the lawyer's office, sauntered along the street towards the police headquarters. He found that walking stimulated his brain; and he had enough to make him thoughtful at this stage in the case. Despite his assertion that pure reason was the only thing that should count in a criminal case, he found that he was giving weight to something which was no more than a. sort of instinctive feeling. He could not shake himself free from the idea that in spite of all the apparent crisscrossing of trails, there must be a single simple solution of the whole problem. And yet, if Groombridge's evidence amounted to anything, here was a second root cropping up in the equation. He had already formulated an explanation which would cover the forgeries; but unfortunately he could not see his way to make the rest of the case dovetail logically into his hypothesis. His mind rejected the view that two sets of criminals had been at work simultaneously and that the interlacing of their doings had been mere chance; and yet, on a basis of pure reason, that hypothesis was the easiest.

Wrapped in his thoughts, he halted unconsciously before a shop-window; and when someone, in passing, brushed against him, he came out of his brown study and lifted his eyes to find a show of glass and china on the shelves before him. He examined the display incuriously until at last his glance lighted on a set of tumblers ranged in a row just above his eye-level. At that, he woke up and studied the pattern etched on the glass. It seemed familiar; and he recalled that it was the same as that on the tumbler found in the drawing-room on the night of the murder. For quite a minute, the Superintendent scrutinised the pattern, as though he had just detected something of importance; then, with a rather less troubled countenance, he turned away from the window and, at a quicker pace, made his way to the police station.

Sitting down at his desk, he took note-paper and wrote a letter to the Canterbury and Mercantile United Insurance Co. asking for particulars of any insurances which had been effected on Mrs. Fenton's life.

CHAPTER XI
THE FINANCIAL SIDE OF THE CASE

When Superintendent Ross called upon Dr. Hyndford next day, he made no previous appointment. On this occasion, he felt, it was inadvisable to put the doctor on the alert, so he selected a time just before the consulting hour, when his quarry was certain to be at home. It was after lunch, and as the Superintendent entered the gate he found Mr. Hyndford loitering in the garden, smoking a cigarette and passing his flower-borders in indolent review. Ross, confronted with an expert, did not exhibit the interest in botany which he had made so much of in the garden of The Cedars. He confined himself to vague praise of some of the most familiar plants: begonias, calceolarias, foxgloves, dahlias, and geraniums; and then despite Mr. Hyndford's evident desire to exhibit his finer specimens, the Superintendent tore himself away and went up to the front door.

Dr. Hyndford received him in no very conciliatory fashion.

"Well, what do you want now?" he demanded. "You've come at an awkward time. I'm just going to see some patients."

"I shan't detain you more than a moment," the Superintendent assured him smoothly. "I only want to ask a question or two."

"Then ask them," Dr. Hyndford snapped. "It's these I.O.U.'s I handed to Corwen the other day, I suppose? Was it you or he who unearthed this mare's nest?"

Ross ignored this sneer.

"The I.O.U.'s are all right," he said, watching the doctor's face keenly. "But everything connected with Mrs. Fenton is of importance now, and I want to understand her affairs as well as I can. What I don't understand is why you lent her such a considerable sum."

"She was . . . an intimate friend of mine," said the doctor, slowly. "She got into difficulties at times with her bookmakers—it wasn't always a case of cash bets, of course, with her—and once or twice I had to come to the rescue. Is that clear?"

The Superintendent nodded.

"You gave her cheques, I suppose?" he asked.

Dr. Hyndford laughed contemptuously.

"Think it's likely?" he demanded. "Would you give a woman your cheque for money of that sort? I'm not a fool, Superintendent. When a man pays over money to another man's wife, he doesn't advertise the business, if he's got any sense. No, I drew the stuff in notes on my own cheque and handed the notes over to her."

The Superintendent allowed a slightly foolish expression to pass across his face. If the doctor was bluffing, he meant to call the bluff; but he wanted to manage it without seeming to use *force* majeure.

"It's a bit awkward," he said clumsily. "Of course, between men of the world, I see your point; but I've got to satisfy my people higher up that I've done my work thoroughly and they'll probably want something more than my say-so to go on. Now your banking account. . . ."

Dr. Hyndford gave a bark of laughter at the Superintendent's obvious reluctance to hurt his feelings.

"One would think you imagined I've something to conceal in this affair," he said, acidly. "Well, I haven't. Strange, isn't it? You can go to my bank and turn up the transactions. I'll give you authority to do it—a note to the manager. Now, is there anything else you'd like to look into? Care to come upstairs and count my shirts, or any little thing like that? I'm quite ready to let you occupy your time with my affairs if you've really nothing better to do."

The Superintendent looked downcast by this comment. He had got his own way so easily that he began to wonder whether it was the right way after all. Quite clearly, the doctor had no fears as to the result of the examination of his banking account.

"Well, it's really hardly my doing, you understand?" he pointed out, rather shamefacedly. "Only, the question's sure to be asked; and I want to be able to answer it. If you'll just give me that note to the bank-manager, I'll be able to certify that there's nothing in the thing. Otherwise, somebody higher up might insist on going into the matter and putting you to a lot of unnecessary trouble, doctor."

Dr. Hyndford sat down at his desk and wrote a few lines.

"That do you?" he demanded. "Now, is there anything else? I've no time to spare."

Ross's mouth seemed dry, and he swallowed once or twice rather painfully.

"If it wouldn't be troubling you," he suggested, "I'd like a glass of cold water. The road up here's very dusty."

Dr. Hyndford seemed to bear no malice.

"A whiskey and soda?" he proposed.

"No," the Superintendent declined. "I'd rather have some plain soda, thanks, if it isn't too much trouble. I'm frightfully thirsty."

Dr. Hyndford rang the bell and gave an order. In a few moments a maid brought a tray with soda and a tumbler. Superintendent Ross fell upon it with obvious relief, poured out a fair quantity, and drank it at a draught.

But as he poured the rest of the soda into his glass, he had to admit that his long shot had missed the mark. The tumbler in his hand had a pattern entirely different from that which he had found in the drawing-room of The Cedars. He finished his soda and turned to meet Dr. Hyndford's pale blue eyes.

"There's just one thing more," he said in a tentative tone, "I take it that you're a loser over these I.O.U.'s. At least, I understand from Mr. Corwen that the estate wouldn't cover one of them, let alone the lot."

Dr. Hyndford's face showed unconcealed annoyance, and his answer indicated its cause.

"You seem to be taking a damned lot of interest in things which I'd have thought were my private business," he said angrily. "What does it matter to anyone except myself whether I drop money or not? But if you're losing any sleep over it, Superintendent, you can calm your nerves. I'm not out a penny on these I.O.U.'s, you'll be glad to hear. It's another of your mare's nests. I hold an insurance policy for £10,000 on Mrs. Fenton's life. Cheer up! That weight's off your mind."

"Well, I'm very glad to hear it," said the Superintendent politely. "What company is it in? I insure with the Bromwich Union, myself."

"Stirring news!" said the doctor, with unconcealed contempt. "My policy's in the Canterbury and Mercantile. And I buy my stamps at the post-office, invariably. Any other bits of information I can give you? If not, I heard a patient come in, and I'd like to get to my work."

As the Superintendent made his way towards the town, he had to admit to himself that Dr. Hyndford had succeeded in mystifying him. The doctor had been far franker that Ross had anticipated. He had thrown open his banking-account and thus saved the police a considerable amount of trouble. And he had admitted without any ado that he held an insurance policy which covered him against all loss through the I.O.U.'s. On the face of things, that looked like a man who had nothing to conceal and nothing to fear through facts coming to light. But, on the other side, these two points could not be suppressed even if Dr. Hyndford had wished to do so. The police have their own methods of gaining information about banking-accounts; and it would be easy for them to ascertain whether the doctor held an insurance policy or not. The most that a criminal could do would be to fight a losing battle on these points; and the fact that he fought at all would be enough to arouse suspicion. It would be safer for him to feign frankness and be done with it.

"If he's not a dark horse, at any rate he's dyed invisible green," the Superintendent concluded, with some natural vexation. "If he was out to mystify me, he's managed to do it so far as the main case goes. But there's one thing. If I can't get him for murder, there's still the matter of these I.O.U.'s that he'll have to clear up. There's been hankey-pankey there, if that man Groombridge is right. . . ."

A sudden flash of illumination lit up the case in his mind from a fresh angle.

"*Now* I begin to see something!" he said aloud in his excitement.

He quickened his steps and soon arrived at the bank. It was after hours, which suited the Superintendent quite well since he was able to gain immediate admittance to the manager's office and could count on being left uninterrupted by clients. He produced his official credentials and his authorisation from Dr. Hyndford.

Laxey, the bank-manager, a brisk grey-moustached man, examined the documents carefully before saying anything.

"You want the record of cash paid in and cheques drawn by Dr. Hyndford?" he asked, when he had satisfied himself. "I can get you that. . . . But perhaps there's an easier way. The doctor's a bit slack with his pass-book. It's never up to date, and he may have left it with us to be written up. It would contain all you want, I expect, if we happen to have it here just now."

"If it goes back three years or so, it would give me all I need," the Superintendent agreed. "At least, it would do for a start. I'll probably want to ask your teller a question or two as well, though."

Laxey summoned a clerk and gave some instructions. As it chanced, Dr. Hyndford's pass-book was in the bank's charge at the moment; and when it was produced, the Superintendent found that it covered the whole period in which he was interested, for the doctor's banking transactions per annum were not very extensive.

A rapid examination satisfied the Superintendent that the entries to the credit of the bank could be ascribed roughly as follows. A monthly cheque of almost constant value he put down as money drawn for the payment of household bills. Sundry items under £20 were probably payments of larger accounts by cheque. Other cheques, running up to a hundred or a couple of hundred pounds in value at each transaction, suggested the doctor's losses on betting. All these the Superintendent left aside, confining his attention to still larger entries which occurred from time to time.

Turning to the other side of the account, Ross ignored the steady dribble of minor increments, which could obviously be identified as cheques from patients. Occasional figures of larger value he put down as representing the doctor's gains in his betting transactions. After eliminating these, a series of figures remained which represented considerable sums. One or two of these the Superintendent left aside, owing to the dates attached to them; and by concentrating his attention on the remainder he began to fit things together. In a very short time he had drawn up a schedule which he copied into his notebook:

		£
26th April	Paid in	300
29th April	Paid in	500
3rd May	Paid in	1,200
9th May	Drew out	1,500
(10th May	I.O.U.	1,500)
13th May	Paid in	1,200
15th May	Paid in	1,300
24th May	Drew out	3,000
(25th May	I.O.U.	3,000)
3rd June	Paid in	700
4th June	Paid in	1,400
16th June	Drew out	2,000
(17th June	I.O.U.	2,000)
30th June	Paid in	2,400
8th July	Drew out	2,500
(9th July	I.O.U.	2,500)

A rather grim smile passed over the Superintendent's face as he checked the figures, which evidently suggested something definite to his mind. He turned over the pages of the pass-book until he came to the period shortly before Mrs. Fenton's death and made a short calculation based on the figures in the book, which showed increasingly heavy withdrawals at short intervals. Evidently the doctor's gambling transactions had been going heavily against him at that period, and he had been steadily raising his bets in the hope of getting square.

The Superintendent glanced across the desk at the bank manager, who had been watching him with unconcealed interest.

"Round about this date," Ross said, putting his finger on the page, "Dr. Hyndford seems to have overdrawn his account pretty heavily—something like £3,000, I make it. I suppose you had some security?"

Laxey hesitated for a moment before replying.

"I suppose I may answer that," he said at last. "Dr. Hyndford got his brother to give security for him. We had £3,000 in bearer bonds to cover ourselves at that period."

"At that period?" questioned the Superintendent. "But there's still an overdraft of about the same amount."

"Quite true. But when Mr. Hyndford wanted his bonds back, Dr. Hyndford deposited a £10,000 policy on Mrs. Fenton's life instead."

"Why didn't he collect the money and be done with it?" the Superintendent demanded. "She's dead, and nobody would dispute it."

"Perfectly correct," Laxey admitted. "But under the Life Assurance Act of 1774, you've got to establish an insurable interest—I mean you've got to prove clearly that you've suffered a pecuniary loss at least equal to the value of the insurance. I understand that Dr. Hyndford is a creditor of Mrs. Fenton's estate and that the estate may not cover the debt. But until they get probate and settle things up, that state of affairs is too indefinite for the Insurance people to act on. The money will be paid eventually, of course; but not till the whole procedure is in order."

"I see," said the Superintendent, thoughtfully rubbing his chin. "A bit complicated, I gather. Now I suppose you've got someone who might remember a few things about the entries in this pass-book.

I'd like to see him—the man at the paying-in counter is the one I want."

"We've got only one teller there. Everything goes through his hands. I'll send for him."

In a few moments the official came into the room, and Ross was relieved to find that he seemed to be uncommonly alert.

"I'd like you to remember, if you can, something about these transactions here," the Superintendent said, opening the pass-book at the proper page. "April 26th. Three hundred pounds paid in by Dr. Hyndford. Was that notes or a cheque? Perhaps you can recall something about it."

The teller glanced at the manager.

"Is this all right, sir?" he asked, evidently doubtful about revealing anything connected with the business. Then, reassured by a nod from his chief, he wrinkled his brow in an effort to recall the transaction. "No, I can't remember anything about it."

"Then this one," the Superintendent went on patiently, pointing to the next item.

Again the teller admitted that he could remember nothing about the payment.

"Well, this one, then. May 3rd. Twelve hundred pounds."

The teller's face showed that he remembered something.

"That was a cheque—Mr. Richard Hyndford's cheque," he stated unhesitatingly. "I remember it because it was the first time Dr. Hyndford had paid in such a large sum."

"And ten days later, another twelve hundred pounds?"

"That was Mr. Richard Hyndford's cheque too. And there was another big one—here it is, £1,300— two days later. I began to notice these figures. They weren't usual in Dr. Hyndford's account."

"Then there's this one—£700 on 3rd June."

"That was in notes. I remember it because Dr. Hyndford made some joke about having done well out of the bookies this time."

The remaining items the teller was able to recall as having been paid over in the form of cheques drawn by Richard Hyndford.

"That's all I wanted to know," Ross said. "You'll be able to remember all that again if we want it? Thanks. And of course this is bank business, so you'll say nothing about it."

Superintendent Ross had got all he wanted now and he did not linger at the bank. His afternoon's work had thrown light on the Fenton case from an entirely fresh angle, and he began to see his way through some parts of the maze. It was too early yet to be confident, however.

At the police headquarters, on his return, he found a telegram from the Canterbury and Mercantile United Insurance Company which helped to make him more certain that he was on the right track. From it he learned that the £10,000 policy had been taken out by Dr. Hyndford almost immediately after Mrs. Fenton herself had insured her life for £500.

"Now's the time to bluff hard," he said reflectively to himself as he put down the paper.

He summoned one of his subordinates.

"To-morrow morning, you're to detach a man to watch Dr. Hyndford. Plain clothes, of course; but you may tell your man that it doesn't matter much if he's spotted. So long as he's not obtrusive enough to give ground for complaint, I don't mind much what he does. If the doctor stays indoors, let your man hang about the road and keep an eye on the premises. . . . Oh, by the way, there's always a chance that Dr. Hyndford may give him the slip by going on the river. Don't worry if he does; but report it to me at once."

He considered for a moment or two, then put a question about Watchet, the estate agent. It appeared that no trace of him had yet been found; but this did not seem to perturb the Superintendent. Dismissing his subordinate, Ross picked up his hat and went to the office of the *Stanningmore Gazette*.

"This is your busy time, I know," he explained to Dorrington when he had found his way to the sub-editor's room: "Don't bother to tell me all about it, for I'm not going to detain you. I just dropped in to let you see I wasn't forgetting you."

"Meaning you want us to do something for you," Dorrington interpreted ironically. "All right. Out with it. I've really no time to spare."

"It's just a titbit for you. You can put in a nice prominent paragraph to this effect: 'The Cedars Mystery. We learn on absolutely reliable authority that the police hope to make an arrest within the next two days.' And of course you can add something about the genius of that deservedly popular officer, Superintendent Ross, if you like; I leave that entirely to your good taste."

The Superintendent's expression showed clearly enough that this last suggestion was not to be taken seriously.

"You've got the murderer, have you?" Dorrington demanded. "Tell us all about it, will you?"

"No, you're very busy," the Superintendent pointed out blandly. "It'll keep for the present. A sort of Surprise for a Good Boy, perhaps, later on."

And without giving the sub-editor time to argue, Ross left the office.

As he walked back to the police station, he conned over some of the facts which he had gathered in the afternoon.

"Three thousand pounds is a biggish sum for a little country bank to handle," he reflected. "He could hardly have avoided including some £100 notes in that lot; and these ought to be traceable if the banks have had their eyes open. That's one possible line to work. Then there are these items in his banking account. He must have taken me for a flat ass, luckily, when he threw all that stuff open to me. It's like Whittaker Wright on a small scale."

As he entered the police station, a fresh idea occurred to him. He went to the telephone and rang up Joyce Hazlemere.

"There's just one question I want to ask, Miss Hazlemere," he explained, when she had come to the instrument. "Can you remember anything at all about where Mrs. Fenton kept her betting-books? She must have had some place where she generally put them."

Joyce Hazlemere's voice betrayed her mistrust of the detective.

"I really can't tell you much," she said. "I do remember once or twice seeing several old ones in a drawer of her writing-desk in the drawing-room. But that's all I can think of."

"You don't know the name of any bookmakers she dealt with?" Ross inquired.

"No. I never took the slightest interest in her betting."

The quiver in the girl's voice touched the Superintendent in spite of his official inhibitions. After all, there was no need to keep the girl on the rack. He had laid his mine now, and it would explode within a day, quite independently of anything that Joyce could do.

"I'm speaking absolutely unofficially," he said, slowly. "You understand that? But I think I can relieve your mind, Miss Hazlemere, if you promise to say nothing to anyone about it. I'm not thinking in the very slightest of bringing a charge against you."

He heard a gasp of relief at the other end of the wire, and felt repaid to some extent for his breach of confidence.

"That's all right," he added, in response to a flood of thankfulness. "Now, remember, Miss Hazlemere. This is for your own information. Not a word to Mr. Corwen, or Mr. Seaforth, or anyone else, please. I'm trusting you."

CHAPTER XII
THE LIGHT IN THE MUSEUM

"Suspicion's one thing; proof's another pair of shoes altogether." One or two failures in the course of his career had impressed this ancient aphorism on Superintendent Ross. In the Fenton case, he felt he had fair grounds for suspecting Dr. Hyndford, but real proofs were still to seek.

If the doctor could be scared into bolting, that would score a point against him; and Ross had put his plain-clothes shadower to work simply in the hope of making Dr. Hyndford nervous. But even an attempted escape could be explained away. Fresh evidence was essential.

Next morning he made a complete review of the case, hammering at his notes one by one in the hope of discovering some overlooked point; and suddenly a spark kindled as he re-read one of Fenton's statements.

Seaforth was the person whom he wanted, but first he saw James Corwen to put a question.

"You've gone over Mrs. Fenton's financial affairs now, I suppose?" he asked. "Did you find any trace of large sums being paid into her account at the bank within a couple of years of her death—figures like £1,500 or £3,000?"

James Corwen shook his head decidedly.

"Nothing like it," he said gruffly. "Her whole estate won't amount to anywhere near those figures."

The Superintendent did not trouble to explain the bearing of his inquiry. After all, there was the possibility that Dr. Hyndford had paid over the cash in the form of notes and that Mrs. Fenton had used the notes in betting, without paying them into her bank account.

"I'd like to consult Mr. Seaforth," he explained, by way of changing the subject at once.

James Corwen rang the bell and sent a clerk to summon Seaforth. When he came into the room, his manner showed his feelings quite clearly; but the Superintendent disregarded the obvious hostility.

"You're Secretary to the Struan Trust, aren't you, Mr. Seaforth?" he asked. "And you manage the affairs of the Museum, don't you? It appears that there was a light seen in the Museum about 11.30 p.m. on the night of Mrs. Fenton's death. Could you find out for me who was moving about the Museum at that hour?"

Seaforth looked down at the floor for some moments before speaking.

"Are you trying to prove that Miss Hazlemere and I came back to The Cedars at 11.30 and went away again?" he demanded at last.

"Good Lord, no!" said the Superintendent, with obviously honest surprise. "I never thought of such a thing. Nothing of the sort. I'm not concerned with you and Miss Hazlemere so far as this side of the thing's concerned."

The sincerity of his tone seemed to convince Seaforth.

"Very well, then. The only likely person would be the keeper, old Jim Buckland. Why didn't you go to him direct?"

"Because," Ross admitted frankly, "from what I've heard, I don't think I'd get much out of him. If you go to him, he'll talk freely. I want the information as soon as possible. Can you get it for me?"

"Jim Buckland's away on leave just now," Seaforth pointed out. "He'll be back to-morrow. That soon enough for you?"

"I don't suppose I can get at him any quicker," Ross agreed. "You'll get hold of him as soon as possible and ring me up? . . . Thanks."

On his return to the police station, Ross found a letter on his desk addressed to *Supperintendant Ross*. He had never derived much assistance from would-be helpers, and he opened the envelope with very little curiosity, though he was careful to avoid leaving prints on the letter-paper itself.

> *Supperintenant Ross* [he read],
> It was Doctor Hyndford that done for Mrs. Fenton he give her the patent medicine bottles for her colds: the parrinax with the poison in it you ask him and see if he can contradict this statement wich is true. He doped her with the verrinal when he was in the house after dinner; came back later and put her lite out.
>
> Yours obediently,
> ONE WHO KNOWS

As Superintendent Ross glanced over this epistle, two phrases caught his eye. He re-read the document thoughtfully, and other points attracted his attention. An application of powder failed to reveal any finger-prints; and the detective smiled when he got the negative result. Taking the paper carefully by its edges, he deposited it in a drawer.

"That fellow Groombridge might try his talents on it," Ross reflected. "I'll show it to him later on. He'll be interested."

He had little difficulty in connecting the arrival of the pseudonymous letter with the appearance of the paragraph about an impending arrest, which had been printed that morning in the *Stanningmore Gazette*. If an informer had a grudge to pay off, now was the time for him to strike, while the police were still apparently hesitating. Ross had planned the insertion of the paragraph with that very object in view; and he was glad to find this confirmation of his reading of the situation.

"Things ought to begin to move a bit, soon," he reflected with satisfaction.

CHAPTER XIII
"KOWTOW! KOWTOW TO THE GREAT YEN HOW!"

THINGS MOVED FAR QUICKER than Ross had expected.

Shortly after midnight, an excited constable roused him from his sleep with the news that Dr. Hyndford had committed suicide. Leaving orders for the police surgeon to follow as soon as possible, the Superintendent was on the scene of the tragedy within a quarter of an hour. In the hall of the house he found his plain-clothes man in charge, whilst Mr. Hyndford, hastily dressed, hovered in the background in a pitiable state of agitation.

"Dreadful business this, sir," the constable explained in a low voice. "He's quite dead—head nearly blown out at the back. He must have had the muzzle in his mouth. I heard the shot and ran up to the door; and after I'd hammered at it for a minute or two, Mr. Hyndford here opened it to me. The maids were in hysterics, so I sent them up to their rooms at once."

The Superintendent turned to Mr. Hyndford for further particulars; but it was clear that the shock of the tragedy had shaken him up badly; and he could furnish only a disjointed account.

"That letter he got . . . I mean, it must have had something to do with it, Superintendent. I knew by his look when he opened it that it must be something rum. . . . But, of course, I never dreamed . . . You see, he didn't show it to me. He was a bit depressed at dinner-time, one could see that. Then he went into his consulting-room. The revolver was there, in one of the drawers. . . . He sat there the whole evening. I suppose he must have been brooding over the business. . . . Then I thought I'd go to bed, it was getting on, half-past eleven, perhaps. So I looked into the consulting-room to say good night. I thought he'd been making up his books, probably, and I hadn't disturbed him. When I said good night, he looked up and nodded, just as usual. I didn't see anything much out of the common. What I mean to say is, he seemed a bit gloomy, but he often was like that, so I thought nothing about it. . . . Then I went up to bed, and as I wasn't very sleepy, I took a book and tried to read myself to sleep. Perhaps I dozed off. . . . Anyhow, I got the shock of my life when I heard the shot. I thought he'd perhaps caught a burglar, or something like that. . . . I mean to say, it never crossed my mind that he'd shot himself. . . . Then someone began hammering on the front door just as I'd jumped out of bed and pulled on my trousers and dressing-gown; and when I got down, there was your constable at the door, wanting to get in. . . . I didn't make it out even then, and I called to Simon. Then we went into the room together, and there he was. . . ."

Superintendent Ross made no attempt to check the flood of information which Mr. Hyndford poured out so confusedly. He waited till it ceased and then spoke kindly but firmly.

"You'd better sit down for a while, Mr. Hyndford. You've had a nasty jar. I'll have to trouble you by and by, but in the meantime, just try to pull yourself together. You'd better have some whiskey, I think. Get the picture of the thing out of your mind if you can. Pictures are the worst of it."

He turned to the constable.

"Now come along. We'll take a look round."

He led the way to the door of the consulting-room and the constable followed, though with obvious reluctance. Evidently he, too, was seeing "pictures" in his memory.

Dr. Hyndford's body was crumpled up in a small arm-chair. Apparently he had shot himself while sitting at his desk; and the old Navy revolver lay on the floor beside him, where it had fallen from his hand. The leaden bullet, entering by the mouth, had shattered the back of the skull in its emergence; and death had obviously been practically instantaneous.

Superintendent Ross stepped over to the desk and picked up a sheet of paper covered with illiterate handwriting very like the script on the pseudonymous letter which he himself had received.

> Doctor Hyndford,
> This is your dead last chance if you dont pay me what I ask I have written to the police about you allready and they will listen to what I say. I saw you in the cedars garden just before Miss Hazlemere came home that night; so even your brothers lying wont help you if I split now. Pay the money the way I directed and I'll keep quiet; but if you refuse, then I'll go straight to the police. It will be £5,000 now, and cheap at the price.
>
> Yours obediently,
> *ONE WHO KNOWS*

The Superintendent put the paper aside and turned to other matters.

Picking up the revolver, he laid it carefully on a book so that he could support it without leaving finger-prints on it; then he carried it over to the desk and pulled down the hanging lamp so as to bring a strong light to bear on the weapon. A brief examination with a pocket lens seemed to satisfy him temporarily; but before putting the revolver down again, he lifted it to his nose and sniffed slowly, once or twice, as he detected a. very faint smell of rubber mingling with the fumes of the burned powder.

He laid the book and revolver on the desk and glanced round the room in search of something.

"Get me that measuring-glass over yonder," he directed the constable. "Got a clean handkerchief? Well, rub the thing with it—hard—and don't leave any of your own finger-marks on the glass. Hold it by the base. That'll do. Here!"

He took the glass gingerly from the constable and again glanced round the room.

"See if you can find some oil or grease—vaseline or olive oil would do. He's sure to have had some stuff of the sort amongst his things."

After a short search, the constable managed to unearth a small bottle of olive oil.

"Take a drop of that on the corner of your handkerchief and rub it on the tips of the last three fingers of his right hand. Then clean off as much as you can with a dry bit of the handkerchief—I don't want more than a film of oil left on the skin. That'll do."

As the constable moved out of the way, Superintendent Ross lifted the dead man's hand and pressed the tips of the treated fingers one by one on the surface of the measuring-glass to register the prints. Then, going back to the light again, he compared the prints on the revolver butt with those on the glass.

"They're the same, so far as one can see," he intimated for the benefit of the constable.

The curtain of the window behind the dead man's chair waved softly in a faint draught, and the constable moved as though he meant to adjust it.

"The window's open?" questioned the Superintendent. "All right; leave it alone."

Putting down the measuring-glass, he passed behind the dead man's seat to approach the window himself; and as he did so, his attention was attracted by a faint grating sensation on his boot-sole. He was about to stoop down and examine the floor when the door opened and Mr. Hyndford's perturbed countenance appeared. Evidently he preferred to face the sight of his brother's body rather than remain alone in the hall.

"Oh, by the way, Mr. Hyndford," the Superintendent demanded. "Where did Dr. Hyndford usually keep this revolver?"

Mr. Hyndford blinked in the strong light from the low-hung bulb.

"He kept it in one of the drawers of his desk, I think. The one with the rubber bandages in it—the second top one in the right hand tier, I mean. He had varicose veins and he kept his elastic bandages there, and the revolver used to lie there too. We never used it. I mean to say, it was an old pistol. I don't remember it ever being fired."

The Superintendent pulled open the drawer and found some rolled-up elastic bandages.

"Ah, thanks. Now I'm afraid I'll have to ask you to go away for a moment or two, Mr. Hyndford. We're busy; and I'd rather not be interrupted."

Mr. Hyndford gave him a pitiful glance as though asking for permission to stay. Quite obviously he yearned for company in his shaken state. But the Superintendent was stubborn, and the little man had to withdraw, closing the door behind him.

As soon as he had gone, the Superintendent hunted through the other drawers of the desk and in one of them he came upon some camel's hair brushes. Arming himself with one of these and taking a sheet of note-paper from the stationery cabinet on the desk, Ross went round behind the dead man's chair and knelt down on the floor, while the constable followed his movements with a bewildered eye.

"What is it, sir?" he ventured to inquire as Ross rose to his feet.

The Superintendent pulled out a pocket lens and examined the powder minutely before replying.

"See for yourself," he suggested finally, putting the paper carefully on the desk and handing the lens to his subordinate.

"It looks just like some sand mixed up with fluff and dirt off the floor, sir," the constable reported with a rather mystified expression. "Is it important, do you think?"

"It's so important that the less there's said about it the better. You're not to say a word about it to anyone, you understand?"

"Very good, sir," the constable acquiesced, though his perplexity was obvious.

"Hunt about and see if you can find an empty pill-box to put this stuff in," the Superintendent ordered. "This place seems to have been both consulting-room and dispensary. There ought to be some clean unused pill-boxes somewhere."

While the constable was searching for the required container, Ross placed the threatening letter between two sheets of note-paper to protect it; and he fastened the edges with adhesive labels which he had noticed in a drawer of the desk, thus ensuring that any finger-prints on the letter would be preserved intact. By the time he had finished this work, the constable had found a clean pill-box, into which the Superintendent swept the dust he had collected from the floor. The revolver gave him more trouble; but at last he managed to wrap it up in such a way as to protect the finger-prints on the butt.

The constable, having nothing to occupy him during these operations, had evidently begun to meditate on his superior's proceedings, for at length he ventured to put a question.

"It's a clear enough case of suicide, isn't it, sir? The muzzle of the pistol was in his mouth when he fired. You couldn't murder a man by shoving a pistol into his mouth. He could struggle and prevent you, easy enough."

"Oh, yes. The revolver-muzzle was in his mouth right enough," the Superintendent agreed. "His cheeks are all lacerated with the sudden rush of gas at high pressure when the shot was fired. That's clear enough."

"And his finger-prints are on the butt of the pistol," the constable pursued.

"Quite obviously."

"Um!" said the constable undecidedly.

He was evidently anxious to know why the Superintendent had swept up the material from the floor; but Ross's demeanour did not encourage further questioning.

"That's about all for the present," the detective said as he completed his task. "You're to stay here on guard until you're relieved. Don't leave the room; and don't let anyone come into it except the police surgeon. He'll be here any minute now. I'll see that someone's sent along very soon to take your place."

Picking up his three packets from the desk, the Superintendent left the room. In the hall he almost ran into Mr. Hyndford, who was pacing restlessly to and fro, as if unable to calm himself sufficiently to sit down. As Ross came thus unexpectedly upon him, he heard Mr. Hyndford faintly whistling an air below his breath; and the Superintendent, with a mental leap backward through twenty years, fitted words to the tune:

Kowtow! Kowtow to the great Yen How!
And wish him the longest of lives. . . .

The Superintendent smiled rather grimly at the irony of the words in the present circumstances.

"Funny tune to be whistling here, Mr. Hyndford," he suggested.

Mr. Hyndford stopped abruptly, evidently disconcerted by having been overheard.

"Poor old Simon!" he said, hopelessly. "It was his favourite tune, that. He and I went together to *San Toy* one night when we were boys. It all came back to me just now. Funny how one's memory works on these little things. I can remember Rutland Barrington playing the old mandarin and ordering people about. Simon always liked that tune; I heard him whistling it this evening, just before that letter came. It runs in my head, somehow. . . ."

His voice broke, and he paused for a moment to recover control of himself.

"This is a dreadful business, Superintendent."

"I see it's upset you," Ross said, kindly. "What you want is a sleeping-draught of some sort. You'd be far better in bed, really. No good sitting up like this—it simply knocks you out next morning, I know from experience."

Mr. Hyndford paid no attention to the suggestion.

"I read the letter that Simon left on his desk," he said in the tone of a man who has decided to make a clean breast of something. "You can't guess who the writer is? No? What I mean to say is, he accuses me of having lied about something. That's not true. At least, I mean, I may have made a mistake in gauging the times I gave you—about when Simon came back that night, you know. But that's not lying. I was giving you the thing as near as I could make it, you understand? I just made the best guess I could."

"It's no matter now," said the Superintendent, brutally. "Any case there was against your brother is over and done with, obviously."

He jerked his head carelessly in the direction of the consulting-room, and Mr. Hyndford winced at the gesture.

"Oh, so you suspected him?" he said dully. "Well, it's all over with the poor chap now. Did you find out that it was he who gave Mrs. Fenton the Paronax bottles? No? Well, he did, I know. He got them from America, direct by post, you know. I saw the parcels once or twice. . . ."

"Just one plain hint, Mr. Hyndford," the Superintendent interrupted. "You're coming very near to making yourself an accessory after the fact, by what you're saying."

He broke off sharply, though his tone, in the last words, suggested that he had meant to say more.

"Now take my advice about a sleeping-draught," he continued in a different strain. "I'm going off now. By the way, would you mind signing these notes of mine—your account of this affair to-night. The constable will witness your signature. The surgeon will be here almost immediately. There's really no need for you to sit up and work yourself into a state of nerves."

CHAPTER XIV
THE EYE IN THE MUSEUM

WHEN HE RETURNED to his temporary rooms, Superintendent Ross unwrapped both the revolver and the threatening letter and tested them carefully with an insufflator; but on neither article could he detect any prints other than those of Dr. Hyndford's fingers.

The powder in the pill-box fell under examination in its turn. So far as he could make out, it appeared to be ordinary sand, such as is used in gardens. The Superintendent tapped the paper on which it rested and noticed with satisfaction that the grains did not cohere to any extent. Evidently the sand had been fairly well dried, either by the sun or by artificial heat.

"And if it had been dried by the sun outside, it wouldn't have stuck to anyone's shoes. So it didn't come into the consulting-room that way," Superintendent Ross inferred. "Besides, there was far too much of it for that. Nobody goes about with half an ounce of sand on their soles."

Instead of going to bed, he sat down in an armchair and considered the Fenton case in all its bearings once again. He had now enough evidence in hand to feel sure that his solution was the right one.

If Groombridge confirmed his views, there was a fair case to take to a jury. But to ensure a conviction the Superintendent wanted more than that; and his summons to old Jim Buckland was in the nature of a long shot which might just hit the mark. If old Jim failed to give him the final confirmation he hoped for, then the case would have to come into court as it stood, except for some further points which could be worked up after an arrest had been made.

Having made up his mind, the Superintendent suddenly realised that he was very sleepy, and with an unsuppressed yawn he went upstairs to bed.

Early in the following forenoon he was rung up by Seaforth.

"I've got hold of the keeper, Buckland, for you, Superintendent. He'll be at our office in a quarter of an hour, if that suits you."

Seaforth's voice was much less hostile than it had been hitherto. Obviously he had inferred that he and Joyce Hazlemere were no longer on the suspect list.

"Thanks," said Ross, heartily. "Now there's just one other thing. I'd like to have a talk with your clerk Groombridge for a few minutes, before I see Buckland. Can you fix that up for me if I come round immediately? . . . Yes, that'll suit. Goodbye."

When he reached the office, he was shown into James Corwen's private room, and the lawyer looked up with a smile as his visitor entered.

"Some more of your graphological inquiries on the carpet, Superintendent?" he inquired, with his usual slight tinge of derision. "I had you shown in here, since I don't suppose you want to thrash these weighty problems out with Groombridge in front of a lot of idle clerks in the outer office."

"Very good of you to think of it," the Superintendent said gratefully. "And by the way, I suppose you still have those I.O.U.'s of Dr. Hyndford's? I'd like to have another look at them."

"I've no objection," James Corwen answered, opening a drawer in his desk and taking out the packet of papers. "But it's beyond me why you worry about the matter any longer. The man's dead, isn't he? You can't bring a case against a corpse—not with any advantage to anyone, so far as I can see."

Superintendent Ross refused to rise to the bait. "One can always learn something by going into things," he suggested, vaguely.

"A bit of private research, eh?" said Corwen, sharply. "You're not going to try any of your cat-hanging tricks in this room, are you? If so, I'll have to think about my duty to my client."

"I'm not thinking of bringing any charge against Miss Hazlemere," the Superintendent said, bluntly. "As to hanging, if one cat's dead, there are always plenty left to hang, either toms or tabbies."

"Oh," said the lawyer, thoughtfully. "A bright idea, perhaps. Or perhaps not so bright. . . ."

"Time will tell," the Superintendent retorted with deliberate sententiousness.

Seaforth came into the room, followed by Groombridge carrying his microscope, at which James Corwen threw a scornful glance.

"So he's committed suicide?" Seaforth said, turning to the Superintendent. "It's all over the town. Great excitement among the populace, I gather. He slipped through your fingers at the last."

Ross ignored the faint tone of sarcasm in Seaforth's voice.

"He's certainly quite dead," he said seriously. Then, as though dismissing that subject, he turned to the amateur graphologist.

"Now, Mr. Groombridge, if you'll be so good as to give me the help of your expert knowledge, I'll he much obliged to you."

Groombridge, unused to treatment so flattering, beamed with pleasure as the Superintendent carefully withdrew some papers from a large envelope and laid them on the desk.

"Here's the first exhibit," he said, handing Groombridge the envelope of the pseudonymous letter addressed to himself. "What do you make of it?"

Groombridge examined it closely for a time, using a pocket lens at certain points. Seaforth and the Superintendent watched him eagerly; James Corwen preserved a certain aloofness which hardly concealed his real interest in the affair.

"There's not much to be made out of that," Groombridge admitted frankly as he laid the envelope on the desk. "It's supposed to be written by a half-educated person, if you go by the spelling. But then the lines of the script are perfectly level although there's been no pencil line drawn to guide the writer. That would be unusual, in my experience of semi-educated scripts. It's been written with a very broad-pointed pen—a blunt-shaped nib, if you see what I mean. That was meant to disguise the writing, so probably the writer uses a fine nib in his ordinary day's work. You can see he wasn't accustomed to the nib he was using. Two or three times, he's failed to get the ink to run, altogether. There's a scratch on the surface of the paper at the S, for instance, made with no ink on the pen. Then he's gone over it again, to ink it in, but the scratch in plain enough. He's been holding his pen at some abnormal slope, I should think, to help to disguise his script; and so he hasn't been able to manage the proper flow of ink."

Superintendent Ross made no comment, but merely handed Groombridge the pseudonymous letter itself, cautioning him not to finger-mark it.

"He spells it 'Supperintenant' this time," Groombridge pointed out. "That doesn't mean much, though. But again you'll notice how neatly he's managed to keep his lines spaced."

"Anything else?" questioned the Superintendent.

"It's a poor attempt," Groombridge commented, with confidence. "He starts off by running two sentences into one with no period or capital. Then he forgets that he's not supposed to know about punctuation, and he puts in a colon. A colon's not very often seen in letters nowadays, or even in printing either, if it comes to that. The colon's gone out of fashion very much. People don't take the pains they used to do with the punctuation of their sentences. Now after that colon, he remembers again that he's supposed to be semi-illiterate, so on he rushes with no punctuation till he comes to 'true.' There he forgets again, and puts a period and a capital at 'He.' And he ends up with a semi-colon and a full-stop in his last sentence. I'd be much surprised if that was a genuine semi-illiterate writer, very much surprised indeed. And, finally, he has a comma after 'Yours obediently.' What half-educated man would know to put that, will you tell me?"

"Anything else?" the Superintendent asked.

"The spelling's interesting," Groombridge pointed out. "He can spell words like 'patent,' 'medicine,' 'contradict,' 'statement,' and 'obediently' quite accurately. And yet he writes 'wich' for 'which' and 'lite' for 'light.' That's a bit far-fetched, in my opinion. It's not conclusive, though."

"Anything more?"

The Superintendent was taking pains to conceal the fact that Groombridge was reaching precisely the conclusions at which he himself had already arrived. He wanted an absolutely independent confirmation of his own ideas.

"Oh, yes," said Groombridge, in reply to the question. "It all tells the same tale. See, it starts ungrammatically. He writes: 'that done for Mrs. Fenton' and 'he give her the patent medicine.' But after that he forgets to be ungrammatical, for the next bits are in plain, straightforward English. Then he suddenly recollects, and he leaves out 'and' or 'then' before the word 'came.' And finally, he winds up with 'Yours obediently.' Semi-illiterates don't use the word 'obediently' much nowadays, in my experience, though it's always a possibility."

"Is that all?"

"No, not quite. There's the phrase 'if he can contradict this statement.' That sticks in my throat, I must confess. It's out of tune with the rest altogether, like 'Yours obediently' or even worse."

"I don't see much display of graphological lore in all this," James Corwen commented in a tone which a grumpy uncle might have used while watching a children's game.

"No, sir. It's just a case of using common sense, so far," Groombridge defended himself, with the air of a rabbit in a corner. "I took it that the Superintendent wanted this."

"Mr. Groombridge interests me very much," Superintendent Ross said, freezingly. "Common sense is rarer than you'd think, Mr. Corwen. Now here's a third document. You might compare it with the last one and tell us what you think about it."

He handed over the threatening letter, supported on a sheet of paper so that Groombridge did not need to touch it with his fingers.

"This is written by the same hand as the other two," Groombridge pronounced. "It's disguised in exactly the same way. Handwriting slope changed from the natural, I should say, and the broad nib used to change the style. Same sort of thing in the punctuation, you'll notice. Sentences run together at the start, when he was keeping the point in mind; and then a relapse into natural ways of doing things at the tail-end. No apostrophe in 'dont,' but one inserted correctly in 'I'll' of the penultimate sentence. No capital or apostrophe at 'cedars,' though. And a semi-illiterate would hardly use the expression: 'Pay the money the way I directed,' would he? And he ends up with the comma after 'Yours obediently.' I'd need to go carefully into it, if you want me to give evidence; but on the face of it I'd say the same man wrote them both."

Superintendent Ross nodded thoughtfully but made no direct reply.

"I've been profiting by your lessons, Mr. Groombridge," he said pleasantly. "Now I want to see if I've picked them up properly."

He handed one of the I.O.U.'s to the clerk.

"You remember you pointed out something about the I and the O in this document," he reminded Groombridge. "Will you look at the I's in that second letter I showed you, and also the O's in the phrase 'ONE WHO KNOWS.' If you use your microscope, take care you don't finger-mark the letter while you're adjusting it."

Groombridge obeyed instructions and made a careful examination of both documents.

"I should say they're both written by the same person," he said at length. "The forger of the I.O.U. has the join of his O at the side; so has the writer of this letter. The capital I in both of them has the strokes made in the same order. The imitated tremble in the I.O.U. doesn't occur in the letter, naturally. But if you'll take the trouble to measure, you'll find that there's roughly the same spacing between the lines of writing in the I.O.U. and in the letter. And what's more, they both have almost the same clear margin on the left-hand side between the writing and the edge of the sheet. That's a point that most forgers forget all about. When they start to imitate another person's writing, they don't mask their own peculiarities in things like that."

"That's good enough for me," the Superintendent said. "It's a fresh bit of information—very ingenious. Now there's just one thing more. I'd like to borrow your microscope for a moment if I may, to examine a powder."

"Here's a slide," Groombridge volunteered, producing it.

The Superintendent brought out a tiny package and strewed some grains on the glass.

"What do *you* make of it?" he asked.

Groombridge peered down the tube.

"Sand, I should say," he decided. "I'm familiar with the appearance of sand-grains, because sometimes I come across it stuck to the ink in old documents—they used sand to dry their ink before blotting-paper was invented, you know."

He looked again through the microscope and then gave up his place to the Superintendent.

"Oh, it's sand, sure enough."

The Superintendent removed the glass slide and tapped the powder off it, back into the original holder.

"That's all the help I need at present, Mr. Groombridge," he explained. "Thanks very much for giving me your assistance. It's been invaluable. And now, would you mind writing down what you've told me, and putting your signature to it?"

Groombridge took this as a sign of dismissal, picked up his microscope, and left the room. The Superintendent turned to Seaforth.

"I suppose you've got the keeper there? Suppose we have him in now?"

Seaforth nodded and went in search of old Jim.

"Very interesting," James Corwen conceded grudgingly when he was left alone with the Superintendent. "But how much of all that stuff would a jury follow?"

"That'll be a matter for the jury," the Superintendent answered curtly.

Before James Corwen could reply, Seaforth ushered old Jim Buckland into the room.

"This is Superintendent Ross," he said to Buckland. "He wants you to answer a question or two, as I told you."

"You're the keeper of the Museum, I believe?" the Superintendent said, formally. "I understand that you were at the Struan Museum on the night of Mrs. Fenton's death. There was a light on in the building late in the evening. I want to know something about that. Who was about the place at that hour?"

"I was, sir. I generally go round the whole place before going to bed, to see that all the fastenings are right for the night. We've so many valuable things there, you see, that it would be a great temptation to burglars if I wasn't most careful. It's a great responsibility, being in charge of a collection like that."

"Can you remember exactly where you were at half-past eleven that night?"

Buckland considered for a moment or two, then his face brightened.

"Half-past eleven, sir? I can tell you that, as it happens. I generally go round the Museum about eleven o'clock, just when I go to bed. That night, I went round as usual, I remember. I was going away first thing the next morning—Mr. Seaforth'll tell you it was under doctor's orders—and after I'd gone round the whole place and seen that everything was safe and fast, I went up into the tower to the *camera obscura*. It's a hobby of mine, that. I like to have a look round the town with it. And as I was going away for a while, I thought I'd just take a last look with it."

"*Camera obscura?*" said the Superintendent inquiringly.

"It's an arrangement that throws a picture on a screen," Seaforth interjected. "By shifting the lenses you can turn on views of most parts of the town—make the places seem quite near at hand."

"Indeed!" The Superintendent was suddenly alert. "And you were having a look round with it, Buckland? But it was night then, wasn't it? How about that?"

"It was a full moon that night, sir. I could see things clear as day, almost."

The Superintendent nodded.

"Well, what did you look at?" he demanded, taking care to avoid leading questions.

"Oh, just round about, generally: Main Street, the Town Hall clock face, because I wanted to set my watch, the Old Bridge, and then up and down the river a bit. That's all I can remember, sir. I was just looking round, just looking round. I knew it would be my last chance for a while, and I spent a while up there. I'm very fond of the *camera obscura*, sir. It's always fresh, somehow. Most interesting."

"Up and down the river, you say. Did you happen to watch any place in particular on the river?"

Seaforth was evidently growing excited, though he did his best to hold himself in check. Apparently he had never thought of the possibilities involved in old Jim's fondness for his toy; and now he was beginning to see what the Superintendent was groping for so cautiously.

"I had a look at Mr. Marton in his garden," old Jim confessed, rather shamefacedly. "At that time of night, there's only a few people about; and it's more interesting to see someone doing something, instead of just looking at the empty streets. Mr. Marton was very busy with his telescope."

"And after that?"

"After that, I turned over a bit and looked at the water-front close by—the bottom of Mrs. Fenton's garden. It's quite close to the Museum, as you know, sir—just down below us. One can see it very plainly with the instrument."

"What time would that be?"

Old Jim considered carefully.

"It was five past eleven when I set my watch by the face of the Town Clock. It might have been five or ten minutes after that that I looked at Mrs. Fenton's garden; five or ten minutes, that would make it ten or a quarter past eleven at the time I'm speaking of. Say ten past, as near as I can remember."

"You saw something there?"

"The first thing I saw was Mr. Richard Hyndford in his canoe, just landing at the bank."

"Ah!" said Seaforth, as though starting to interrupt; but the Superintendent stopped him with a glance.

"Mr. Hyndford it was," old Jim continued. "What struck me about him at the time was that he lifted his canoe out of the water and carried it round behind some bushes. It's a light little thing, easy to lift about. I thought perhaps he was afraid someone might come along the river in a boat and steal it, if he left it there; a very natural precaution to take at that time of night, you can understand, sir."

"And after that, what did you see?"

"I didn't bother much about it, sir. I turned the lenses and looked at something else for a while—the New Bridge, I think, if I remember right. You see, sir, I'm in a sort of position of trust in the Museum. The *camera obscura* was never meant for spying on people; Mr. Struan would have been greatly horrified if he'd ever imagined it could be used in that way; and I've always been most careful to do nothing of the sort. When you can overlook people in that way, you're more or less on your honour not to abuse the instrument, that's how I look at it."

"Very sound," said the Superintendent in a distinctly disappointed tone. "Did you happen to see anything else?"

"Well, sir, after a time—perhaps a quarter of an hour or so, but I can't tell you exactly—I bethought me that I might keep an eye on Mr. Hyndford's canoe for him while he was in The Cedars. I could see if anyone touched it, you understand. That wasn't spying or anything like that—a quite justifiable use of the instrument. So I turned the lenses round and had a look for the canoe. But by that time it was gone. Just to make sure everything was all right, I ran the garden across the screen. The Museum looks slant-ways down, you understand, and one can see the back of The Cedars owing to a slight curve in the river. I saw a man's figure at the French windows of the house, kneeling down as if he was trying to look into the room."

"Could you recognise him?"

"No, sir. His face didn't show up. I didn't like the look of his doings, as you can well understand, sir; and I was relieved when he got up to his feet and went away from the house, across the garden. It didn't look well, sir, I thought; and I watched him off the premises. So far as I could see, he was doing no harm, though it seemed a funny thing to be after, at that time of night. He walked away up the road finally, and I didn't trouble to keep him in sight longer."

"And you saw nothing else of interest?"

Old Jim glanced rather apprehensively at Seaforth.

"Well, sir," he said, hesitatingly, "I did turn back to The Cedars again just for a moment later on. It was just a sort of precaution, you understand? I wanted to see if that man had come back again, because I hadn't quite liked the look of his doings. And just as I got The Cedars on the screen again, I saw Mr. Seaforth here in his canoe with Miss Hazlemere, coming in to the bank at the foot of the garden. So I turned away at once, knowing that they wouldn't care for me to be overlooking them just then. Besides, with Mr. Seaforth there, The Cedars was quite safe and there was no need for me to be keeping an eye on it any longer."

"What time was that?" the Superintendent asked in an indifferent tone.

"It would be a minute or two after midnight," old Jim answered readily. "I remember quite well now that the Town Clock struck twelve just before that, and I began to think it was quite time I was in my bed, seeing I had an early start and a long journey before me next morning."

"What I don't understand," said the Superintendent, "is why you haven't come forward with all this evidence long ago. You must have known it was important."

Old Jim was plainly taken aback by this.

"Me, sir? But how could I have come forward with it when I knew nothing about Mrs. Fenton's death?"

"It was in all the newspapers," the Superintendent pointed out brusquely.

"But I never read a newspaper, sir. Haven't done that for years. They don't interest me. Mrs. Buckland reads them now and again and tells me things, but mostly I hear all I want just by talking to people, people that come to visit the Museum and some of the friends I have in town. A newspaper's the last thing I'd think of looking at, sir."

"But surely your wife must have mentioned the case in her letters?"

"What letters, sir? She and I never waste time in writing letters. I sent her a picture postcard when I got to Broadsands, sir, just to let her know I'd reached there safe. I'd never expect her to sit down and write to me. She's no hand with a pen, any more than I am myself. It's the plain truth, sir, I never heard a word about this murder case till I got back home again; and the first thing after that was Mr. Seaforth telling me you wanted to see me and that I was to say nothing to anybody till I'd seen you. I couldn't think what you wanted, that's honest, sir."

The Superintendent, without comment, added a few jottings to his notes, read them over to old Jim, and got him to put his signature at the foot.

Seaforth had followed the interview with undisguised relief, and now his repressed feelings found vent in chaffing the keeper rather grimly.

"You'll have another curiosity to show the visitors now," he pointed out to Jim Buckland, "something to match Mr. Struan's Eye."

"Indeed, sir?" the keeper asked in mild surprise. "And what will that be? I don't quite see what you mean."

"Your own eye, Buckland. Perhaps it's cleared up The Cedars case, for all one can tell." He glanced at the Superintendent for confirmation, but got no response. "You'll need to leave it to the Museum when you die—a second historical specimen."

Old Jim appeared to have no relish for this rather morbid suggestion.

"I think, sir, that Mr. Struan's Eye stands by itself. I shouldn't dream of such a thing as you say."

James Corwen ignored this by-play completely. He turned to Ross.

"It doesn't take X-rays to see through this part of the business, Superintendent. Am I right in supposing that you have no intention of bringing any charge against my client now?"

"No immediate intention, certainly," Ross qualified the statement, though his smile showed that it was purely for form's sake that he did so.

"Ah, then I shall have to consider the question of my fees for my trouble in the matter," said James Corwen. "You've given me a lot of bother with these cat-hanging notions of yours, Superintendent."

"I found your reminiscences of great assistance," Ross acknowledged in a tone which was half grateful, half quizzical. "One of them, in fact, turned out to be the key to the whole affair."

He broke off, as though his mind had been switched on to a fresh line of thought; and in his apparent absorption he whistled absent-mindedly below his breath. James Corwen pricked up his ears.

> Kowtow! Kowtow to the great Yen How!
> And wish him the longest of lives. . . .

The lawyer smiled in his usual bleak fashion as he appreciated the adroitness with which Ross had conveyed his meaning without enlightening the other two people in the room.

"I had a suspicion all along that you'd find something to interest you there," he said, unemotionally. "I was thinking along the same lines myself. I suppose you hit on the veronal? It put me on to the sequence of events."

The Superintendent made a gesture admitting this.

"Without the veronal, there would have been a struggle when she was attacked," he said. "Therefore on the face of things the veronal was a crucial factor in the business. The fact that Miss Hazlemere once had a dose of veronal in her possession complicated things for me a bit, though."

James Corwen's facial expression betrayed little of his feelings, though his words carried something of annoyance.

"You gave me a lot of trouble," he said. "But I suppose I shouldn't complain. I started with the handicap of knowing Miss Hazlemere well. She wouldn't commit a murder on that provocation. You knew nothing about her when you started; so I suppose you had to begin without that assumption to help you. Naturally I did my best for my client by giving you other fish to fry."

CHAPTER XV
THE RACE TO THE SEA

WITH HIS CASE practically completed, Superintendent Ross's next step was to procure a Justice's warrant. He was fairly sure that he had excited no suspicion in Richard Hyndford's mind, so nothing would be lost by observing every tittle of the legal formalities. The murderer was not likely to take fright and make off at this stage in the affair. Ross contented himself with setting a plain-clothes man to keep a close watch on the suspect; and this time his instructions were to make the supervision effective and unobtrusive.

In timing his arrest, the Superintendent was influenced mainly by ulterior factors. Once he had Richard Hyndford in his grip, he meant to get a statement from him if it was humanly possible without violating the forms of the law; and the longer his prisoner could be kept awake, the better chance there was of breaking down his resistance. For that reason, it was expedient to make the arrest as late in the evening as possible without having actually to drag the man from his bed. Ross fixed on ten o'clock as being the best time; and, wishing to be comparatively fresh himself when the trial of endurance came, he slept for a couple of hours in the afternoon.

As he and an attendant constable drew near the gate of Hyndford's house, the plain-clothes man on duty came cautiously up to them.

"He's in the garden, sir, wandering about and pottering with the flower-beds. He doesn't suspect anything yet; I've been watching him through the hedge most of the time, and I've kept well out of sight."

"You wait here," the Superintendent ordered. "No use taking a small army along for a job like this. Two of us are more than enough. You can come if you're called for."

Followed by the uniformed constable, he pushed open the gate and entered the garden. The open garage with the car ready in it attracted his attention; but almost at once his glance, ranging through the dusk, caught the figure of Richard Hyndford at some distance down one of the walks. The Superintendent moved leisurely in that direction and at the sound of his steps, Richard Hyndford glanced round. Seeing the Superintendent, he walked towards him, apparently quite unsuspicious.

"Richard Hyndford," said Ross, "I charge you with the wilful murder of Evelyn Fenton. Do you wish to say anything in answer to the charge? You are not obliged to say anything unless you wish to do so, but whatever you say will be taken down in writing and may be given in evidence."

With strict adherence to the Judges' Rules, the Superintendent omitted the final words: "Against you" from his caution, though in this case he knew he was not dealing with an innocent person who might be terrified by the implication.

Richard Hyndford seemed dazed by the words.

Then suddenly, taking the Superintendent by surprise, he sprang.

Ross, taken completely off his guard, went down under an attack which combined complete novelty and scientifically produced agony. His head struck the hard-rolled path and for a moment or two he was half-stunned. He heard the constable make a rush in support; then came a slight crack like the sound of a breaking stick, a yelp of pain, and the swift patter of light footsteps down the path. Nearly sick with the anguish of the blow he had received, Ross forced himself up to a sitting position.

"Cut him off from the garage!" he shouted.

The clang of the iron gate, dashed violently open, told him that the plain-clothes man had heard and acted on the order. Ross looked up and found the uniformed constable standing beside him, his face a mask of amazement and pain and his right arm dangling helplessly at his side.

"He's broke my arm," the constable volunteered.

"He knocked me out," Ross said. "Jiu-jitsu, apparently. What a fool I was not to remember that he's lived in Japan."

"I'd never have thought he could settle both of us like that, a little devil like him," the constable said wonderingly.

Ross got to his feet and stood for a moment unsteadily, shaken with pain.

"You wait here," he said. "You're no use with that arm. I'll go after him. Which way?"

The constable, taking his left hand from his wounded arm, pointed the road; and Ross walked with an effort after the escaping criminal. Twenty yards down the path, he came in view of the river and realised that the fugitive had found a surer instrument of escape than the car. Just visible in the dusk, a canoe with a man's figure in it was sliding swiftly out from the bank toward midstream; and beyond it lay the dark outline of the motor-launch moored in the fairway.

"We'll get him yet!" the Superintendent promised himself as he turned and moved laboriously back to his subordinate.

"He's off in his launch," he explained.

And at that moment the roar of the motor broke on the stillness of the evening.

"Go into the house; ring up headquarters; tell them to send a car with four men in it along the other side of the river—the *other* side, you understand? They're to keep that launch in sight and nab the beggar if he tries to get ashore."

With less pain, he moved again down the path till he could see the water. The launch was slipping away from her moorings, heading down-stream as he expected.

"Down-stream, they're to go," he instructed the constable. "And tell them to send up someone to fix that arm of yours. You'll have a compound fracture if you aren't careful of it. Now hurry—as fast as you can go."

He himself made his way to the garage, where the plain-clothes man was waiting.

"Get into the car," Ross ordered. "Or, wait! Fill up the tank from some of these tins there. We can't risk running short."

He climbed painfully into the driving seat, and, as soon as the tank was full and his subordinate was aboard, he drove out of the garage. As he did so, the wounded constable appeared.

"It's all right, sir. They're sending the car at once. Good luck, sir! I hope you'll nab him."

Ross nodded as the car slipped past. For the first mile or more, the route lay out of sight of the river; and the Superintendent, having no idea of the speed of the motor-launch, let the car out as much as he dared. But the road was sprinkled with courting couples sauntering in the cool of the fine evening; and he could not take too great risks. At corners, the yarr of his horn drove startled couples in haste to the safety of the wayside; and in the long straight stretches the white faces and dazzled eyes of lovers lit by the glare of the headlights, gleamed and were gone like moths in a beam. These grew fewer as the car sped on and left the town behind; and at last Ross was able to put the accelerator hard down.

Soon the motor swept round a long turn and came in sight of the river. The Superintendent slowed down and at last brought the car to a standstill.

"See any signs of him?" he demanded.

The constable gazed up and down the visible reach of the river for a moment or two in silence.

"I can hear her all right," the constable answered—rather superfluously, since the thuttering of the launch's exhaust, though distant, could still be heard above the tick-over of their own engine. "Ah! there she is, sir! Just rounding the bend ahead of us. She must have a fair turn of speed."

Superintendent Ross grunted by way of reply and let in his clutch again. From that point onward, the road ran like a towing-path beside the river; and now he felt sure he could keep in touch with the launch, even with night falling. Richard Hyndford could not silence his engine, and the exhaust would give him away so long as he was moving.

"You're not thinking of pulling up and telephoning ahead to get him stopped," the constable questioned, after a moment or two.

"No, I'm not," said Ross irritably. "He's only got about ten miles to the sea now, and we'd lose touch with him if we knocked up someone to get at a 'phone. Chances are we couldn't raise more than a single constable at the best; and all that he could do, we can do ourselves, easier. Besides," he added viciously, "I want to take him myself."

After a moment's thought he spoke again. "Can you swim?"

"Yes," the constable assured him. "I'm quite a good swimmer, sir."

"You may need to be, before long," Ross commented.

A fresh thought struck him.

"See any signs of the car on the other bank—glare of its headlight, or anything?"

The constable turned round in his seat and scanned the dusk for a time in vain.

"There's a headlight away behind us, sir. The car seems travelling at a fair old lick. P'raps that's them."

"We'll get a bit ahead of the launch, then," Ross explained, as he speeded up the car. "Once we've got him between the two of us, we can afford to play tricks."

In a short time they pulled level with the launch and then shot ahead. A few minutes later, the Superintendent reversed the car, so that its headlights pointed towards the position where he expected his supporting motor to be found.

"There's their light, if it *is* they," he said, with some relief as the glare of the big lamps shone on the further side of the river. "Now, Heaven send that somebody on board knows Morse fairly well."

He bent forward and, using the switch, sent a message in longs and shorts by flashing and dowsing his headlights.

"They've seen it," the constable exclaimed in high delight. "They're pulling up and signalling back."

"Well, you don't expect them to drive when their headlamps are jumping like a guttering candle, do you?" growled the Superintendent, whose temper was impaired by the pain he still felt. "Of course they've stopped."

He signalled again, watched the response, and then swung his car round to face down-stream.

"I'm going to let her out, get well ahead, and see if we can pick up a boat anywhere. We'll need to try to board the launch somehow, though it's a poor chance."

Leaving the launch far in the rear, the car rushed ahead, whilst the constable kept his eye open for any boat which might be lying by the river-side.

"Stop!" he cried at last. "We passed one there, sir. If you go back a bit we can have a look at it."

Ross reversed the car and in a few moments they were both running a light skiff into the water.

"No oars, of course," said Ross, as they thrust the boat into the water and jumped in. "Take up the floor-boards and paddle like blue blazes. It's a narrow bit here, and we may just manage to get in his way."

Hardly had they got near the middle of the river than the launch was upon them, its exhaust roaring in their ears. At the stern sat Hyndford's black figure, outlined against the dull light of the sky. Suddenly they were dazzled by the glare of a projector unexpectedly switched on; the black bow of the launch swung slightly as it came down upon them; then their frail skiff, clean hit, was stove in by that swift-flying stem; and they found themselves in the water, grasping haphazard at the smooth sides of their destroyer.

The Superintendent had the luck to get a firm grip on the gunwale and for a moment he had hopes that he might scramble aboard; but Hyndford, leaving the tiller, sprang forward. Ross felt a hand on his face; a ruthless thumb searched for his eye; and just in time, he dropped back into the tumbling wash of the launch as it swept ahead into the gloom.

"I'll have him yet!" Ross assured himself as he swam for the shore. "I hope that constable's got clear."

He had been carried further downstream than his companion, and when he ran back to the car, he found the constable was there before him.

"All right, sir?"

"All right. Get in."

Ross had little fear of meeting anything on that road at this hour of the night; and he let the car out on full throttle, taking risks as they came. Soon the launch was left behind once more; and still they flew on through the dark behind the long cones of the headlights. Suddenly an exclamation from the Superintendent startled the constable.

"I have it!"

And shortly afterwards he was again amazed by a swift application of the brakes as they tore past a wayside cottage.

"Out you get— There's a clothes-line in that garden. I saw it against the sky. Cut twenty feet off it—if there's as much. Hurry!"

Far behind them they could hear the throb of the launch's exhaust; and in the distance an occasional flash showed the movement of the companion car keeping level with the fugitive. The constable dashed back along the road, entered the garden, cut off the clothes-line, and raced back to the car with his prize.

"Got it?" the Superintendent demanded. "Good. Then get over that wall and bring me up two or three stones from the bank of shingle at the waterside. Two or three pounds weight each stone. And see they're of a shape that you can tie the rope securely on to them. Hurry!"

Completely mystified, the constable did what he was bidden. When the car was again coursing through the night, the Superintendent gave instructions that a stone was to be tightly tied to each end of the rope.

"What are you going to do with this, sir?" the constable ventured to inquire at length, when he had completed his task.

"Dodge out of *The Swiss Family Robinson*," Ross said shortly. "I used to practise with it when I was a kid, thank goodness. One never knows what'll turn up useful."

Again he let the car out. They were near the river-mouth now, and the constable completely failed to understand the Superintendent's plan of campaign.

"Lucky that beggar has no firearms," Ross reflected aloud.

He slowed the car slightly.

"There's a group of fishermen's huts just ahead," he explained. "I know one of the men, so there'll be no trouble. As soon as I stop the car, your job is to unship the headlights so that you can move them about freely. Mind you don't snap the wires. I'm going to use them as search-lights. I want them kept on the launch so that I can see what I'm doing. I'll get you a man to handle the second one. That's all you've got to look after."

He swung the car sharply onto a little quay beside the road and left it pointing riverwards. Then, jumping down, he ran to a cottage near by and hammered on the door. The constable, busy with the headlights, heard an answer and a sharp interchange of talk. Then the Superintendent ran over to where some fishing nets were hanging up to dry, and began to pull them down. Almost at once he was joined by two men from the cottage; and the three took the nets down to a boat for which one of the fishermen procured oars.

"Got those lamps off?" the Superintendent demanded, as he came back to the car. "All right. Here, Bob! You take one of these lamps and do as the constable tells you. Harry and I will handle the boat."

He bent over the car, snatched up the rope and stones, and hurried off to where the boat was launched and ready. He and the second fisherman jumped aboard and began to row out into the stream.

The constable and his companion, keeping their lights on the boat, could see the whole manoeuvre almost as clearly as if it had been daylight.

"Puttin' the nets afloat in the fairway—see the corks?—to tangle up the launch's screw, see?" the fisherman explained. "Fair ruination of the nets, though. They'll have to pay for them; good nets, too."

He listened for a moment or two.

"Here she comes. I hear her sputterin'."

The Superintendent and his companion, having completed their task, let their boat drop down slightly below the line of nets. A shouted order from his superior made the constable swing his lamp upstream, ready to pick up the fugitive as soon as he came in sight. The fisherman followed his example with the second lamp.

"Here she comes!"

The throbbing of the exhaust grew louder and all at once the boat itself appeared in the beams of the lamps. On she came, spectral in the glare, with the bone in her teeth flashing as it divided into twin waves along her sides. In the stern they could see the figure of Hyndford, crouching at the tiller with something in his hand, something which looked like a bar.

"Keep the light square in his eyes if you can," the constable urged.

He had no idea of what the Superintendent meant to do; but it was obvious that a dazzled man would be at a disadvantage against one whose eyes were tuned to the dark.

The launch was almost level with them now, every detail of her clean-cut against the gloom of the further shore. With the tail of his eye, the constable took in a movement on the Superintendent's boat. Hyndford rose to his feet at the tiller, holding his bar ready to strike. As he did so, the launch rushed into the invisible trap. She checked, wrenched clear, checked again, and slowed down as the drag of the nets stopped her way. The engine, baffled by the fouled propeller, coughed and stopped, the failure of the exhaust coming with surprise on the ear.

Then, suddenly something happened which the constable could only stare at in amazement. Full in the beam of the twin searchlights, with no one visibly near him, Richard Hyndford suddenly staggered and began to struggle with some unseen assailant. Before he had time to free himself, the fisherman had pulled alongside the launch and the Superintendent was aboard.

"They've got 'im! That's a good job!" the fisherman commented at the constable's elbow. "Eh! but what a mess o' these nets that screw'll have made!"

The slightness of the struggle on board the launch surprised the constable. Apparently the Superintendent had got the better of his man almost instanter; for they could see that Hyndford was quite helpless as he was lifted into the rowing-boat. The launch was left to look after itself for the time being, and the boat made for the shore.

As it came in just below them, the constable saw in the light of the lamps that Hyndford seemed to be swathed in rope which pinioned him.

"Come down here and give me a hand," the Superintendent called to his subordinate as the boat touched the shore.

As the constable stooped over the form of their prisoner, he saw to his astonishment that the two stones were still attached to the ends of the rope which restrained Hyndford.

"Not see how it was done?" the Superintendent asked in surprise. "Simple enough, if you've had any practice. You swing one stone round your head—like swinging a lasso—until it begins to hum. Then you let go. And if you aim right, one end of the thing swings round your man; and then the other one, as soon as the first one's checked, winds round and round the fellow until he's nearly smothered in it. And to-night I swung it for all I was worth, so that it nearly squeezed the life out of the brute. He caught me napping with his jiu-jitsu tricks. And he tried to gouge my eye out. I wasn't anxious to take any further risks with him. And if it comes to surprises, I think my string-and-stone stunt gave him as much of a jar as his jiu-jitsu dodges gave me."

A search through Hyndford's pockets brought to light a bulky package which the Superintendent opened.

"Three thousand pounds' worth of bearer bonds. I thought he'd have them with him."

Between them, they fastened up their prisoner so securely that he could hardly move a finger.

"He won't find much chance of using his Asiatic games now," the Superintendent commented as he examined the result. "Just dump him into the back of the car. You can sit beside him. Put your thumb in his eye if he gives trouble. I've discovered that it has a wonderfully calming effect. Bob and Harry will see to the launch. We needn't wait."

"Do you think he expected to get clean away, sir?" the constable asked. "Or was it just a last gamble?"

"A bit of both," said the Superintendent. "If he'd got clear of the river mouth, he could have gone along the coast for a good bit—

that launch has a fair turn of speed. Then he could have got ashore, turned the launch's head out to sea, and let her go under full power. That would have left no trail to show where he'd landed; and he might have dodged us. But I think he imagined he'd thrown dust in our eyes completely, and a bolt was the last thing he thought it would come to, though he had his bearer bonds in readiness if the worst came to the worst."

He suddenly remembered the second car.

"Hold up that lamp, constable. Point it across the river."

And, manipulating the switch, he flashed the news of the capture across the water to their auxiliaries.

CHAPTER XVI
THE CASE FOR THE PROSECUTION

WITH ALL HIS NOTES on the desk before him, Superintendent Ross lit his pipe and prepared to draw up a preliminary account of his case for the official in charge of the prosecution of Richard Hyndford. Since the arrest, he had re-examined all the relevant witnesses to make certain of details; but he had discovered nothing which he had not already suspected. His case was now complete, and with an occasional glance at his notes, he began to write.

> Dear Sir Henry,—At our interview yesterday, you asked for a general outline of the Hyndford case, with notes of the names of the witnesses who should be called to prove the various points. This I shall give below; and I enclose herewith copies of the witnesses' evidence to amplify the narrative.
>
> 1. Fifteen years ago, Evelyn Hazlemere married John Fenton, and they bought The Cedars, where Mrs. Fenton lived up to the date of her death on 3rd June, 1928. Mrs. Fenton had no private fortune; but her husband lodged £10,000 with trustees who were to pay over the income to her as long as she lived. The marriage was not a success. One cause of trouble was Mrs. Fenton's intemperance. Two years ago, Mrs. Fenton's niece, Joyce Hazlemere, came to live under Mrs. Fenton's charge. Shortly after that, matters

became acute, with the result that Mr. Fenton separated from his wife and left Stanningmore. Mrs. Fenton was addicted to betting.

(Witness: John Fenton.)

2. Up to 1926, Mrs. Fenton's health was quite normal. Her indulgence in alcohol had no marked effect on her constitution.

(Witness: Dr. Hubertus Platt.)

3. Between April and July, 1926, a series of transactions took place, involving the bank accounts of the accused and his brother, the late Simon Hyndford, M.D. The accused banked with Leiston's Bank, whilst his brother had an account with the North-Eastern Midland Bank. The accused drew cheques in favour of his brother. Dr. Hyndford cashed these cheques at the North-Eastern Midland Bank and took notes for them. These notes were then passed to Richard Hyndford, who paid them into his account at Leiston's Bank. A fresh cheque in favour of Dr. Hyndford was then drawn by the accused, and the process went through the same cycle. By this means, with a capital of £3,000, it was possible to simulate a transaction putting Dr. Hyndford in possession of notes to the value of £9,000.

(Witnesses: Frederick Richmond of Leiston's Bank and James Laxey of the North-Eastern Midland Bank.)

4. A series of four I.O.U.'s form part of the exhibits. These documents purport to be drawn up and signed by Mrs. Fenton on 10th May, 25th May, 17th June, and 9th July, 1926. The dates interleave with the above-mentioned banking transactions. Thus on 9th May, Dr. Hyndford drew £1,500 from his bank; and

the first I.O.U. is dated 10th May and is of the value of £1,500. The suggestion obviously was that Dr. Hyndford lent the £1,500 to Mrs. Fenton in return for the I.O.U., whereas actually he handed the notes to the accused, who paid them into his own banking account. These I.O.U.'s are forgeries prepared by the accused.

(Witness: Laurence Groombridge, N.P.)

5. On 10th August, 1926, Mrs. Fenton took out a £500 policy on her own life with the Canterbury and Mercantile United Insurance Co. Two days later, Dr. Simon Hyndford took out a £10,000 policy on Mrs. Fenton's life with the same company, relying on the same medical examination and producing as proof of his interest in her life the various forged I.O.U.'s amounting to £9,000. He was informed that in case of death he could collect only the amount of his actual loss from the company and he professed himself satisfied with this. He suggested that he might have to lend further sums to Mrs. Fenton, which would bring the total up to the insured value.

(Witness: Gerard Coxwold of the Canterbury and Mercantile United Insurance Co.)

6. If Mrs. Fenton had actually received these sums and had gambled them away, some trace of the transactions would have been found in her betting-books. No betting-books have been found which relate to her last two years' betting, though she kept books.

(Witnesses: Superintendent Ross and Joyce Hazlemere.)

7. Shortly after the £500 insurance policy was taken out, Mrs. Fenton began to suffer from intermittent heart-trouble, the symptoms of which were akin to

those produced by digitalis poisoning.

(Witness: Dr. Hubertus Platt.)

8. No preparation of digitalis was prescribed by Dr. Platt or supplied by Mrs. Fenton's druggist in this period.

(Witnesses: Dr. Hubertus Platt and John Knowle, M.P.S.)

9. According to a statement by the accused after his brother's death, Dr. Simon Hyndford was supplying Mrs. Fenton with bottles of a drug Paronax, a cough-and-cold patent medicine.

10. The last of these Paronax bottles, found in Mrs. Fenton's possession after her death, was found to contain digitalis, a drug which is not a component of Paronax as sold in the open market. Digitalis can be extracted from the common foxglove.

(Witness: Duncan Holland, F.I.C.)

11. There is a large bed of foxgloves in the garden of the house occupied by the accused and Dr. Hyndford.

(Witness: Superintendent Ross.)

12. From the middle of 1927 onwards, Dr. Simon Hyndford had an overdraft at his bank amounting to £3,000 at times. As security for this, the accused deposited £3,000 in bearer bonds with the bank.

(Witness: James Laxey of the North-Eastern Midland Bank.)

13. On 30th May, 1928, John Fenton returned to Stanningmore temporarily, taking a room at Hollingworth's Hotel. On 3rd June, he met the accused in the street; and the accused invited him to

come and see him that evening about 9 p.m.

(Witness: John Fenton.)

14. The moon was nearly full that night. This was an awkward time to select for the commission of the crime, owing to the chance of discovery in the moonlight. But by choosing that particular night, it was possible to take advantage of John Fenton's presence in Stanningmore, in order to throw suspicion upon him. As this chance might not recur, the accused and his brother took the risk of the moonlight.

15. At 7.30 p.m., Mrs. Fenton and Joyce Hazlemere dined. Both partook of the same food. Joyce Hazlemere felt no ill-effects. Joyce Hazlemere went on the river after dinner with her fiancé, Leslie Seaforth, in a canoe.

(Witness: Joyce Hazlemere.)

16. According to the statements of the accused and the late Dr. Simon Hyndford, Dr. Hyndford at 8.45 p.m. went across the river and visited Mrs. Fenton. This was just after Joyce Hazlemere had left the house. Dr. Simon Hyndford entered The Cedars by the French window of the drawing-room, which was then open.

17. The house-parlourmaid at The Cedars had left in the drawing-room, as was customary, a tray with a whiskey decanter, two half-bottles of soda-water, and two tumblers. (Witness: Lucy Stifford.)

18. The case for the prosecution will be that Dr. Hyndford had a drink with Mrs. Fenton and seized the opportunity to administer a dose of veronal in her whiskey. Veronal is a scheduled poison which

Dr. Hyndford might have had in his possession. No veronal was ever supplied to Mrs. Fenton by her druggist.

(Witness John Knowle, M.P.S.)

19. Except some blurred ones left by the maid in lifting the bottles on to the tray, no finger-prints were found on either of the soda-water bottles. Both these bottles were open; and any person unscrewing the stoppers in the normal way would have left prints on the glass. Dr. Hyndford had a habit of swathing such bottles in his pocket-handkerchief when he opened them, which would account for the absence of the opener's finger-prints in this case.

(Witness: Superintendent Ross.)

20. At 9.15 p.m., whilst Dr. Simon Hyndford was at The Cedars, John Fenton called on the accused at his house. He drank a glass of whiskey and soda with the accused, leaving his finger-prints on the tumbler which was of a common pattern. Fenton left at 10.45 p.m.

(Witnesses: John Fenton and Isaac Bourton, dealer in glassware and china.)

21. At 10.47 p.m., Dr. Simon Hyndford left The Cedars by the front door. Mrs. Fenton accompanied him into the hall. The case for the prosecution will be that he waited with her till the dose of veronal was taking effect, so that she would fall asleep almost as soon as he was off the premises.

(Witness: Joshua Marton.)

22. At 11.10 p.m., the accused crossed the river to The Cedars in a canoe, which he proceeded to conceal behind some bushes in the garden of The Cedars.

(Witness: James Buckland.)

23. The case for the prosecution will be that he entered the house by the open French window, found Mrs. Fenton asleep under the influence of the veronal, and killed her by applying pressure to the vagus nerves and internal carotid arteries. He had brought with him the tumbler used at his own house by John Fenton. This he had kept free from other finger-prints, and he now exchanged it for the tumbler on the tray which his brother had used, taking his brother's tumbler away with him. He then secured Mrs. Fenton's betting-books from the drawer in the writing-desk where she kept them usually. After this, in order to delay the discovery of the body as long as possible from anyone entering the house from the river, he went out on to the terrace and closed the catch of the French window behind him by means of a loop of thread passed over the end of the lever handle. The two free ends of the thread were slipped under the door; and when the two valves of the door were closed, the lever was pulled down by tugging on the two ends of the thread. When the catch was in place, a pull on a single end of the thread brought it away from the catch and under the door, so that no trace was left of any closing of the valves from the outside.

24. At about 11.30 p.m., John Fenton was in the garden of The Cedars and made his way to the French window.

(Witness: James Buckland)

25. John Fenton, looking through the curtained window, saw his wife's feet and ankles on a settee. His evidence suggests that by this time she was dead.

(Witness: John Fenton.)

26. Shortly after midnight, Joyce Hazlemere returned, found the French window closed, and entered the house by the front door. She discovered Mrs. Fenton's body in the drawing-room, recalled Leslie Seaforth and brought him to the house. Leslie Seaforth then rang up Dr. Hubertus Platt.

(Witness: Joyce Hazlemere.)

27. Dr. Platt came at once and found life extinct.

(Witness: Dr. Hubertus Platt.)

28. A post-mortem examination showed the following. The stomach of the deceased contained a non-fatal dose of veronal and also some material which gave the effect of digitalis. On the neck of the deceased, just over the most accessible positions of the vagus nerves and the internal carotid arteries, were two faint pressure-marks. Pressure at these points was believed to be the cause of death. There was no sign of constriction of the windpipe such as an ordinary person would use to kill a victim. The pressure on the vagi and carotids could have been applied only by someone with special knowledge, either a medical man or someone trained in jiu-jitsu (since these points are attacked in one of the jiu-jitsu holds).

(Witness: Amyas Keymer, M.D.)

29. The accused resided in Japan for years and had the opportunity of learning jiu-jitsu.

(Not contested.)

30. Immediately after Mrs. Fenton's death, the accused removed his bearer bonds from the North-Eastern Midland Bank and Dr. Simon Hyndford substituted for them, as security for his overdraft, the

£10,000 policy on Mrs. Fenton's life.

(Witness: James Laxey of the North-Eastern Midland Bank.)

31. On 27th June, a letter signed "ONE WHO KNOWS" reached Superintendent Ross. The letter accused Dr. Simon Hyndford of the murder of Mrs. Fenton.

(Witness: Superintendent Ross.)

32. This letter was written by the same person who forged the I.O.U.'s purporting to be signed by Mrs. Fenton.

(Witness: Laurence Groombridge, N.P.)

33. Shortly after midnight on 27th June, information was received that Dr. Simon Hyndford had committed suicide. On examination it was found that he had been killed by the firing of a heavy-calibre revolver with a leaden bullet. The muzzle of the revolver had been inserted in the mouth of the deceased at the moment of firing, as was shown by the tearing of the tissues around the mouth. The back of the skull had been almost blown out by the discharge. On the desk beside the body was a letter signed "ONE WHO KNOWS" and containing a blackmailing demand for money in connection with the murder of Mrs. Fenton. On the floor at the back of the deceased's chair, some sand was discovered. The only finger-prints on the revolver were those of Dr. Simon Hyndford. The revolver smelt of rubber, and the accused explained this by saying that the weapon was usually kept in a drawer containing rubber bandages.

(Witness: Superintendent Ross.)

34. This second letter signed "ONE WHO KNOWS" was written by the same person who wrote the previous one and who also forged the I.O.U.'s purporting to be signed by Mrs. Fenton.

(Witness: Laurence Groombridge, N.P.)

35. The case for the prosecution, if this second crime is charged against Richard Hyndford, will be that while his brother was seated at his desk, the accused came behind him and struck him on the back of the head with a bag or stocking filled with dry sand, to stun him. In this operation, some sand escaped from the bag or stocking and fell unnoticed on the floor. The accused then put on rubber gloves, took out the revolver, impressed his victim's fingerprints on the butt, and then, after placing the pseudonymous letter on the desk, he fired the revolver with its muzzle in the mouth of the stunned man. This simulated a case of suicide, since no one could contrive this state of things against a resisting man, especially as Dr. Simon was a powerful person whilst the accused is of feeble physique. The damage to the back of the skull done by the lead bullet was quite sufficient to destroy any traces of the previous sand-bagging. The only motive which need be suggested to the jury to account for this crime is as follows. This simulated suicide, coupled with the pseudonymous letters, tends to prove that Dr. Simon Hyndford was the sole author of Mrs. Fenton's death, and that when he discovered that the author of the letters was on his track, he preferred to commit suicide rather than to run the risk of exposure and hanging. In this way, the part played by the accused would be completely hidden.

36. Since the forger of the I.O.U.'s was obviously one of the Hyndford brothers, and since Dr. Simon Hyndford clearly did not write the second letter signed "ONE WHO KNOWS," it is evident that the accused must have written it; for the I.O.U.'s and the two letters were written by the same person. This proves that the accused was clearly implicated in both these crimes, since he must have been at least an accessory before the fact in the murder of Mrs. Fenton, even if the actual murder cannot be brought home to him.

I am

Your obedient Servant,
John Ross.

CHAPTER XVII
THE SPRINGS OF ACTION

"So Dickie Hyndford didn't manage to slip through your fingers after all?"

James Corwen's voice had something in it which sounded like a tinge of regret.

"If he'd got past us at the river-mouth, he might have led us a dance for a while," the Superintendent admitted. "He meant to coast along the shore in one direction or the other for the best part of the night, then land and send the boat off again straight out to sea with the engine running. That would have covered his trail temporarily; and I expect he might have got away by rail if he'd chosen his landing-place skillfully. But we'd have had him in the end."

"I suppose so," Corwen agreed.

"And of course he had about £3,000 worth of bearer bonds on him when I arrested him—enough to give him a fresh start somewhere."

James Corwen reflected for a moment and changed the subject.

"It was the veronal that gave me the first inkling of the possibilities of the case," he said, inconsequently.

"I'd like to hear just how much you guessed, if it's no trouble to you," Ross suggested.

James Corwen's gesture seemed to disclaim any special merit in the matter.

"Oh, I didn't make much of it, really," he acknowledged frankly. "The veronal was what made me think, to start with. Veronal's a scheduled poison—even I knew that. Therefore it could have been procured only by some authorised person, and it could have been administered only by Mrs. Fenton herself or by someone who was in the house that evening."

"Yes?" prompted Ross.

"The only people likely to have veronal in their control were: a druggist, a doctor, and a research chemist. There was no research chemist on the scene at all; so I ruled that out. The druggist had no interest in Mrs. Fenton's death; so he was off the map. That left a doctor. There were two doctors in Mrs. Fenton's circle: Platt and Hyndford. Platt had no interest in her, except a professional one; Hyndford . . . well, he might have had some reason for wanting her out of the way."

"You didn't stop there, of course?"

James Corwen carried the chain on to another link.

"At that point, the method of killing took my attention. The effect of pressure at that point in the neck was new to me. It was a case of special knowledge. Who had special knowledge of that sort? A doctor or, possibly, a jiu-jitsu expert. Simon Hyndford was a doctor; Dickie had been in Japan. Either of them would have the information. Eliminate everyone else who had either no access to veronal or no special knowledge of this sort, and it leaves you with Dr. Hyndford as a residuum. He had both the qualifications needed by the criminal."

"There was no apparent motive. That's what held me up for a while," the Superintendent commented.

"I think we were looking for different types of motive," James Corwen explained. "But what held me up at that stage were the finger-marks on the tumbler. Anyone could see that they gave you some trouble; and if they'd been Simon Hyndford's you would have identified them easily enough."

"The finger-prints on the tumbler were Fenton's," the Superintendent disclosed. "I nearly fell into the Hyndford trap there. Finger-prints are generally taken as sound evidence that the owner of the fingers made the marks at the place where they're discovered. Here was a tumbler in perfectly natural surroundings—a tray, a decanter, soda, another tumbler of exactly the same pattern—

and at the start I assumed that the man who left his prints on the tumbler had actually made the marks in the drawing-room. Then, one day, I happened to notice a tumbler of that very pattern in a shop-window; and that threw fresh light on the thing. It's easy enough to substitute one tumbler for another—a tumbler isn't a fixed object like a window-pane or a mantelpiece. Suppose Fenton had made the marks on the tumbler *outside* The Cedars?"

"I see what you are driving at," James Corwen interrupted. "The Hyndfords knew the pattern of Mrs. Fenton's tumblers. They bought a couple of the same pattern, offered Fenton a drink at their house, took the tumbler he had used over to The Cedars and planted it on the tray as evidence that Fenton himself had been in the drawing-room that night. Was that it?"

"Precisely. Richard Hyndford and Fenton both told me that they had a drink that evening at the Hyndford house. That was when Fenton left his prints on the tumbler which turned up later in the drawing-room of The Cedars. And of course, since this connected Richard Hyndford with the Fenton case, I began to open my eyes to his part in the affair. It was then that I recalled what you'd told me about the relations between the two Hyndfords—though that didn't help me much at the time."

"And the digitalis question?" James Corwen catechised sardonically.

"Anyone who had foxgloves in their garden could make a tincture of digitalis, if they knew how," the Superintendent answered. "There were foxgloves in the Hyndfords' garden and also in the garden of The Cedars. Miss Hazlemere *might* have prepared a tincture; Dr. Hyndford certainly had the necessary knowledge for the job. Veronal, vagi, digitalis: Simon Hyndford fitted all three. But still there was no motive that I could see."

"I suppose you got on to the betting-book question about that time?" James Corwen questioned.

"Those missing betting-books gave me a lot to think about," the Superintendent admitted in a reflective tone. "The first thing I thought of was that Simon Hyndford had been betting with Mrs. Fenton and had made heavy losses which would be recorded in her books. That would be a sound reason for the books being removed. Then, I turned the thing outside in, for change. Suppose that these betting-books didn't contain something which *ought* to be in them, according to the murderer's planning. That would be an equally sound reason for their disappearance. I puzzled at it for long enough, but I couldn't see it. Then you brought up the matter of the I.O.U.'s. . . . By the way, was that a deliberate move on your part?"

James Corwen's face showed his derision at the suggestion that his move had been accidental.

"Of course," he said, curtly. "The I.O.U.'s gave the key to the disappearance of the betting-books. Where had that £8,000 gone, if Hyndford really lent it to her? Gambled away, of course. That was the only hypothesis that would hold water. And her betting-books had to be destroyed, because they would have given the show away. That was as clear as crystal, to my mind. So I dropped the I.O.U.'s in your way—made it seem quite casual—and let you draw your own inferences. If I'd forced the I.O.U.'s on you, most likely you would have discounted that as a mere blind put up to divert suspicion from my client."

"There's something in that," the Superintendent acknowledged without malice. "Then your man Groombridge came in neatly with his graphology stunt; and that brought something like true perspective into the case, so far as I saw it. And then up there came in my mind the fact that Richard Hyndford was involved to some extent through the tumbler and the finger-prints. The whole Hyndford evidence was suspect, if they were both in it up to the neck. But I got stuck over the tale you told me about the relations between them when they were youngsters. It didn't seem to fit, somehow. Why should Richard Hyndford come home and stay in the house with a brother who'd treated him like that when he was a boy?"

James Corwen's lips curved in his characteristically chilly smile.

"That was the very question I asked myself when Dickie came home from the East," he cxplained. "Knowing something of Dickie's tenacity, it seemed strange to find him letting bygones be bygones.

Of course one finds these 'undying grudges' oftener in fiction than in real life. Very few people cherish really dangerous hatred for any length of time. But this, you see, wasn't a case of normal affairs. Simon had made his mark on Dickie through nearly ten weary years, just at the period in a boy's life when he is most receptive and when his memory is most retentive. It was a lasting impression. If I had been a friend of Simon's, I should have felt rather perturbed when Dickie settled himself down in that house in preference to anywhere else. There was something unnatural about it; one couldn't help feeling that, when one had an inkling of the early history of the two."

"You mean you suspected the grudge was still there, under all the surface amiability?"

James Corwen agreed with a nod.

"My impression of Dickie Hyndford, Superintendent, didn't fit in with his doings. If you change a single word in one of Byron's couplets, you get a picture of Dickie as I believed he really was:

> He was a hater, of the good old school
> Who still become more constant as they cool.

Perhaps now you will be able to see how I looked at the Fenton case from the start. It was a play within a play, like that scene in *Hamlet*. The superficial part of it was the murder of Mrs. Fenton; that was what you saw. But the latent part of it was the manoeuvring of Dickie Hyndford towards his revenge, the final squaring of an account that he'd kept open for the best part of a quarter-century. Mrs. Fenton was a mere pawn in that game."

"And you saw all this?" the Superintendent demanded.

"Not all at once," James Corwen admitted. "One thing fitted in after another. And of course I had no proof; it was merely suspicion. All I could do was to give you a bit of information now and again without seeming to do so. I trusted to you to find your way to the solution eventually."

"I got the impression you rather liked Richard Hyndford."

"My business was to get my client off," James Corwen pointed out. "And the surest way to manage that was to turn your attention elsewhere. But if I had shown animus against *both* the Hyndfords, you would probably have discounted my information."

"That's true enough," said Ross reflectively.

"Then I suppose you had some theory about the whole affair?"

James Corwen seemed to have no objection to putting his cards on the table at last.

"Here is the outline of the affair, as I saw it," he began. "First of all, you have Dickie Hyndford, a sensitive clever child, blackmailed and terrorised by Simon through the whole formative period of his life. Whenever he tried to find his way out of the maze, the shadow of Simon lay across his road. He was fond of his father—and Simon managed to embitter even that side of existence by his continual dripping of suggestions. Oppression, repression, a sort of miasma of meanness and unscrupulousness which clouded everything in life . . . ten weary years of it would be enough to give a permanent twist to most people's characters, I think. 'Some day I'll get square with that swine!' must have been the only beacon ahead through all that ugly experience. That's how I would have felt myself, I think, if I had been put through the same thing.

"But if I had gone through it, I doubt if it would have affected me permanently. You have to bear in mind that tenacity I spoke of before. That was the keystone of the whole affair. He came back from the East, still with that grudge against Simon, and with the firm intention of paying the account. Simon, for all that cheap subtlety of his, didn't see what was afloat. He was a coarse-fibred animal, and I really doubt if he was capable of understanding what he had done to his brother. He imagined that bygones were bygones, when Dickie came back. And Dickie didn't trouble to undeceive him.

"Then, I expect, Dickie saw some glimmerings of a plan. Simon was making a mess of his betting, and money was becoming very tight. My belief is that Dickie lent him money from time to time until he had Simon fairly in his grip. Then he must have propounded the scheme that led to the Fenton case: get Mrs. Fenton to insure herself for a small sum; and at the same time effect a £10,000 insurance on her life in Simon's favour. That demanded some proof of interest; and so you get the forged I.O.U.'s. Dickie was evidently the forger. He would be clever enough to see that Simon would expect both of them to be in the thing up to the neck, so as to avoid either of them turning King's evidence and saving himself.

"That gives you the forgery of the I.O.U.'s and the fake insurance. The next stage is the attempt to poison Mrs. Fenton with digitalis extracted from foxgloves. That smacks a bit of Simon's mentality, I think. By that time Dickie had evidently got him into his debt so heavily that Simon had to make some show of an effort towards paying up; and he could pay up only by collecting the Fenton insurance money. Hence the Paronax business.

"But the Paronax failed in its purpose, and Dickie grew more pressing in his demands for repayment. At last, when Simon was at his wits' end in the matter, Dickie produced his second scheme—the thing that culminated in the real murder. My impression is that in the original draft of this, Simon was cast for the murderer's part and Dickie meant to stand aside and blow the gaff on his brother when the deed was done. But Simon was not absolutely a fool. That subtlety of his came to the rescue. He insisted on a modification of the scheme. (I'm giving you the thing as it appears to me, merely.) Dickie was to be as deeply involved as Simon—more deeply, indeed. He was to do the actual murder; Simon was to be accessory before the fact. That put a rope round both their necks; and Simon thought he had got Dickie under his thumb by that.

"Dickie had probably thought out things a good deal further. All he wanted to do was to clear Simon off the board—nothing else counted. He could not see his way to straight murder in Simon's case. But if he could involve Simon in a charge of murder, then suicide on Simon's part would seem natural enough. That was what Dickie was working towards; and of course Simon never saw it.

"The Fenton murder went through according to plan. Then Dickie arranged matters so that you were on the edge of arresting

Simon. And just at the last moment, he shot him himself and left the forged letter beside him as evidence in explanation of a suicide.

"So far as could have been foreseen, that left Dickie on velvet. Everything concentrated on his dead brother and he himself would be outside suspicion. He had nothing to gain over the business, since the insurance policy was not in his name. There was no visible motive connecting him with the Fenton case. That's how I see it, at any rate."

"And but for two bits of bad luck, I expect he'd have pulled it off," the Superintendent admitted. "One was the chance that Groombridge happened to be a bit of a graphologist. The other was old Jim Buckland's eye, up there in the Museum. Neither of them singly would have helped much. But the two of them put together were enough to clear up the case. There's always a lot of luck in this detective business."

COACHWHIP PUBLICATIONS
COACHWHIPBOOKS.COM

ISBN 978-1-61646-329-8

Coachwhip Publications

CoachwhipBooks.com

ISBN 978-1-61646-332-5

Coachwhip Publications

Also Available

ISBN 978-1-61646-326-7

Coachwhip Publications
CoachwhipBooks.com

ISBN 978-1-61646-274-1

Coachwhip Publications

Also Available

ISBN 978-1-61646-275-8

Lightning Source UK Ltd.
Milton Keynes UK
UKHW022258020219
336590UK00001B/360/P